LIAR GO ROUND

MADISON RUPP

MONARCH
Publishing

Publishing

NONARCH PUBLISHING
Copyright © 2025 by Madison Rupp
All rights reserved.
ISBN 979-8-9909535-4-3 (print)
ISBN 979-8-9909535-5-0 (ebook)
First Edition

Cover artwork by Katt Phatt

ALSO BY MADISON RUPP

Liarland

Liarland

Liar Go Round

Death Dates

LIAR GO ROUND

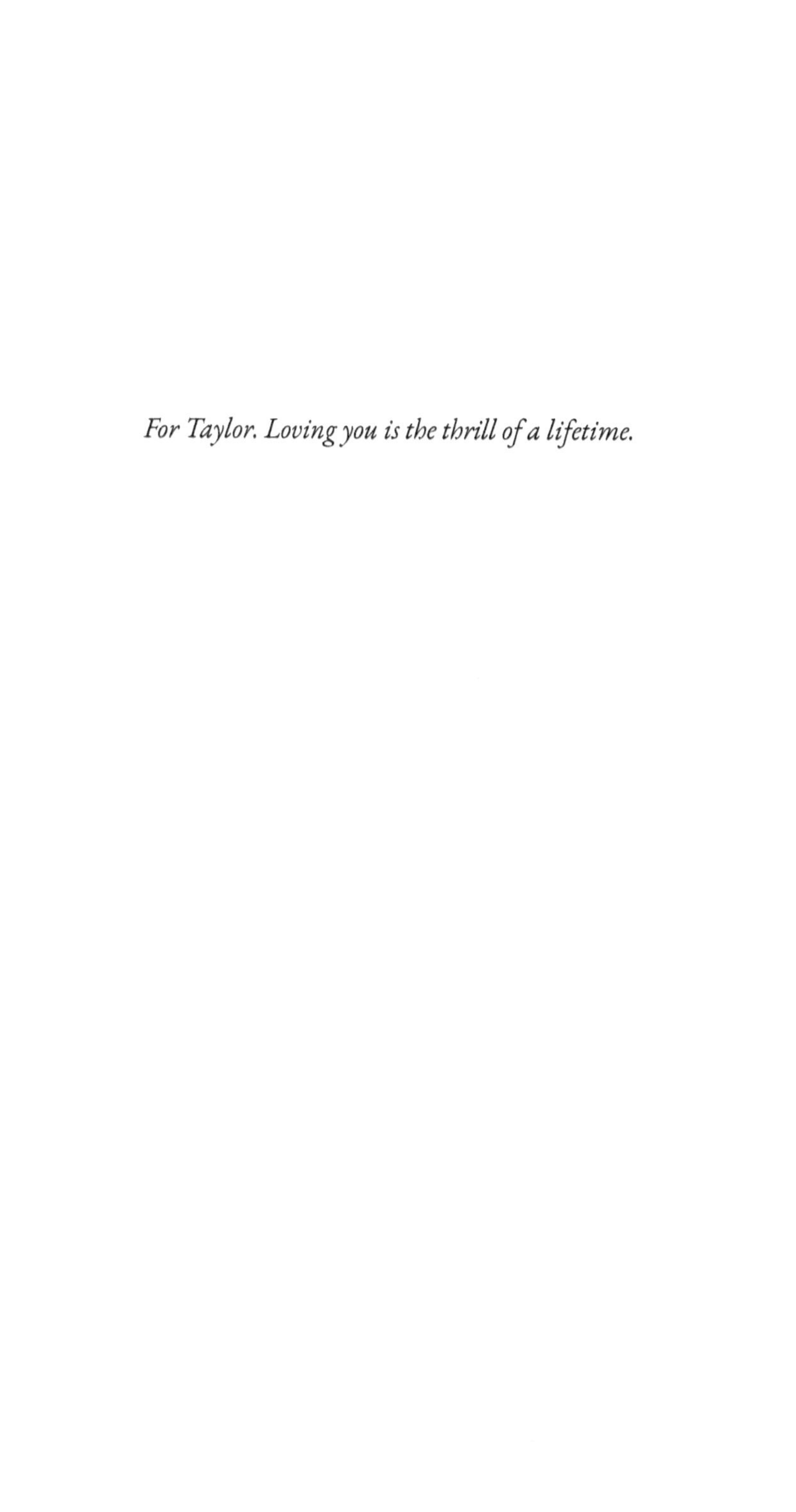

For Taylor. Loving you is the thrill of a lifetime.

CHAPTER
ONE

THERE ARE screams all around me.

Although, I guess that's kind of the goal. Screams. The more horrified, the better.

I know I've done my job when they're loud, piercing, and accompanied by guests scrambling to grab hold of each other.

The sound used to bother me, but I'm getting better at tuning it out.

Jumping around the wall concealing me from guests, I lunge at a trio of teenage boys, baring my teeth and clawing toward them with scraggly fingers. Their shrieks are higher than I'm sure any of them would care to admit. Lucky for them, I don't recognize their terrified faces. They must be from out of town.

Their screams aren't real, of course. It's amusing to feel afraid. To yelp and squeal, like they're actually in danger. They can't help wanting to experience a night of fear this time of year. But that doesn't stop me from resenting them.

These lucky fools wouldn't know real danger if it held a knife to their throats. Even then, they might be so preoccupied with their *fun* that they don't even realize they're about to die.

Advancing toward the boys once more for good measure, I

chase them into the next room of the haunted house. And then, not feeling as satisfied as I should, I slink back into my dark hiding spot, waiting for the next wave of petrified guests to walk past.

Crouched against the flimsy plywood wall, I attempt to keep my disgust in check. As easy as it is to forget, these guests are innocent customers. Sweet folks who drove to Pineland for a night of fall festivities. They don't mean any offense by prancing and screaming all around the site of four brutal murders.

Or maybe they do. After all, it sure is thrilling to be where it happened.

Not for me.

Last summer, my classmates turned out to be lying, scheming serial killers paid by the former park leaders to make salacious headlines to sell more tickets. That sort of scenario would mess with even the calmest person's head, especially when one's best friend is involved.

Ex-best friend.

Valerie Ross, the ex-best friend in question, used me to absolve herself from being implicated as a murderer. She played mind games with me and used my loyalty in her favor.

After that experience, I'm not sure I can find anything in this theme park thrilling. Least of all, a Halloween event celebrating everything that keeps me up at night.

The sound of heavy footfalls approaching promises the next round of fear-seekers will be a large group. Why anyone would pay money to be scared is beyond me, but judging by the packed park, I'm in the minority with that mindset.

Pull it together. Collect your paycheck and get out.

I contort my face into a wicked expression. Wide eyes, menacing grin. My costume is pulling a lot of the leg work here. A sleek, silver wig hangs to my waist, covering a good portion of my face. Unfortunately, that didn't stop the makeup artists from plastering a crooked prosthetic nose over my real one. The best part of the night is ripping that dang thing off. It makes it nearly impossible to breathe. Maybe another tragic death inside the park is their goal. Who's to say?

The skittish guests round the corner, braced for something to startle them. I remain crouched in my hiding spot, waiting for them to exhale a sigh of relief like suckers.

The little room of the haunted maze called "*Flytrap*" is themed to look like the inside of a witch's gardening shed. There's a workbench littered with overturned pots, fragrant soil, and glow-in-the-dark seeds. It's all part of the story of the Mad Witch living in the woods surrounding Pineland. She's hard at work, nurturing a deadly plant that feeds on humans. Fake poisonous flowers and herbs hang from the low ceiling, forcing the guests to push them out of their way for a clear view of the room.

By the time they reach me, guests have journeyed through the actual forest that surrounds the theme park, following glowing plants that seem to snap at their ankles (thanks to committed crew members hiding in bushes with puppets), and finally, they've stumbled across the Witch's lair. Their hearts are racing as they pray to make it out in one piece.

I grab a prop trowel, tightening my grip around the handle, as I wait one last second. Long enough for these guests to think they're safe.

No one's safe at Pineland. The sooner they learn, the better.

Mustering my deepest growl, I jump out from behind the plywood wall, catching the group by surprise.

There's five of them. Two couples holding hands and a poor fifth wheel trailing behind. Her arms are crossed over her chest and she's the only one who doesn't scream her head off. It's just as well. I was going to leave her alone anyways.

"Oh my gosh," one of the girls giggles, tugging on her boyfriend's arm. "I think that's her!"

Eyes wide, she stares right at me, making it abundantly

clear she knows exactly who is hiding beneath all the prosthetic warts and silver hair. It's the girl from the news and the memes. The one who played right into a pretend serial killer's hand. Gwen Gardner, the most gullible girl in the Midwest.

I freeze, like I do every time someone has the gall to talk about me like I'm a caricature of a human. As if I can't understand what they're saying. Their inability to remember I'm an actual person with feelings will always take me by surprise.

The fifth wheel groans at her friend. "Will you stop with that already?"

"Chill, Nicole," the friend scoffs. "It's just a joke."

Her callous tone snaps me out of my daze. Why can't these people just leave me be? How much longer is this going to continue? I'm trying to carry on with my life.

Suddenly motivated to get them out of my sight, I target the lovebirds, pretending to stab them with the sharp tip of my trowel while threatening to turn them into fertilizer for my beloved plant. My advance is closer than they expect, and they clutch each other with terrified screams. The sight is oddly therapeutic.

The single girl snorts as the others scramble out of the shed. At least she's enjoying herself. Not that it becomes much cheerier from here.

Jenna Thatcher is waiting in the next room, wearing the same Mad Witch costume as me and cackling as she feeds a mannequin into the blood-dripping maw of an enormous Venus flytrap.

My arms drop to my sides as soon as the group escapes. I allow them to evaporate from my thoughts, as well. They're not my problem anymore.

I don't mind the repetitive work of performing the same scare all night. It comes with the territory of working in a theme park. But when I agreed to work night shifts at Hauntland, the park's brand-new Halloween event, I didn't expect it to turn me into an actual witch. But every scream of manufactured horror makes my bitterness bury deeper into my soul.

I probably wouldn't be so resentful if the whole world wasn't screwing with me.

At first, my role in last summer's scandal didn't make the news. Not until a Michigan-based reporter, Abigail Herron, wrote a tell-all and named me in it multiple times. She called me "Pineland's final girl" because I was the only one who made it out with my reputation—and my life—seemingly intact. It's kind of ironic her article would be the thing to change that.

When school started, the piece went viral. As it would seem, the masses found my involvement pretty pathetic. Only an utter fool would fall for such ridiculous lies and not run straight to the cops. They're right, of course. I was a fool. But I didn't need them telling me to know. It brought countless trolls out of the woodwork. Their accounts were throwaways, with ominous profile pictures and handles, but the DMs were all the same.

No one I love is safe.

Someone is going to attack Pineland.

If I don't help, they'll come after me.

The messages were reminiscent of the ones I received from Valerie, back when she was pretending to be kidnapped and masquerading as her kidnapper, Ride or Die, in my DMs.

Hathaway Police Department stopped taking these new threats seriously after I cried wolf one too many times.

I can't win. Last summer, I should've immediately divulged the dangerous messages I was receiving. Now, I'm reporting too much. Eventually, Nora Pierce, the police captain, recommended to my parents that I seek counseling. Because in these parts, honesty is cause for concern.

I wound up deleting my social media altogether. If no one wanted to care about the warnings sliding into my DMs, I no longer needed to receive them.

The sound of boots thudding on wood alert me to an approaching party. They're far quieter than normal. Not screaming or gasping for breath. It makes me wonder if they're a party of one.

Freak. Who would come to a place like this alone?

Chewing the inside of my cheek, I fight the urge to break character and tell the sick guest off.

I need to calm down. Maybe they became separated from their group. Or their best friend betrayed them so coming alone was their best option. After all, even in its inaugural year, Hauntland is already considered the premier Halloween event in Michigan.

Readying myself to provide a decent scare, I listen carefully for when the footsteps are almost outside my hiding spot.

Three, two, one...

I spring out at the guest, snarling a threat about feeding them to my precious plant while prodding my trowel in their direction.

The guest doesn't yelp or scurry away. They don't even startle.

So, they are a freak, I confirm. A repeat visitor who has clearly been through this haunted house a dozen times. How else would they know to brace for my scare?

The guest is a few inches taller than me, wearing a black hoodie that's pulled up over their head. In the low light, I can't see their face below the shadow of the hood. Realizing they have me stunned, the guest releases a patronizing laugh.

"Hey there, Gwen Gardner."

The hair on the back of my neck stands on end as I search for any discernible details of their identity. Thanks to their bulky attire and hooded head, I'm unsuccessful. But that doesn't stop me from mentally filing away what I can for a potential police report. Slender build. Stands at about five-feet-nine-inches. Male, I think?

"Do I know you?"

"Not yet." His voice is unusually low, and I wonder if he's intentionally deepening it to disguise his true tone.

If my mother was here, she'd remind me to stop looking for tells that people are lying. I know she's worried I'll stop believing anything is true. Mom's been reading all sorts of self-help books as of late, and because our family insurance doesn't cover a therapist, she considers the written advice to be the next best thing to help her traumatized daughter.

The shadowy stranger simply stares, giving me no real reason to fear them. They're not coming at me. All they are doing is observing. Waiting for some kind of reaction.

My jaw clicks as it hits me. This is just another troll. Someone who glorifies the Pineland murders and anyone involved. A Ride or Die fanatic. I bet this stranger thinks it's *hilarious* that I fell for my ex-best friend pretending to be a victim, when in actuality, she was the reason everyone died in the first place.

"Move on," I say gruffly, hoping they'll get the message. "Find another horror to obsess over. Pineland is through with tragedies."

"Is it?"

The question hangs between us, making the cool air go still.

"You need to leave me alone." I hate how my voice shakes.

They shrug. "Whatever you want, Gwen. Sit back and enjoy the show."

"What's that supposed to mean?"

The stranger disappears deeper into the haunted house without another word. I'm left to stand dumbly in the empty room, surrounded by an ominous soundtrack that plays on a loop and walls that seem to press in.

I want to call after him. Chase him down and demand an answer. I could report him to park security or the police, but what good will that do? No actual threat was detailed. My report would be flimsier than any of my previous ones.

Realizing I'm standing in the middle of the shed like a fool, I finally creep back into my hiding spot. Crouching, I press my back against the plywood wall and attempt to settle my nerves. Instinctively, I begin anxiously twisting the silver ring around my middle finger. I'm not supposed to wear it while playing the Witch, but fiddling with the gift from my boyfriend, Dev, feels like the only thing keeping me sane. It has a knot in the middle of the band. Dev says it's supposed to be a reminder that no matter how tangled life gets, we'll always be tied together. I never thought I'd be the kind of girl who found something that cheesy so comforting.

It's just a prank, I remind myself with a deep breath.

Yet, those six words ring in my ears with foreboding. *Sit back and enjoy the show.* I can still hear the confidence in his voice. The glee. He knew those simple words would rattle me because I'm the girl who cries wolf. The one who falls for the horrors in front of her, even when they're nothing more than scary costumes and fake DMs.

Whether I want to admit it or not, this stranger knows me well, because, of course, I'll believe him.

Despite what the park's new owner might want to believe, Pineland will never be free from tragedies. It's built into the very DNA of this theme park. Disaster after disaster. It was only a matter of time until the next one occurred.

Sit back and enjoy the show.

The stranger got what he wanted: my attention. Now all I can do is wait and pray that it's the only item on his agenda.

But who's to say with Pineland? Every visit to this park could be the best day ever. Or it could be someone's last.

CHAPTER
TWO

Panic begins to creep through my veins, and I allow the next group of guests to make it through the room without a scare. How can I go after them when I'm equally as petrified? It's highly probable that I'm more scared than any of these paying customers will be all night.

I have every right to be terrified.

Does this count as a "genuinely serious" situation worthy of a call to the police? Or will they shoo me away again with a shake of their heads?

But what if this *is* genuine and serious?

What if someone dies?

Stop. Get a grip on yourself.

He was just a troll. A creep craving something to boast about to his fellow freaks. No one is going to die. The park now has proper security measures in place. Cameras, careful bag checks, and patrolling guards. Nothing bad happens here anymore, despite what my inner monologue might try to tell me.

A wave of frustration replaces my fear. These people need to leave me alone. How much more of this parasocial attention can a person endure?

"Gwen?"

I shoot a foot into the air as a tall figure pokes his head around the plywood wall. Although, this is the last face that should frighten me. My chest heaves at my foolishness. I really do need to get a grip.

Dev's dark eyebrows raise at my reaction. "You good?"

It's not so difficult to feel okay now. At the sight of my boyfriend, all my bitterness begins to melt away like a forgotten blue-raspberry slushy outside of an attraction. Everyone else in this park might disgust me—but not Dev. Never Dev. He's as sweet and safe as they come.

"I'm good," I say after a deep breath, taking his outstretched hand and allowing him to pull me to my feet.

Judging by the concerned look creasing his forehead, we both know I'm lying. But Hathaway residents are obliged to a white lie every now and then. The truth always comes out eventually.

"B Cast is waiting," he murmurs knowingly. "And unless you're planning to skip our only break..."

"Let's get out of here."

A loud voice calls from the corner, "You sure you don't want to stay?"

Peering around Dev, I spy Estelle, a sophomore at Hathaway High, waiting in an identical costume as mine. She's the Garden Shed Witch on the B Cast. We switch on and off throughout the night.

"Here's your trowel," I reply, holding it out to her.

The girl sighs, flicking long strands of her pale wig from her face before taking it. "Halloween can't come soon enough."

The holiday falls on a Saturday this year. A week from today. After performing the same scares repeatedly, we're all ready for the season to end. Our bodies ache and our sleep schedules are completely out of whack. After finishing tonight's shift, we have a few days to rest before tackling the final weekend of event nights. Then, on the first of November, we're free until Pineland reopens in May for the summer season.

Cast changes must be quick. Wendy Thatcher, Pineland's new owner, doesn't like the line to be paused too long. After all, we want to keep our rabid, death-complacent guests happy.

As Estelle gets into character, Dev nabs the long, black robe that hangs on the backside of the wall I hide behind and drapes it over my shoulders. I have to wear it, so no one recognizes I'm a performer when I walk through the park to the break room. After pulling the hood over my wig, he gently glides a hand down my cheek, giving my chin a squeeze.

"Can you two find a different room?" Estelle groans at our affection.

"Our bad," Dev apologies, not sounding sorry at all. His hand wraps around mine, guiding me through the rest of the house. It would likely be a far-creepier stroll had we not spent the last three weeks trapped inside this haunted house.

Or maybe, we're immune to all horrors after last summer. We've already seen the worst this park has to offer.

My cloak flows behind me as we dart in and out of the showrooms. Dev doesn't have one because he's not wearing a costume. Assigned to the crowd control team, it's his job to keep the guests moving through the house and ensure everyone is on their best behavior. This means he isn't dressed in some ridiculous getup. He gets to wear his usual khaki pants, but his blue polo has been exchanged for a neon-green event crewneck.

We hurry through the final scene, which is intended to feature a cackling witch ushering human sacrifices through a doorway decorated to appear like the plant's open mouth. The Finale Witch, Cassidy, leans against the plant, enjoying her final few minutes of break by scrolling on her phone. She nods at us as we pass through the plant and back into the open air.

Three scare zones loom between us and the break room. *Scout Stabbers*, *Forest of Fears*, and *Lair of the Dogman*. Plus, a few attractions with horror overlays, like the *Scary-Go-Round*, where you ride the carousel with a bunch of creepy clowns. But it's not the fake knives, killer squirrels, or famed Michigan cryptids that disturb me.

It's the people who relish them. Anyone who enjoys that which is sick and twisted can't be that far off from becoming sick and twisted themselves. And those are the people I refuse to trust. If there's one thing I've learned after last summer, anyone—even the most unsuspecting of souls—is capable of truly horrible things. And like hell am I going to get caught up in that again, no matter how hard they attempt to search me out and involve me.

I know I'm testing fate by continuing to work at Pineland. At least, that's what my parents think. But Wendy Thatcher's late-night pay was too tempting to ignore. I may have been awarded last summer's Park Ranger scholarship on a technicality, but it's not enough money to put me through four years of school. When Wendy announced the park would remain open through the fall, I recognized staying was my best opportunity to save up more.

I used to be saving for out-of-state college tuition. Now, as my grades haphazardly slip and my old dreams of studying environmental science grow fuzzy, I'm not sure what I'm saving up for. But I'm a Gardner through and through, so all I know is that I need to save for something. I'll be happy I did when I finally figure out what I want to do with my life. Until then, I'll continue to clock-in for the best-paying job in town and hope I clock-out unscathed.

If I stick close to Dev—the only person in Hathaway I can wholeheartedly trust—I know I'll be okay.

In its decades of operation, this is Pineland's first autumn season. But following the headlines of three murders in the park, Wendy Thatcher would be remiss not to capitalize on the newfound audience: horror fanatics. Give the people what they want. If Pineland wants to be known as the murder-theme-park-capital of the world, so be it. They charge the freaks a premium to be in the park where it happened. Their inconsequential screams can follow our real ones. Surely, there's nothing messed up about that.

Dev and I traverse through a patch of artificial fog, which makes the crisp, late-October air thick and damp. On the other side of the cloud, a tall figure lunges at us with a snarl.

To my credit, I don't jump. However, Dev likely lost feeling in his fingers from my tightening grip.

"Seriously, dude?" My boyfriend groans.

"Oh shit," Weston McCray grunts in a way that he hopes sounds apologetic but never does. "I didn't realize it was you two. My bad."

A fellow crew member, he's outfitted in ripped cargo shorts with a padded muscle shirt that gives him the torso of a hairy wolf. Prosthetic ears and fangs complete the look of the monstrous legend, The Michigan Dogman.

"Whoa," I hear Dev say. "You okay?"

Glancing up at the blond boy, I find his face peaked. His eyelids hang heavy, and from the way he's swaying, I worry he might pass out in front of us.

Dev immediately releases my hand and loops it around Weston's forearm. "Let's get you backstage."

"I'm fine," Weston mumbles unconvincingly.

"This place isn't worth it," I tell him, wrapping my arm around his free one. "If you're not feeling well, you should go home."

"Wait, you guys don't think," he says, his eyes bugging out, "that someone poisoned me, do you?"

If anyone else had said it, we'd leave them to pass out in the middle of the park. But this is Weston, which means the remark isn't poking fun at my fears. Ever since he was framed for Luca Mendes' murder last summer, Weston's been on edge. He's always suspicious that someone is targeting him. I can't blame him, really. We're both learning to live with our new scars. Although, I'll admit, tough guy Weston McCray is the last person I expected to share my trauma.

"I think you're dehydrated," Dev reminds him, keeping his voice even and calm. Out of all of us, Dev's the one whose best kept his wits about him. He's the steadiest person I know. "Let's get you some water inside."

Without further argument, Weston allows us to guide him through the park. This proves to be no easy feat because the muscular hockey player weighs more than Dev and I do combined. We dodge teenagers who are having a fight with kettle corn and cozy couples who can't keep their drinks from sloshing over the edge of their souvenir cups. Hannah Flannigan, the newly-reinstated-but-still-as-uptight-as-ever entertainment manager, will kill us if we ruin our costumes.

Everyone expected Hannah to keep her distance after her Pineland-executive father was arrested for hiring teenaged-hitmen to create bad publicity for the park. But Hannah isn't the type to let anything go easily. No one was going to derail her career at Pineland. Not even her father. I guess her determination paid off. Wendy Thatcher rewarded her loyalty with a promotion.

That feels like the trend around here. Those of us who suffered the most last summer are now seeing reparations. Not that it makes up for anything. I don't care if I get the nicest hours or a comfortable indoor position. I've already lost everything. My best friend. My reputation. My sanity.

All I have left is Dev, but that's enough for me.

"Give us some space." My boyfriend fends off a particularly rowdy group of teenage boys who are sprinting away from a short performer dressed as a nature scout. The performer wields a dagger almost as long as them. The boys narrowly dart by us, and I'm treated to a whiff of B.O.

As we cross through the park's kiddie area, *Sapling Spring,* the horror-movie soundtrack stops abruptly. This is the only part of the park free from scares.

There are only a few guests back here, taking refuge from the horrors scouring the rest of the park. Maybe they've come to their senses and realized that glorifying all things dark and sinister might actually be a pretty messed up thing to do.

Careening around a large wall that separates the park from backstage, we hold our breaths past dumpsters and hurry into the welcoming heat of HQ. We pause a few feet into the doorway, allowing the warmth to toast us through. Michigan winters seem to arrive earlier every year. Even now, as October comes to a close, the awaiting season can't wait to make its presence known.

Crew HQ has seen quite the face-lift under new management. I'm not sure where Wendy Thatcher found it in her budget, but now, the atrium is properly furnished. The large room used to simply serve as a hub to the crew member locker rooms, costuming, offices, and cafeteria.

But Wendy had a new vision for the space. One that invites crew members into work and makes them want to linger after a shift. Now dubbed the "Crewmunity Hall," comfy armchairs cluster in small groups, as do standing tables. The walls are now decorated with large photographs of current crew members performing their job. There are also frequent morale-boosting pop-ups, like free hot chocolate and Halloween candy.

It's hard not to wonder how things would be if Wendy Thatcher had bought the park ages ago like she wanted. There certainly wouldn't be any dangerous PR stunts to sell tickets. I'd be different, too.

If last summer hadn't happened, you wouldn't be dating Dev.

When the "what-ifs" start to plague my mind, I've learned to remind myself that some of these scars were worth earning. My life shines tremendously brighter with Dev in it.

"Are you sure you don't want to go to first aid?" Dev warily eyes Weston.

However, the fluorescent lights in the atrium seem to be enough to return the boy's senses. Weston blinks against the harsh, pale light before rubbing the heels of his hands into his eyes.

"Must be the exhaustion," he mutters to himself before glancing between us. "I had a pretty intense workout before my shift."

"Let's get some water and sit down," I say.

Weston's teeth chatter in agreement. He still has all of them, which is a testament to the large helmets youth hockey players have to wear. "Damn, it's cold out there."

"Some hot chocolate, too," Dev suggests, his eyebrows raised again with concern. What hockey player feels the cold that easily? Not one at the top of his game, that's for sure.

"Yeah, that sounds good," Weston says, his face so pale that I worry he has a fever. "Let me meet you in there. I need to pee."

Dev immediately offers, "Want me to come with you?"

"To pee?" He bites back, suddenly sounding like his old, snarky self. "I got it, bro."

My boyfriend raises his hands innocently. "Just looking after you."

"Sorry, I know." Weston rubs his hands down his face. "Man, I'm tired."

"You sure you don't want to leave?" I ask. "They'll survive without you for the night."

"I'm sure they would," Weston dryly agrees before turning toward the locker rooms.

Dev and I stare after him, waiting until he disappears before blinking at each other with sober expressions. Weston's always been a weird guy, but we know his current oddities aren't anything he can control. We all have our new habits after last summer.

"Poor guy," Dev mutters after him.

"Let's go find a table."

Sometimes, I think the best thing we can do is pretend like we don't understand the root of all our problems. It might not be the healthiest approach, but when we're in the middle of a shift at Pineland, it's certainly the easiest.

In agreement, Dev pulls me through the Crewmunity Hall and into the cafeteria, where the quirkiest assortment of individuals reside. There're the usual weathered crew members who operate rides and handle park cleanliness. Then there's the monsters, demons, and hags mixed into the bunch, all sporting outlandish costumes and makeup. As a whole, we've become the cast of a horror movie.

Not that we weren't already living one.

After grabbing paper cups filled with water, Dev orders a hot chocolate from the woman working the counter.

"Did you want one?" he asks me, but I shake my head. Pineland makes their hot chocolate too sweet. As good as something warm sounds, my shift is only halfway over and I don't want to make myself sick. There's nothing worse than performing a repetitive scare with a churning stomach.

Our usual booth in the back corner is empty and we slide into the vinyl seats with the beverages. Dev graciously slides the cup of hot chocolate in my direction, nodding for me to wrap my hands around the warm container. As soon as I do, a soothing heat spreads through my veins.

Dev waits until the color returns to my cheeks before finally asking, "Are you sure you're okay?"

My eyes meet his and I slide the drink back across the table. Ever since we were kids, Dev's always had the keen ability to see right through me. Even during that strange period last year when we pretended to not be friends, he remained one of the few people in this miserable town to make sense of me.

"Something happened in the house," I whisper, and he

immediately leans over the table. Beneath it, I feel his foot come and rest next to mine.

"What?"

My heart rate picks up as I recall the hooded figure and the way they just stood there, staring at me like they knew my deepest fears. Somehow, they were fully aware of how their actions would make me feel. And they did it anyway.

"Did you see a hooded guest come through?" I ask. "They were alone."

Dev is usually stationed toward the entrance of the house, making sure guests are pulsed through in appropriate group-ings. He frowns as he tries to recall this particular guest before shaking his head apologetically. "I'm sorry, but no one stood out to me. A lot of people wear hoodies this time of year."

"But not the actual hood. It was right at the end of our set. This guest—I couldn't see their face—came into my room and called me by name."

Dev's eyes widen. "They knew who you were?"

I nod. "I figured they were one of those online freaks. You know, the ones who are still obsessed with the deaths from last summer. But when I told them to move on, they alluded to something dangerous on the horizon."

"Like what?"

"They didn't go into detail, Dev. They just questioned Pineland's safety before moving into the next room."

That's when I see it. The minuscule waiver of faith in Dev's gaze. It glints over his midnight eyes like an eclipse, dark-ening them for a moment. And then, in the blink of an eye, the look is gone. But the damage has already been done.

My insides sink. If Dev doesn't believe me, who will?

"That was really uncool of them."

"Uncool?" I snip. "I'd say it's a lot more than that. It's threatening."

His brow furrows. "Did they threaten you?"

"Not exactly," I say, hurriedly continuing when I see the

seriousness of his expression start to dissipate, "but they tracked me down for a reason. They wanted to scare me!"

"And it looks like they succeeded." Dev's hand reaches for mine over the table. "Jeez, babe, I wish I had been there. That freak probably thought they were being funny."

"But how do they know where I work?"

"They're probably one of the regulars who go through the houses nonstop. The wig doesn't hide your face completely. If you know who you're looking for, it's not hard to find you."

"Is that supposed to comfort me?"

His head shakes. "Of course, not. I'm just trying to make sense of what probably happened. If they didn't have an exact threat or anything—"

"Uh-huh?"

"I think we should tell Hannah and ask for you to be moved for the final weekend. The closer we are to Halloween, the worse it'll get."

"So, you think we should tell Hannah and not the police?"

He sighs and another splinter pokes into my heart. "If there wasn't a concrete threat, I don't think there's anything you can report to HPD."

"Seriously?"

He offers me a pleading look. "Babe, I know you're not happy with how I'm responding—"

"Because I'm not."

"—but we've run into Captain Pierce's office a dozen times. If we keep going in there with every message you receive—"

"This message was delivered in person!"

"—they're not going to believe you for much longer."

"Dev."

"Gwen."

"Please," I insist, "this felt different."

He sighs with a helpless shrug. "Then we can report it. But

know that they might not take any future reports as seriously. Are you absolutely sure this is worth it?"

Before I can answer, his phone lights up on the table with a new text. We both catch sight of the name on the screen, our eyebrows raising in unison.

"Why is Jenna texting you?"

Jenna Thatcher. Our boss's daughter. Dev's ex-girlfriend. The accomplice of my ex-best-friend, Valerie. It's convoluted, but such is life in a small town. All I do know is that she has absolutely no business messaging my boyfriend.

Dev shrugs, clicking his screen off. I know he's trying to make me feel better by showing me the message doesn't matter to him, but I'd almost prefer it if he'd just read it aloud now. I'd rather know what she texted than pretend like she hadn't said anything at all.

"She probably forgot which piece we're supposed to rehearse for orchestra by Monday."

I frown. "Why not ask her stand partner?"

"I don't know, but why else would she message?"

"You tell me?" I sound more upset than I should be, but my frustration from our previous topic is running over.

"Gwen," Dev moans, his expression growing desperate as he pleads for me to get a grip. He's the only one brave enough to douse me with a dose of honesty, and normally, I appreciate it. "Please, you're spiraling."

I want to snap that I'm not, but we both know it would be a lie, and I've told enough white lies for one night.

"Can you blame me?" I mutter instead.

"No, I can't. You have every reason to be upset right now. What can I do to help?"

I stare at him blankly, at a total loss for words. I want to tell him to hold me. To help me convince the police nothing is okay. To quit with me. But none of that is going to get us anywhere, and so, all I do is let my shoulders rise and fall.

"Nothing? Are you sure?"

"Let's just get through Halloween and then we can be done with this park until next summer."

Dev clicks his tongue. "Or until Ms. Thatcher thinks we should stay open for the holidays, too."

"I'll tell her I'm hibernating."

"If that's the case, I'm hiding away with you."

At that idea, warmth returns to my cheeks. There's nothing I'd love more than to hole away with Dev and forget the outside world for months on end.

There's a long silence as we imagine what life would be like if we weren't stuck living here. It's not hard to allow our minds to wander with the possibilities. We are two months into our senior year. After graduation, the world is full of endless options for us to explore. I'm sure there are countless places Dev and I could find to hibernate together.

"I should go check on Weston," Dev says finally. "He's taking a while."

"Yeah, that's probably for the best."

Still, I don't miss how swiftly Dev tucks his phone into his back pocket as he slides out of the booth. He's trying to make a point that he doesn't care about Jenna's text, but I know his curiosity will get the best of him. He'll likely read the message on his way to Weston. Which means it'll be up to me to ask what it says.

"Everything's fine, babe," Dev says, seeing the worry on my face. "Don't let yourself go there."

He's too good at reading every thought that crosses my mind.

Not wanting to allow my anxiety to win, I release a shaky breath. "Sorry."

"You don't have any reason to apologize, Gwen," Dev assures me. "Everything is going to be okay. I promise. I'm going to make sure those freaks stay far away from you."

I want to believe him. I really do. But it's like I've lost control of my brain. It's easier to maintain a sense of reality when Dev is nearby, reminding me of the truth. But as I watch his retreating figure, it becomes difficult to ignore the whirlpool of terrifying thoughts swirling through my mind.

"Sit back and enjoy the show," echoes around my brain. What show? What if they aren't satisfied with simply scaring me? What if this is the freak to take things too far?

Our break ends before Dev and Weston return. I loiter around Crew HQ for as long as I can, clutching the now-luke-warm cocoa, but it's no use. I either need to return to my post or face the wrath of Hannah.

Texting Dev about heading back into the park, my lips purse when he doesn't immediately read the message. What could he possibly be doing?

Trying to convince myself that nothing is amiss, I trudge back through Pineland. I keep my head down with the hood of my cloak pulled over as far as possible, so none of the other weirdos in the park notice me while I'm alone.

With every nervous step, I remind myself there is likely a reasonable explanation for the entire situation. Perhaps Dev decided to take Weston to first aid after all. But that doesn't explain him not messaging me back. Why not keep me in the loop? He knows I'll be worried.

It feels well within my right to stew on the matter for the entirety of my final set. Sure, I pop out at guests and give them the scare of a lifetime, but my thoughts are far from the Witch's shed. I'm simply going through the motions and doing my job. The only thing placating me is coming up with a thousand-and-one possibilities as to what could be keeping my boyfriend from responding to me.

I want to believe this has nothing to do with Jenna. I can't let myself go there. An anxiety spiral is dangerous enough without intertwining a thread of jealousy. It's better to let that theory lie and not hurt my own feelings.

After the final guests exit the haunted house and all who remain are crew members with sore backs and throats, genuine panic sets in. Dev missed the rest of our shift. The boy starts sweating if he thinks we're going to be tardy at school, but now he can suddenly play hooky like it's nothing?

"Have you seen Dev Vishwakarma?" I ask the other crowd attendants as I hurry back toward Crew HQ.

"No," a girl named Alison grumbles bitterly.

"Dev left us to fend for ourselves all night," Evan, another crowd control crew member, adds with a roll of his eyes. "He's lucky if we don't report him to Hannah."

Hannah's reaction will seem saintly after mine.

I march into the atrium, blinking against the bright lights as I scan the room for any sign of my boyfriend. Nothing.

Unable to go much further in this horrifying costume, I hurry into the women's locker room to change into my street clothes.

Leaving the wig pinned to a mannequin head, I swiftly change into a black sweatsuit and sneakers. Not minding that my cropped hair is a mess from the wig, nor that my makeup is still ridiculous, I speed walk toward Wardrobe to return my costume. Tossing it into the dirty laundry bin, I turn and nearly run into the last girl I want to see.

"Whoa, someone's in a hurry."

Valerie Ross looks flawless despite working a late-night shift in a theme park. Her long black hair is still sleek and straight, her dark skin isn't oily, and her eyeliner isn't smudged. But that's just Valerie's way. She's always put-together. Even while ruining my life, she's managing it in a full face of makeup and her cutest fit.

After last summer's scandal, Wendy Thatcher thought it best for Valerie to remain out of sight of guests. The boss couldn't keep her own daughter employed and not also extend the same opportunity to her accomplice. Besides, Wendy didn't want Valerie's talents to go underutilized, because wouldn't it be a waste to not ignore our town's greatest actress? Valerie's spending the season as "Polly," the mascot dolly in the haunted house themed to be a creepy, life-sized dollhouse, aptly titled, *Play With Us.*

Ironically, Valerie is the last girl I want to play with. Not anymore.

"Happy to go home," I bite back.

"Since when?"

I frown at the girl. She lost the right to act like she understands me after she pretended to be kidnapped and then proceeded to bribe me into helping others believe her story. We are never going to be the same after that. Cordial, maybe. Friends, never.

I spare her an eye roll and pray she'll take the hint.

But once I slip past her, she calls after me. "I heard you were looking for your boyfriend."

Grinding my teeth, I turn back around to face the girl who used to know me better than anyone. She still knows me well enough, I guess. I mean, she knew what to say to capture my attention. "Have you seen him?"

"When I was on break, I saw him head toward the parking lot."

"With Weston?"

Valerie shakes her head. "Nope. He was with Jenna."

CHAPTER
THREE

Despite my better judgment, I accept a ride from Valerie.

What else am I supposed to do? It's midnight and my normal ride is missing in action. Dev left me no choice but to find a ride or walk home. My mind was made up as soon as I could see my breath. I'd freeze before making it back to my house.

I numbly climb into the back seat of Valerie's beat-up sedan while she chit chats with her new girlfriend, Milly Dillard. It's a miracle I even fit back here, seeing as the seat is littered with seemingly every possession Valerie has ever owned. The used car was acquired after our friendship ended. Frankly, I'm shocked Valerie's father permitted her to purchase a car after she ran away a few months ago. It must be a test.

I snap back to attention when the girls lean over the center console to gape back at me.

"So," Milly begins, flicking one of her purple braids over her shoulder, "it's been a minute, Gwen."

"Uh-huh."

Valerie says nothing, allowing her girlfriend to navigate these treacherous waters.

Milly clicks her tongue. "Why do you think your boyfriend left the park with his ex-girlfriend?"

My eyes narrow. "Oh, so we're hopping right to it. No 'how have you been?' or 'have you decided what schools you're applying for yet?'"

Milly breathes out a laugh. "Do you want me to ask those questions?"

"No."

"That's what we thought."

We. Valerie and I used to be a "we." Now, she's no more than a stranger behind the steering wheel. It's scary how fast you can go from sharing every bit of your life with a person to nothing at all.

Still, Valerie must remember some things about me because she turns her key in the ignition, bringing the car to a rumbling start and this awkward conversation to a close. There's a part of me that resents her for knowing how to save me from this uncomfortable discussion. I don't like that she knows I need saving at all. But that's the consequence of sharing yourself with another. There's a chance they'll never forget how you tick.

We pull out of the glowing Pineland parking lot, tires crunching over gravel as Valerie steers us toward the exit. I pathetically search the lot for Dev's truck, hating that its disappearance confirms a portion of Valerie's story.

Did he really leave with Jenna? Why wouldn't he say anything? Where did they go? What are they doing?

A whole new thread of anxiety has wound itself around my mind, twisting alongside my earlier fears of murder-fanatics and their ominous threats. I'm not sure how much of this my head can take before it combusts.

We fall into silence, allowing the pop radio playing softly through the speakers to fill the car ride. We leave Pineland behind as Valerie steers toward town. In the intermittent glow of the streetlights, I catch her eyeing me in the rearview mirror. Shifting myself toward the window, I pointedly avert my gaze.

Dev isn't cheating on me—of that, I am confident. He would never. Could never. The boy is way too honorable and honest for that. But then why not tell me where he's going? All this could be cleared up with a simple text explaining why he left me stranded at Pineland. He should know I'd realize something was wrong when he wasn't present to drive me home. It's not like his absence would go unnoticed.

None of his actions this evening is representative of the Dev I know. Or the Dev I *think* I know. My hands run down my face, like they'll scrub that terrifying notion away.

Suddenly, the car lurches toward the left as Valerie dramatically turns.

"Babe?" Milly asks as we career toward Pineland's sister water park, Wetlands.

Valerie doesn't have to explain herself though. We all can see Dev's truck haphazardly parked between two spaces in the middle of the lot.

The pit in my stomach doubles in size. Why the hell is he here?

Valerie stops next to the empty truck. Throwing her car into park, she fully turns to look back at me, making it abundantly clear I'm the playmaker.

"Do you want to go find them?"

Fidgeting with my ring again, I study the shadowy water park with its sloping slides and water tower centerpiece. After Wendy Thatcher bought Pineland and merged the once-competing parks into one entity, I've grown to appreciate the wide variety of free admission offerings for crew members. Now, I'm on the brink of swearing off water slides for good.

"Park's closed for the season," Milly says, earning blank stares from both Valerie and me.

Like a closed sign has ever stopped us before.

Valerie turns back to me, raising her eyebrows in question.

"Yeah," I confirm, even though she already knew the answer. "Let's see what they're doing in there."

My ex-best friend offers me a wicked grin before yanking her key from the ignition. There's nothing Valerie loves more than finding trouble. Lucky for her (and unlucky for the rest of us), she has quite the knack for it.

We slink through the parking lot, toward the front entrance of the park. It's no secret countless security cameras cover every inch of this place. There may not be a security guard on the premises, but one is definitely watching the feeds from the park across the street.

"We're seriously going to hop the gate?" Milly asks, likely thinking about her father who is in the middle of campaigning for reelection as mayor of Hathaway.

She's already on thin ice after aiding and abetting Valerie's crew over the summer. Milly Dillard might not have been an inner member, but that didn't absolve her from tampering with security logs and cameras. Needless to say, Wendy Thatcher moved Milly's job out of the security department and into a less-risky team—costuming. It was a mercy Ms. Thatcher had to extend, especially after the park president didn't fire her own daughter from committing murder in the park. Sure, it was technically self-defense, but it was then preceded with the covering up of multiple other murders.

"We're going to walk right through the front entrance," Valerie corrects her girlfriend, gesturing toward the already-open security gate meant to cover the main entrance turnstiles.

Apparently, Jenna Thatcher has a key.

I'm already preparing a list of excuses should we be caught.

"We were worried about Dev and Jenna, so we went in after them."

"We didn't think to call the cops because we assumed the daughter of Wendy Thatcher had permission to be in Wetlands after it closed."

It shouldn't be this easy to explain away extremely out-of-line actions, but around here, you take what little wins you can.

One by one, we slip through the opened gate, all putting on our best concerned expressions for the cameras.

"We won't have long before security calls this in," I mutter as we hop over the turnstiles and enter the park.

"I doubt anyone was called before we got here," Valerie remarks dryly. No one in security is going to tattletale on the boss's daughter for sneaking into a closed park.

Milly rubs her arms as a chilly breeze blows past us. "Let's make this quick."

Forget the horrors of Hauntland. I can't think of many places creepier than a shuttered water park in late October. Bulky towers of inner tubes hide beneath dark tarps. Chaise lounges are stacked preciously high, as well. Everything feels like it could topple over and crush you without warning.

We cross a wooden bridge over the lazy river, which is drained for the season. Everywhere there should be water is dry, leaving empty cement basins filled with fallen debris. I'm immediately reminded of a skate park.

We wander deeper into the park without any real aim. The walkways bask in a white glow from the floodlights. The further we trek, the worse I begin to feel.

Where are they?

Suddenly, we all come to a halt, our ears pricking at a sound coming from the distance. Listening closely, I realize it's the soft cries of a girl. *Jenna.*

"Wave pool," I mouth to the girls, already heading toward the attraction at the heart of the park.

"Gwen," Valerie hisses after me, but I don't stop my pursuit of the sound. I have to know what's making Jenna cry. Is it Dev? What did he do?

Fear pulses through me as I sprint past artificial palm trees and shadowy water slides. Finally, just as a stitch is beginning to plague my side, I crash into the clearing.

Resting far below Wetlands' iconic water tower is a wave pool. Like everywhere else, the pool is completely drained, leaving an enormous cement pit. The far side of the basin is lined with fake cattails and tall grass. Nearest us, a persistent puddle of muddy rainwater stands near where the pool levels into a zero-depth entry. A few feet of cement walkway turns into a large sandy bank that's missing its fleet of lounge chairs.

A single work light illuminates the scene in a hazy, white glow. My boyfriend and his ex stand where sand meets cement, his arm around her shoulder. Jenna cries into his chest.

At what? They broke up months ago. Why did they need to come here to hash it out?

Neither seems to have noticed my presence, and suddenly, I'm embarrassed to interrupt them. This feels like far too intimate of a moment for me to crash.

No, it's not. Dev is your boyfriend. You deserve to be in the loop.

My sneakers sink into the soft sand, and before I can change my mind, I call, "Um, what's going on here?"

My voice makes them jerk away from each other, earning me a better view of the wave pool. Immediately, my lips part as I take in the horrible sight before me.

The dark puddle isn't rainwater.

It's blood.

CHAPTER
FOUR

THE BODY LIES face-down at the edge of the wave pool. Blood pools around a deep head wound and a small handgun is within reach of her awkwardly contorted arms.

"Gwen," I hear Dev call, but his voice is muted as I struggle to stay on my feet, "please look away."

I want nothing more than to comply, but my eyes refuse to cooperate. All I see is blood. Blood and a gun. The first I've seen far too many times. The latter is a new nightmare unlocked. My skin starts to itch as a thousand imaginary spiders dance up my arms and legs. It's a sensation that's haunted me ever since I found Chase dead on top of the Old Wheel in Pineland.

Behind me, there's a scream.

"What the hell?" Milly cries, falling to her knees in the sand.

Valerie drops to grab her. "Who is that?"

Unable to see the body's face, I take in the mass of long-and-frizzy chestnut curls that are matted with blood, and realize this girl isn't from Hathaway. I'd remember anyone with that much hair. It's not hard to stand out in a small town.

But it doesn't matter where she's from.

What matters is that she's dead.

She's dead—and somehow—Dev and Jenna knew.

"Gwen!"

At this, my eyes finally snap away from the body and onto the boy I considered my biggest ally. His face is slack with terror as tears trickle down his cheeks. He stumbles toward me, flinching when I take a step back.

"It's not what it looks like."

My mouth is still too dry to speak, so Valerie takes the liberty to do it for me. "Then tell us what we're looking at!" She scrambles to retrieve her phone. "I'm calling the cops!"

"Wait!" Jenna cries from the shoreline.

"Excuse me?" Milly demands.

Jenna turns away from the body, wiping tears from her face. "We all need to just wait a minute."

"Sure we do," Valerie scoffs. "I turn eighteen in two weeks. Like hell am I getting caught up in whatever you two did."

"We didn't do anything!" Dev insists, not taking his eyes off me. "I swear."

"Then why are you here?" I ask desperately. "With *her*?"

Dev falters, and I see him glance at Jenna from the corner of my eye. There's a long, horrible pause before he finally mutters, "Just an inkling."

And there it is. An actual lie between us. I hope the words taste like a rotten candy apple on his tongue.

Disappointment plunges deep into my heart. I trusted Dev to be the one person who'd never lie to me in a town full of deceit.

How could he?

He's keeping a secret for Jenna. Is it criminal? Knowing that girl, nothing is too far-fetched.

"Why don't you want to call the cops?" Valerie presses Jenna when it's obvious we won't glean any valuable information from Dev.

"Because what if someone is trying to set us up!" Jenna gestures wildly toward the body. "She was here when we arrived!"

"And you arrived at a closed water park in the middle of October because…"

"Because it's none of your business, Valerie!"

"Fine." Valerie's phone illuminates as she begins to dial. "It can be the police's business."

"Wait!" Jenna takes a frantic step toward Valerie, whose thumb still hovers over the screen, daring anyone to give her a reason to complete the call. Jenna's hands are raised, as if she's approaching a live bomb. "Just think for a second. We're all here. We all found the body."

Valerie actually barks out a laugh. "Don't try to rope us into this!"

"I'm just stating a fact," Jenna continues, still cautiously approaching with her hands up. "Whether you like it or not, the five of us are at the scene of the crime. Again."

"How do we know it's a crime?" I sputter. "This looks self-inflicted."

Jenna has the audacity to roll her eyes. "Lesson one in getting away with murder is making it look self-inflicted."

"You would know, wouldn't you?" Valerie snaps back.

Jenna might have killed Luca Mendes, the real murderer behind the other three headline-making deaths at Pineland, but she only fessed up after she was thrown under the bus by her accomplice, Valerie.

I hate how I'm already growing numb to the presence of a dead stranger. What does that say about me?

A lot, unfortunately. This is unlucky Body #3 for me, and I've grown accustomed to the sight of them. Hardened. Emotionless. Perhaps it's the adrenaline keeping my wits about me, and once I'm at home in solitude, I'll crumble.

"We're about to graduate," Milly reminds us of the obvious. "We can't keep secrets from the authorities anymore.

There are scary, real-life consequences if we do. After last summer, I thought we all understood that."

Before I can consider Milly's warning, a far-more terrifying thought enters my brain.

A stranger sought me out during my shift and all-but-prophesied that something bad was going to happen very, very soon. Is this it? The show I was supposed to sit back and watch.

And I said nothing. The one time I exercised self-restraint and didn't run straight to the police. Now, there's a body in the middle of the wave pool.

There's nothing you could have done. You didn't have enough information to be of any use.

But I knew something. What if it was the missing piece the Hathaway Police Department needed to stop this from happening?

What are they going to do to me when they find out I didn't report this straight away? Will I get in trouble?

Get a grip. Someone is dead. That's the real issue at hand.

"Enough." Dev finally finds his voice. He drags his phone from his pocket and dials three numbers. "We have nothing to hide. This person probably has people wondering where they are."

Another dagger to the heart. Their poor family.

"And we're sure we don't know them?" Despite my better judgment, I glance over to the body. A part of me wants to investigate for myself, but Dev grabs my hand and keeps me in place.

"We're sure." His midnight eyes meet mine, imploring me to believe him. "You don't want to go over there. Trust me."

Trust him. The liar.

Stop spiraling. This is Dev. He's the most stable person I know. There must be a reason he ditched me without warning, but before I can plead with him to explain, I hear an officer answer his call.

"Hathaway Police Department, please state the nature of your emergency."

Dev spares all of us a glance, giving anyone a final opportunity to speak up.

Everyone holds their peace.

"My name is Dev Vishwakarma. I'm currently in Wetlands and there's a dead body here."

This is met with a long pause. Finally, the voice on the other line remembers their training. "Officers have been dispatched to your location. Are you secure?"

"Yes," he speaks for us. "We're safe."

Are we? Another strange death has occurred, and someone tracked me down to warn me it would happen. Nothing about this scenario seems safe.

Lost in my thoughts, I miss what the operator says next, but Dev is ensuring them we'll remain where we are as long as the status quo remains the same.

Sirens begin to wail in the distance. A perk of a small town. Help is never far away.

Although, *help* is rather subjective when one considers how long it took Hathaway Police to figure out what was going on last summer. Not that I can blame them much, when half of the pieces to the puzzle were held out of reach by every female still alive in this water park.

Dev was all I had left. The only one who never lied.

Now, the only person in the vicinity who has never lied to me is the dead body lying in the wave pool.

CHAPTER
FIVE

THE WORST PART of going to the police station is that they call your folks. It's pretty hard to explain to your panicked parents that you're not under arrest but were simply a witness at the scene of the crime, which just so happened to be a locked-up water park. It's even harder when the cops attempt to explain all this on your behalf.

Maybe most parents are understanding when on the receiving end of that sort of call. Mine? I'm confident they spent the seven-minute car ride to the station plotting ways that'll teach me to stay out of trouble. It's a shame they'll never realize I learned it from them.

But when Jonah and Sally Gardner march into the station and their furious expressions are not directed at me, I realize I'm not the one in for it tonight. It's the poor officers of the Hathaway Police Department.

This newfound family-first mentality continues to take me by surprise. If my younger brother, Gil, wasn't sleeping over at a friend's house, I'm sure my folks would've dragged him along to the station with them. The Gardeners are a united front now. Not just for appearances sake, but behind closed doors, too.

A year ago, I'd be grounded for a semester if I wound up at the station. But after I endured a supposed-serial killer sliding into my DMs, their priorities reconfigured. So, while I wouldn't wish my parents' wrath on anyone, it's sort of nice to have them on my side.

My mom flicks the bangs of her bottle-blonde bob out of her eyes as she stomps straight to the officer sitting behind the counter. "It's about time you took my daughter's tips seriously."

"Mom," I stop her from my seat in the waiting room. I appreciate my mother's belief in me but now is not the time to demand a written apology from the police.

My folks protectively settle into wooden chairs on either side of Dev and me. His parents are away in Columbus for an education conference this weekend. They had to call Mr. and Mrs. Vishwakarma for their approval before collecting Dev's statement unchaperoned.

The cops are interviewing us separately. They started with Jenna, whose mother was called first, seeing as it was her water park. Milly followed shortly after, her head low as she trailed behind her furious father. My folks sniffed in disgust at the mayor's inappropriate priorities. I guess he shouldn't count on their votes.

Valerie is next. No surprise there. After being at the center of the park's last scandalous death, it's best to get her statement taken down as soon as possible. When her single father arrived at the station, he offered my family a curt nod before finding a seat on the other side of the room with his daughter. He's well aware of where Valerie and I stand.

When Dev finally returns from his interview, he appears more at ease than when he went in. We pass closely as we switch places.

"Were the cops lucky enough to get the whole story out of you?" I snip.

The worry returns to his face. "I'll wait out here for you."

"Will you?"

"Please, Gwen—I'll explain everything."

I don't have time to make any further snide remarks before my parents and I are ushered into the small interrogation room in the back of the station. It's a real shame how familiar this setting is starting to feel.

"I thought we'd seen the last of each other, Miss Gardner," says the middle-aged man with a bushy, brown mustache on the other side of the heavy metal table.

"It's good to see you, too, Detective Weegan," I return. "Though I didn't expect either of us to be back here so soon."

Detective Weegan works in Ann Arbor and is only called in to support extremely demanding investigations. I wonder how long he's been in town. Did he drive over after we called in the body or was he already here?

His presence means we're dealing with something far worse than initially expected. Or perhaps, Hathaway Police wants to get ahead of the potential matter now, instead of waiting for things to get worse.

Beside him, sits Captain Nora Pierce of HPD. After arresting her then-boyfriend and former owner of Pineland for approving a deadly marketing scheme to sell more theme park tickets, the Captain's hair is more silver than black. The bags under her eyes appear to have become a permanent feature. I can't imagine she's thrilled to be investigating yet another death at a Hathaway tourist trap.

"Captain Pierce," my parents greet her tersely.

"Good evening, Gardners," she begins. "Thank you for staying with us so late."

I don't need to glance over at my parents to know what they're thinking. The Gardeners are quite familiar with being shoved to the back of the line. Though, in this case, not being the most-pertinent interview might be more of a blessing than a curse.

"How are you doing?" The captain directs this at me.

After a long pause, I answer honestly. "Not well."

"It's natural to seize-up when faced with an upsetting situation. You, specifically, have already witnessed so much for a girl your age."

"She has," my mother curtly answers for me.

"Gwen," Detective Weegan prompts, "if you're ready, can you detail your account of what occurred tonight?"

I'm ready to get out of the station, so I cooperate. "Sure, though it's probably pretty similar to what you heard from Valerie and Milly. At least, I hope it is."

The detective raises his eyebrows at me. I respond to the gesture with a small shrug. We both know those two girls have a track record.

"Dev was supposed to drive me home from my shift at Hauntland," I explain, "but he wasn't around at the end of the night."

I feel my parents twitch on either side of me, disappointed by this revelation. In their eyes, Dev Vishwakarma is the poster child for a Hathaway youth. Bright, honorable, and loyal. Ditching their daughter without a ride home is going to dock him a few points, but Dev did it to himself.

"That's when Valerie mentioned she saw him leave with Jenna."

"And how did you know they went to Wetlands?"

"When driving home, we spotted Dev's truck in the parking lot and wanted to make sure everything was okay."

"So, you three chose to enter the closed water park?"

"That sounds like an accusation," Dad pipes up. "Do I need to call a lawyer?"

Captain Pierce leans back in her seat and crosses her arms. "Wendy Thatcher is not pressing charges."

"I should hope not," my mother barks. "A body was found in *her* park. Her team should have found it, not these kids."

"For the record," the detective points out, "Wetlands and Pineland now have state-of-the-art video surveillance."

"And yet, no one noticed a body?"

"There was a temporary issue with Wetlands' feed thanks to a storm that rolled through a few nights ago. Wendy Thatcher was waiting on repairs."

"Convenient."

The captain clears her throat before changing the direction of the conversation. "Are you aware as to why Mr. Vishwakarma and Ms. Thatcher went into Wetlands in the first place? Did something or someone tip them off?"

"Nope," I say with a cynical pop of my lips. "I don't know what made them go into the park."

Captain Pierce leans over the table. "Gwendolyn, are you still receiving unsavory messages?"

The air in the room suddenly grows still and I realize this is the question they've been waiting to ask.

"No, I deleted my social media after you asked me to stop filing unnecessary police reports."

To her credit, the woman doesn't waver. "We still asked for you to share any seemingly credible threats."

I shrug, waiting for the next question.

"So, there aren't any messages we should know about?" She sounds almost exasperated at having to ask the question.

My mind races back to the stranger who tracked me down. If I share now—in front of my parents—they'll make me quit working the event. It's the best paying job in town. Even if I'm lucky enough to be accepted into college, I still need to be able to afford it.

But I don't want to be a liar anymore. I can't have the guilt eating me away. There's already so little of me left after last summer.

And so, despite the consequences, I reveal everything about my earlier encounter at work, not withholding a single detail. I don't hesitate when I feel my parents tense up on either side of me. The truth matters too much. I know that now. I just wish everyone else in my life did, too.

The pair across the table take diligent notes, but their faces remain unreadable.

"I'm sorry for not saying anything sooner," I conclude, meaning every word of the apology. "I figured it was another hoax and didn't want to cry wolf again."

Every adult in the room stiffens.

After clearing her throat, Captain Pierce finally says, "You have nothing to apologize for, Gwendolyn. The tip wouldn't have pointed us to Wetlands."

But my parents are still caught up on the concerning detail of someone finding me at work.

Dad is practically shaking with frustration. "What are you two going to do to keep this stalker from further harassing my daughter?"

This takes me by surprise. I risk glancing at my father out of the corner of my eye. It doesn't sound like they're making me quit my job to hole up inside the house forever. Suddenly, I don't dare to even breathe, like any movement might return my parents' senses.

"Our daughter has endured enough," my mother says, protectively gripping my arm. "She's a senior in high school. It's not fair for her to hide away because she cannot trust the people in this town to keep her safe."

Now *that* I didn't see coming.

"I can assure you," Captain Pierce says firmly, "your daughter's safety is of our utmost priority."

"Then prove it, Nora," my father challenges her.

In awe, I gape at the adults in the room. Maybe I should try telling the truth more often, and if I'm lucky, perhaps my boyfriend will feel inspired to do the same.

CHAPTER
SIX

Dev is the only one still lingering around the waiting room.

At the sight of me, he jumps to his feet. "Gwen, is it okay if I drive you home?"

"Now you're available to drive her?" Jonah Gardner pointedly interjects, his eyes narrowing at the boy who lives a few doors down. Never once has Dev disappointed my parents. Not until now.

Dev's shoulders droop as he nods meekly. "I couldn't be more ashamed of my actions tonight. If it's okay with you both, and Gwen, of course, I'd love to explain them to her first."

My parents direct their attention to me, making it clear this is my decision.

Still getting used to this kind of autonomy, I shrug indecisively. I want to hear Dev's side of the story, but only if it's the truth.

Leading the group out of the station and into the dead of night, a shiver works its way through my limbs. Silently cursing the windchill, I pull the sleeves of my sweatshirt over my hands.

When we reach our cars, I find Dev's eyes trained on me,

watching my every move like a hawk. When he realizes he has my attention, his expression turns to a pleading one.

Please, his eyes read. *Give me the chance to explain.*

I do want to know. Maybe whatever I hear will be enough to put my mind at ease. Life was just finding its rhythm. I don't want everything to go downhill again. Especially not with him.

"See you two at home," I say to my folks. "Thanks for being so understanding back there. And now, too."

My parents pull me into their arms. Another thing I'm having to get used to—group hugs. We seem to do them all the time now.

Mom tucks a lock of my dark brown hair behind my ear, but the cropped strand slips right back to my cheek. "You're kind to hear the boy out."

"We'll wait up for you." The promise makes my father's voice crack, and I only squeeze them tighter before finally stepping back.

Dev's shoulders rise and fall with relief as he dashes ahead of me to open the passenger door. He extends his hand out for me—and although I don't want to take it—we both know it requires two people to hoist me into his unnecessarily-tall truck.

After seeing that I'm settled, he carefully closes the door beside me. I wish I could fault him for being so polite because he knows he's in the doghouse, but this is Dev's usual demeanor. It's one of the many reasons I finally succumbed to my feelings for him, after resisting his affection for months. Dev is the best guy in Hathaway. I hope nothing more than to go to bed tonight still believing that to be true.

Outside the vehicle, I hear him thank my parents for still trusting him and promising he won't ever let them down again. My father's response is too quiet for me to catch.

Judging by how fast Dev is behind the wheel, the boy sprinted around the back of his car to join me inside.

Fumbling to fit his key into the ignition, he backs out of the parking spot before clearing his throat uncomfortably. He got me into his truck. Now comes the hard part. It's time to explain what on earth he was doing with Jenna Thatcher and a dead body in the middle of Wetlands.

I refuse to budge on my silence. He's the one who needs start the talking—and it's not like we have a lengthy drive for him to take advantage of. My position is clear as I shift to stare out the window, taking in the sleepy town we've never left. The people of Hathaway have no idea they'll wake up to another crime scene in the morning.

Hot air blows from the vents, making the evergreen-scented air freshener I strung around his rearview mirror smell even stronger.

"Listen, Gwen, I know you're pissed."

I confirm this with my continued silence.

"But there is an honest explanation for everything, I swear. Everything."

"Let's hear this honest explanation," I bite back.

His jaw clicks but there isn't time to mince words. We're already halfway through town and nearing the neigh-borhoods.

"Jenna pulled me aside during our break. I guess the same freak who taunted you said something to her, too."

"They did?" I gasp. "What did they say?"

"The same thing they said to you. Some ominous line about something bad happening and to enjoy the show."

I bristle. "And you took her concerns more seriously than mine?"

Expecting this, Dev sighs. "No. I tried to comfort her with the reminder that this was likely a troll, but I guess she heard they were having issues with the security cameras at Wetlands. She was going to check things out with or without me. I figured it would be better for her to not go alone."

Chewing the insides of my cheeks, I hate how I can't argue

this. No matter how much I might have liked for him to tell Jenna she's on her own, Dev's moral compass is one of the many reasons I adore him.

So I pivot and ask, "Why not call her mom? Or security? Or the cops?"

His grip on the steering wheel tightens as he scoffs. "Because they've taken your reports so seriously in the past. Plus, if security didn't think a missing feed was a concern in the first place—"

"Captain Pierce and Detective Weegan took everything I said today very seriously," I curtly retort.

"That's a first." Dev's eyes cut to me. "You told them everything?"

"Everything."

He blows out a breath, returning his attention to the road. "I assume your parents are making you quit?"

"Surprisingly, no, but I'll explain that after you finish with your part." I'm not letting him move on so easily.

"Well, historically, Hathaway Police hasn't been too concerned with random hunches, and it's not like we broke into Wetlands assuming we'd find a body. Jenna just wanted to make sure everything was okay," Dev continues. "She feels like she owes it to her mom to make sure nothing bad happens. If Jenna had it her way, I bet her mother wouldn't have even been at the station tonight. It's better for the brand if Wendy isn't involved with this sort of thing."

"A dead body is pretty bad for the brand's image," I sarcastically agree.

For anywhere else, maybe. But not for Pineland. It's the reason we stay in business.

Dev simply shrugs at this, driving under the last stoplight in town and heading toward the quieter, residential side of Hathaway.

"And so…" I prompt, because I'm still waiting for Dev to explain why he ditched me without a word. I might adore his honor, but I still want him to articulate that he knew this decision would upset me. At the bottom of all this, that's my real issue.

"And so, she asked me to go with her."

"Why you?"

Dev glances at me helplessly, begging me to not make him say every little detail aloud. But I need to hear him admit it.

"Because she didn't want to go alone and she trusts me."

"You don't think she's still in love with you?"

Finally, I say the question that's been itching to escape my mouth since he and I started dating. Jenna only broke up with him to save him from being sucked into her illegal mess. Now that she's in the clear, who's to say she doesn't want him back?

"I understand why you would think that, but trust me, she's not. Like at all."

"And you know that because..."

"Because Jenna is as tired of Hathaway as you are."

My lips purse. I don't want to have more in common with Jenna Thatcher than I already do.

We fall silent again as we pass the wealthier neighborhoods nearest to town. Ample streetlights illuminate the roads and elegant, brick houses covered in ropes of ivy. It only gets darker from here on out.

I glance at my boyfriend to find his gaze also flicking over to me, anxiously anticipating my response.

"So, that's it?" I scoff. "Jenna asks you to go investigate something potentially dangerous with her and you just up and go without warning?"

His shoulders slunk helplessly, but he had to know I would be upset. Leaving me was uncool. Leaving me, without a word, to go play detective with his ex-girlfriend? Unacceptable.

If Valerie were here, I know exactly what she'd say.

"You don't deserve to put up with his antics. You broke your

rule of not dating Hathaway boys because Dev promised he was different. And now look—he's no better than the rest of them."

I shake her knowing voice from my head. This is Dev, the boy I grew up alongside. I've always known he was one of the good ones. The only reason I rejected his initial advances was because I was worried any sort of romantic relationship near graduation would wreck any chance I had of leaving Hathaway. Couples around here have the habit of sticking around, buying a house near their parents, having babies, and the cycle repeats.

I refuse to get stuck in that loop. Dev knows this. He swears it won't be our fate, and thus far, I've believed him.

We're good together because we push each other to examine different opinions. I no longer loathe our hometown, even if I have no intentions of remaining here my entire life. He used to talk about securing a job as a music teacher at Hathaway High. Now, he's plotting to take his talents as a cellist to a philharmonic in a grand city.

Apparently, challenges about determining our future should be the least of my worries. I never anticipated something like this would rock our relationship so early on. We've only been dating a few months. A simple "here's what's happening" text shouldn't slip his mind.

Turning into our neighborhood, Dev shakes his head guiltily. "I knew what I was doing was going to worry you, and I'm so sorry for that, Gwen. The plan was to skip a bit of our shift to pop over to Wetlands, then be back before anyone was the wiser. I was going to tell you everything afterwards. I knew if I told you beforehand, you'd get lost in an anxious spiral until I got back. I was trying to protect you from that."

I have no choice but to bite my tongue. He knows me too well.

Maneuvering down our cul-de-sac, we both stir, realizing our time to talk face-to-face is nearly up. There's no way a conversation like this gets better over the phone.

"You were being considerate until you never came back."

Clearly growing tired of my unrelenting tone, Dev cuts back, "Finding a dead body will kinda throw you off."

"Yeah, I'm sure you and Jenna are going to be trauma-bonded for life now." The horrible words slip out of my mouth before I can help myself.

This makes him snap. "Are you listening to yourself, Gwen? You're more focused on me and Jenna than the literal corpse we stumbled across. Do you not care that someone is dead? That I was the one to find them?"

My voice raises, too, as anger numbs my common sense. "It's pretty hard to be fazed by a dead body after literally falling on top of one in a Ferris Wheel."

"The only reason that happened is because you were so obsessed with hunting down the truth that you never stopped to think if the answers would be worth it."

My head rears back. "Not worth it? I was tricked into thinking a serial killer had kidnapped Valerie. What kind of person would I be if I didn't try to find her? But don't worry —I now know how stupid I was to believe those lies. The rest of the world won't let me forget it."

Dev pulls into my driveway without a word.

"And, of course, I care that someone is dead," I tack on. "It's awful, whether it was by their own hand or—"

He throws his truck into park. "*Or*? That was clearly self-inflicted. Probably one of those sad murder fanatics who took paying homage to the Pineland murders a little too far. One of their sick friends clearly knew and decided to use it as an opportunity to scare you and Jenna."

Between the stranger who visited me at work and the body at the bottom of the wave pool, these murder fanatics seem closer and closer every day.

I jump when the loud garage door croaks to life and my parents pull straight in. Climbing out of my dad's old car, they both offer Dev a wave before heading inside. The garage door is pointedly left open, making it abundantly clear that our time is up.

"Please, Gwen," Dev whispers. "Tonight was a series of disasters. Every decision I made was wrong and I have to live with that."

"So do I."

He winces. "And so do you. For that, I'm unbelievably sorry."

I glance over at him, my eyes suddenly wet. My thoughts are in pieces as I try to wade through my emotions.

When it's clear no words will leave my tongue, Dev's jaw clenches before he nods sadly. "I have no right to be frustrated."

"You witnessed something terrible tonight," I say, not wanting this conversation to end without acknowledging that reality. He has every reason to be emotional, too. "It's late. We're tired. We owe it to ourselves to stop this conversation before tonight can get any worse."

Dev nods with relief. Enough damage has been done. Sliding his hand across the center console, he hesitantly reaches for me. Soon, his warm fingers are woven in between mine, and he gently brings the back of my hand to his lips.

"Despite the odds." He peppers my hand with more kisses once he knows I won't pull away.

Neither of us have yet to profess the big, four-letter L-word to the other, but we've picked up the habit of saying this phrase in the interim. It's our reminder that despite everything that stood in our way, we still found our way here. Together. And so far, it's been worth it.

"Everything will be better in the morning," Dev assures the both of us.

This is another little lie. We both know that no part of tonight will simply blow over when the sun rises. There's a body to identify. A cause of death to discover. Trauma to unpack. Trust to rebuild. Promises to uphold.

"Goodnight, Dev," I murmur, petting the side of his face. He leans into my hand, allowing his eyelids to close. I'm instantly struck by how selfish I was earlier. Nothing that happened tonight was his fault. He tried to do what was right and got yelled at for it. Now, he has to go to sleep with a new horrifying image to haunt his dreams. As I shouted earlier, it's a feeling I unfortunately know all too well. "I'm sorry, too."

"We'll be better in the morning."

This isn't a lie. It's a guarantee. One I know both of us want to uphold.

Giving his hand a squeeze, I press my lips to the backside of his palm. "See you then."

Tomorrow is Sunday. We have the day off, and if I know us like I think I do, we'll be spending it making up for the foul turn tonight took.

"Race you there."

Finally untangling our hands, I pull myself away from my boyfriend and hop out of his truck. He waits in my driveway until I'm safely inside the garage. We exchange waves and blow kisses after the door starts lowering.

Everything will be better in the morning. Maybe if I repeat the little lie to myself enough, it'll manifest into a truth.

And then my phone vibrates.

Retrieving it from my pocket, my stomach sinks when I glance down at the screen.

I might not know how things will be in the morning, but apparently, the night is about to get a whole lot worse.

CHAPTER
SEVEN

THIS NIGHT IS NEVER ENDING. I'm running out of emotional bandwidth to handle every plot twist thrown in my direction.

Valerie must sense my hesitation because another message appears.

She's gonna have to wait. I have my parents to deal with first.

The garage enters straight into a tight kitchen with out-of-fashion brown cabinets and a white laminate countertop. My dad sits at the round table. Mom's busy at the counter, pouring steaming water from a kettle into a pair of mugs. Each is treated to a chamomile tea bag. That's a good sign. It means this conversation won't be long. Dad must be up for work at his laundromat in a few hours. He likes to launder the soiled costumes brought in from Pineland before opening the machines to the public. It's probably for the best that Gil is at a friend's tonight. We've all done our best to shield him from the onslaught of terrors our town experiences.

"Did you want a cup, hun?" Mom asks over her shoulder.

"No, thanks. The sooner this day ends, the better."

My father makes a grunt of agreement from the wooden table.

I'm still getting my bearings on this new relationship with my parents. It's grown a lot since last summer. We've always been brutally honest with each other, but now, it seems like we share the common goal of being honest for the sake of strengthening our family, not cutting it down.

However, the conversation ahead still feels like uncharted waters. I admitted to being stalked at work. Their perspective on the situation very well could've changed since leaving the station. Whether any of us want to admit it or not, I still need the paychecks from Pineland. We all know my parents want me to go to college, but taking out student loans is only going to hurt us as a whole. The less money I borrow, the better.

Not that you'll ever get into a good school with your grades plummeting downhill faster than the drop on Deciduous Divers.

I shake the anxious thought away. There are too many other relevant fears to plague my mind instead.

"About this weirdo who found me at work—"

My parents share a glance. I remember a time when they could barely stand to look at each other, let alone me.

"—and while I obviously don't like that they knew where to find me, there's a very good chance their vague threat has nothing to do with what happened at Wetlands."

Their eyes dart to each other again, and I hurriedly tack

on, "I swear, I'm not looking for trouble anymore, but I had to make sure Dev was okay."

"We understand why you ran into Wetlands," my mother says quietly, and I wonder if she's thinking of the reckless decisions she made for my father back when they were dating in high school. "Though, I do wish you and those girls had called the cops before going in."

She says "those girls" like one of them wasn't my dearest friend who practically used to live here. I don't think my folks will ever forgive Valerie for what she did to me, and I can't say I blame them.

"Don't worry," I mutter, "we are not friends again. Valerie was the one who offered me a ride home after..."

Both my parents nod, though they look anything but pleased.

Dad sets me with an intense state, and I realize this is the question with the most important answer. "You really believe it was a prank?"

So, there is a chance they will make me quit. Their attitudes back at the station were to twist the arms of the cops into taking me seriously. I should've known they would never actually let me clock back into a theme park that continues to threaten me.

But quitting feels like an act of letting my fears win. If I succumb to my anxiety, who knows what'll become of me. It already feels like there is so little of me left.

My parents are the type to let fear win. It's not an insult. In fact, it's likely the correct course of action in this situation. But I can't.

But I'm not going to lie to my parents, either. I'm past that.

"I can't be sure," I admit. "I really hope it was a prank, but Dev thinks they might have been a friend of the girl who died. I doubt I'll ever learn the truth. All I do know is that I don't want this stranger to win."

"Win?" my mother voices softly, clutching her mug.

I nod. "They wanted to scare me, and I'm embarrassed to say that it worked. But it's like you said at the station—it's not fair for me to hide away. I'm supposed to have my whole life ahead of me."

There's a long pause while they evaluate my words.

Finally, my father breaks the silence. "We trust your judgment on the situation."

I hate how his voice shakes, like he was braced for the worst. Rightfully so, I guess. The worst always seems to happen to the Gardners. So long as we stay in Hathaway, things won't be easy. I'm starting to realize it isn't for anyone who lives here. Though we may hide it well behind our forced smiles and fast-moving roller coasters, this town is cursed with misery.

Mom's head shakes at my father helplessly. "She's too young to constantly be exposed to this sort of thing."

"I turn eighteen in a few months."

Her attention snaps to me. "I'm forty-one, and I haven't seen half the stuff you have."

"I'm going to be okay," I insist. "I *am* okay."

This is the first genuine lie to slip out of my mouth all night. I'm not even on the same planet as "okay." But this is my new reality. The taunting, the trolls, and the night terrors. All I can hope is that they don't stick around for the rest of my life.

Dad inhales the final glugs of his tea, wincing as it burns down his throat. "Let the kid go to sleep, Sally. She needs it. We all do."

My mother still appears uncertain, but we both know my father has the final say in the matter. The conversation is done. We're moving on.

"That poor girl," Mom murmurs into her mug. It's clear she isn't talking about me. "She must have felt so lost and alone to do that to herself."

"That or she was a sick fanatic who thought her death would get herself added to the long list of theme park tragedies making the news."

"Jonah," she admonishes him. "Have a little respect for the dead."

"I don't respect anyone—living or dead—who traumatizes my daughter."

"I'm not traumatized."

Dad tosses me a skeptical look. "Sure, kid. Whatever you say."

"Will the both of you stop talking about trauma so late at night?" Mom intervenes. "It's going to keep me up."

Dad snorts. "You were planning on sleeping?"

Dumping the rest of her tea down the drain, Mom leaves her mug in the sink. "I'm going to try my best. As should the both of you."

Not having to be told twice, I dismiss myself from the kitchen. "Night. Love you both."

"We love you, too!" Mom calls after me as I hurry up the stairs. I'm still getting used to hearing that regularly from them. Not that I didn't think they loved me before, but now, we're all fully aware of how important it is to remind each other of it.

I take the steps two at a time, only to reach an abrupt stop at the top of the stairwell. Why am I hurrying to get on the phone with Valerie?

It's been very peaceful—healing—not having her as a key player in my life. It's like I'm finally free to walk my own path, not the one she deems best for me. As pathetic as it is to admit, I hadn't realized how much of my hopes and dreams weren't actually mine.

Sure, I still want to experience more of the world than just Hathaway. But my detest of this place isn't as concrete as once before. Maybe that's more to do with the current state of my household and my relationship with Dev, but it's hard to miss the timing of Valerie's disappearance. Things are just easier without her calling the shots.

And so, despite thinking I would eventually come to fully forgive Valerie's past transgressions, I realized it was better to keep her at arm's length. I'm far happier this way. And it's not like she hasn't found her own way without me. She's with Milly now and seems very content with the new attention that comes with dating a small-town influencer.

But I would be lying if I didn't acknowledge the crater she left in my heart. There's something irreplaceable about the friendship we shared. I'm not sure anything or anyone will ever compare.

It's that feeling that has me pulling out my phone and giving her a call as soon as I'm in the safety of my bedroom.

Valerie answers on the second ring. "Hey, I didn't think you would call."

"I said I would." The words come out stiff and cold, establishing a tone for this conversation. This isn't old times, and our chat won't be turning into a gossip session.

"Yeah, but I didn't think you'd actually do it."

"Fair."

There's a long pause where both of us try to determine who will talk first. Whether she likes it or not, it's going to be her.

"I just wanted to talk about tonight," she finally concedes. "Are you doing okay?"

"Uh," my forehead scrunches as I situate myself on my bright-blue bedspread, "as good as one can be after seeing their third dead body in like five months."

"That's valid."

Could this be any more awkward? It's like talking to an ex. I guess, in a way, that's exactly what she is. Not a romantic ex, but certainly a platonic one.

Leaning back against the headboard, I clear my throat. "How about you?"

"Yeah, all things considered."

"That's good."

"Uh-huh."

Another uncomfortable lull occurs. This is getting painful. I'm not sure how much more of this I can endure.

I begin, "Is there a reason—"

"I think they're lying," Valerie confesses at the same time.

Sitting back upright, the obvious question tumbles out of my mouth. "Who's lying?"

"Oh, if you weren't already thinking it—"

I immediately catch her meaning. "You think Dev and Jenna are lying?"

Another brief pause. "Uh-huh."

"What about?" The words stick to my tongue as my mouth grows dry.

"Maybe this wasn't a good idea."

"What do you think they're lying about, Valerie?" I ask firmly. I'm not playing games. It's been too long of a day, and our history is too messy.

She releases a sarcastic laugh. "Everything?"

My eyes squeeze shut as I slip down to rest my head against the pillow. Sure, my gut reaction was to also suspect Dev of masking the truth about how he wound up in Wetlands with Jenna Thatcher. But hearing Valerie make the same assumption is in no way comforting. She may make rash decisions and mistakes, but her intuition is rarely incorrect. If something is wrong, it's wrong.

And what sucks is that deep down, I know it, too. Dev's apologies may have sounded sincere, but it's obvious I'm missing something, and whatever it is, Dev doesn't want me to know.

"You okay, Gwen?"

I breathe out a helpless laugh. "No?"

I'm tired of having so many difficult conversations in my childhood bedroom. This is supposed to be my safe haven. A place where I play with toys found at garage sales, stay up too late reading library books, and learn how to braid my hair. But when I finally move out of this room, I fear all I'll remember are the nights I fell apart in here.

"Again, valid," she says. "I'm not asking you to believe me or to do something drastic."

"Then why bring it up at all?"

"Because I think you need to be careful."

The concern in her voice does anything but settle me. "Careful of what? We both know Dev isn't dangerous."

"But Jenna is."

"She killed Luca in self-defense," I remind Valerie, though I'm not sure why I'm defending Jenna. Probably because clearing her name means Dev is completely off the hook, too.

"Sure, but that doesn't take away the fact that she was capable of finishing the job."

"You don't think you could have?"

Valerie scoffs. "You really need to ask? Did you erase everything you know about me from your brain?"

"Sorry," I mutter, not sure why I'm the one apologizing.

"It takes a special kind of person to kill a stranger—let alone someone you know in real life."

"It's probably a lot easier when they are trying to kill you first."

"Maybe."

"So," I bring the conversation back to its main point, "what do you think they're lying about?"

"I'm not suggesting they killed that girl or anything, but they are 100% leaving something out of the story. Like sorry, you don't just waltz into Wetlands and stumble across the body of some rando."

Valerie has a point, unfortunately. This girl is a complete stranger to us. Pineland is a small enough park that it's easy to remember the faces of the frequent visitors. The superfans existed long before the murders ever happened. This girl isn't a local or a regular.

But the reason Dev and Jenna *waltzed* into Wetlands wasn't random. Jenna was visited by the same freak as me. They scared her so much that she went to check the park.

"You just went quiet," Valerie accuses me. "What do you know that I don't?"

I sigh. It's annoying how well she still knows me.

"It's fine if you want to keep secrets," she chirps casually. "Better you than me when the cops start asking questions."

Pinching the bridge of my nose, I exhale another deep breath before telling her about the person who visited me and Jenna at work.

"And for the record, I already told the police," I tack on once I'm finished.

After a long pause, Valerie finally says, "You're scarily honest now."

"I'm tired of lying."

"Most people don't want to lie," she points out. "But sometimes it's the only option."

I'm in no mood for this debate, so I guide us back toward the real matter at hand. "The point is that Jenna was freaked out and asked Dev to accompany her to Wetlands."

"And he dropped everything—including you—to do so?"

My lips pinch at the blatant disgust in her tone.

"Dev and I are working through that," is all I say. Valerie should not be in the business of giving relationship advice after her last suitor turned out to be a blood-thirsty murderer.

Mercifully, she takes the hint. "So, who's the freak that tracked you two down?"

"No clue."

"And who do we think the dead girl is?"

"Again, no clue."

Through the phone, I hear the telltale screech of wood on wood as Valerie yanks open the drawer of her bedside table.

She's probably reaching for one of her pens so she can click it while she thinks.

"My money is that one, or both, of our persons of interest are one of those weirdos who idolize Luca."

I hear the unmistakable sound of a pen clicking. My accurate prediction doesn't make me feel any better. It's impossible to forget everything about a person who's exited your life.

Just like it's hard for Dev to forget Jenna.

I go to fiddle with my ring, but it only makes me wonder if he ever gave her such a beautiful gift. So instead, I start gnawing on my inner cheek. Only when I start tasting blood do I snap out of my daze.

Valerie's still making predictions as her pen clicks away. "I bet the poor girl didn't even mean to die but danced a little too close to the sun for her own good."

"Yeah, I assume that's what the cops think, too. That this is a freak accident."

Valerie laughs at this. "You and I both know there's no such thing as freak accidents in Hathaway."

"But what if there is?" I hear myself ask, because deep down, I need this to be one big coincidence. If it's anything but, I fear I may fray away into a tangled mess.

Valerie scoffs at my naivety. "You start dating a Hathaway boy for a few months, and suddenly, you start believing in this place?"

"No, but I'm not thrusting myself at the center of every conspiracy theory," I bite back.

"Did that dead girl look imaginary to you, Gwen?" Valerie asks pointedly. "Because the blood looked pretty real to me."

"Looked like an accident," I firmly assert.

"That's what they want you to think."

"Are you the one who knows more than they're letting on?"

"Come on, Gwen."

"It wouldn't be the first time, Valerie."

"You've made your point," she snaps back, and I can tell our call—this night—is finally ending.

There's a small part of me that almost wishes it would go on for a little longer. For a moment there, it was sort of nice to speak with the girl I once considered my dearest friend. Like rediscovering a part of myself that ran away.

"And Gwen? I know you don't want to hear it, but someone needs to tell you to watch your back."

"Nothing bad is going to happen, Valerie. This isn't some elaborate plot about to spin out of control. Not this time."

I might not be 100% confident, but all I can hope is that by speaking it aloud, I'll manifest it to be the truth.

"You better hope you're right."

CHAPTER
EIGHT

DESPITE ENDING the night with an ominous phone call, a Jane Doe in the morgue, and a ridiculous number of questions, Sunday morning arrived with one answer. Though it came by way of a text message from the last girl I wanted to hear from moments after waking up.

VALERIE ROSS

thought you'd want to read this

It was followed by a link to an article from the local paper, the Hathaway Harold.

BODY OF TEEN GIRL FOUND AT LOCAL WATER PARK

HATHAWAY, Mi. — Hathaway Police Department is investigating a body discovered at Wetlands on Saturday night, October 24th. The body has been identified as sixteen-year-old Alice Crane of Tristan, Ohio. Crane was in town with her parents and twin brother to visit Hauntland, the inaugural Halloween event at the adjacent theme park, Pineland. The county coroner ruled the death as self-inflicted. However, local authorities plan to conduct a full investigation. This is a developing story.

Alice Crane.

Her name echoes around my mind, but no connection forms. A photo wasn't printed alongside the report, likely out of respect for her family. This isn't an obituary. Not yet, at least. It's a "developing story." I should be thankful our names weren't included.

It's not uncommon for out-of-towners to come into town for the weekend. Over the years, Hathaway has cemented itself as the cheapest-but-still-sort-of-nice getaway in the Midwest. Attractions and lodging aside, the colorful autumn leaves alone make the drive worth it. Dev likes to call the ruby-and-orange treetop display "better than any fireworks show." I wonder if he ever said this to Jenna's mother, because allegedly, the park president has an autumnal firework spectacular cooked up for the final night of Hauntland. Maybe that's where she got the idea.

I shake the uncomfortable thought from my mind, only for another to take its place.

Why is HPD still conducting a full investigation?

Probably at the insistence of Wendy Thatcher. Alice's death might have an explanation, but the owner likely wants to know how the girl broke into her water park in the first place. Security will need to be upped. Ms. Thatcher can't have something this horrible to become a habit.

I wonder how long it'll be before the media swarms our small town again. No one will want to be late to the story this time—if there is a story, that is. Bitter visions of Abigail Herron swirl through my head. I wonder how the reporter will ruin my life this time.

Another text from Valerie appears, snapping me back to reality.

Alice Crane sure doesn't sound like a girl who would care about Pineland's dark history. Is that why Valerie is giving me a rundown of her academic accomplishments? To prove something's off?

The ellipsis says everything Valerie doesn't want to type out.

I can practically hear her nagging voice in the back of my mind. *"You know who else is in the orchestra, Gwen? Ding, ding, ding! Dev and Jenna!"*

And those commonalities point right to my boyfriend.

Starting to feel queasy, I toss my phone to the foot of my bed and sink below the covers. How does this keep happening? I can't have the people I care about the most in this world mixed up with another deadly scandal. I barely survived last summer with my head still screwed on.

My sweet, honest Dev can't be involved. I cannot handle another betrayal of that magnitude.

And yet, one question pulls at the back of my mind, like a loose thread that threatens to unravel me entirely. *What if he is?*

Up until June, I thought I knew Valerie Ross.

What if I don't know Dev as well as I think, either?

What if he knows Alice?

What if he and Jenna—

Stop, I plead with my spiraling thoughts, begging them to not go any further. Dev told me why he went with Jenna. He's given me everything I need to know to believe him. But should I?

The answer might not be the correct one, but it's the one I need. *I have to believe Dev.* Thinking otherwise would be giving into my demons. I'm not letting my anxiety steal him from me, too.

When my phone vibrates near my toes, I groan loudly. That girl is tireless.

Throwing the covers off me, I nab my phone, fully prepared to tell Valerie to back off. I need her out of my head. She no longer has any sway on my thoughts and opinions. I'm better off reaching my own conclusions.

My brow furrows when it's not another text from Valerie, but an unknown number.

UNKNOWN

You thought that was the entire show?
Darling, it was only Act 1.

The hair on the back of my neck stands on end.

This message doesn't feel like any of the other threats I previously received before I deleted social media. Those were all vague, nonsensical messages from dumb trolls who have nothing better to do than bother a teenage girl for a momentary chuckle.

But this is neither vague nor nonsensical. It's the continuation of a conversation. One that I had with a stranger last night.

Who was that? What do they want?

I press the E-stop on every single one of my questions. I am *not* going down this path. This isn't any different from the messages online. It's just a freak who is taking advantage of the timing of Alice's death. They probably read the same article I just did.

But what if it's the same freak from last night?

I force myself to remember the exact advice I gave Valerie earlier. It's easier to find a connection when you're looking for one. I need to stop hunting for an explanation. It's only giving this person what they want. Attention and fear.

I'm no longer a desperate girl who makes rash decisions. I used to solve problems myself or run right to the cops. Now, I just block.

UNKNOWN

Don't bother blocking my number, Gwen Gardner.

Thumb hovering over the Block button, my mouth grows dry as I reread their message. It's like they know me—and that realization does nothing but piss me off. I'm so sick of being yanked around by the people who are supposed to look out for me.

GWEN GARDNER

You think you know me?

UNKNOWN

This isn't about you. It's about me.

GWEN GARDNER

Someone who is too afraid to send a text from their real name?

UNKNOWN

But where's the fun in that?

GWEN GARDNER

I'm not playing games.

UNKNOWN

This isn't a game, Gwen.

I disagree. This definitely seems like a game and I'm starting to feel like a toy. After last summer, I made a promise to myself that I would never be a pawn ever again.

Next?

Alice was killed… apparently, by someone I know.

A chill shoots up my spine. This can't be happening again.

I have to tell someone. This isn't a hoax or a joke. I'm not making irrational leaps. This person killed Alice Crane and staged it to look like she took her own life. They're planning to kill again.

Halloween. My mouth grows dry. That's six days from now.

As the back of my neck begins to prickle, I'm suddenly overcome with the horrible sensation that I'm being watched. The blinds may be closed, but they're doing a poor job of keeping the pale light from illuminating my room. I don't have to open them to know it'll be another gray day in the Midwest.

This unknown contact might not be literally watching me. No, the circumstances are far more serious than that.

They're in my head. This monster doesn't just know me. They know me *well*. There are few things more powerful than being understood so intimately. Usually, it's a comfort. Now, I can't think of anything more terrifying.

Before I can think of anything brave to say back, they text again.

It's said with such finality that I understand if I were to say something back, I wouldn't receive a response. They've made it perfectly clear I have absolutely no control over the situation. The only move I have is what I do next.

Do I inform HPD and endanger their next victim? Or do I try to find their identity and turn them in before they can hurt anyone else?

Either way, someone I know might die. Hathaway is a small town. It could be anyone. My parents. My little brother, Gil. Dev. A crew member at the park. A classmate.

What's worse—this unknown messenger has effectively given me nothing to worth with. There are no clues to decipher or hints at who might be their next target. I mean, the first one was a complete stranger.

What am I supposed to do?

The answer that pops into my head first isn't the right one and I know it. What I should be doing is reporting this to the cops. They can try to find the messenger—although, if they're good enough to disguise a homicide, they're probably smart enough to use a throwaway phone.

Curses fill my thoughts. Am I really going to do this? Try to hunt down another killer? I didn't exactly knock it out of the park last time.

But what choice do I have? This isn't Valerie masquerading as Ride or Die in an attempt to sell more theme park tickets. This murderer doesn't have any obvious cause.

They just want to kill—and to have a little fun while they do it.

In the end, the best choice is clear. I don't have the luxury of taking my time to decide what to do. Halloween is only a few days away.

Before I can further waver, I unlock my phone and type out a response.

GWEN GARDNER

Game on.

CHAPTER
NINE

WHEN I ASK Dev to meet me at the pizza parlor in town, he responds almost immediately.

I immediately feel guilty for being hesitant to accept the ride. At my core, I know Dev isn't violent. But if I learned anything from last summer, it's that the people you know best can surprise you in some truly horrible ways.

Still, I shouldn't push away the only person I can sort-of trust in this town, so I accept the offer.

His truck is pulling into my driveway a few minutes later.

"That was quick," I remark as he helps me climb into the passenger seat.

His shoulders shrug with relief. "I'm just glad you want to see me."

Chewing the inside of my cheek, I buckle my seatbelt as Dev hurries to the driver's side. I need to keep my head screwed on straight. Snap judgements and fear-fueled assumptions are a surefire way to alienate the kindest person in my life.

I'm confident it will be easy for Dev to clear his name from the list of people I know who might be the murderer. Then we can start working together to catch this freak. The clock is already ticking, and I'm going to need all the help I can get. As soon as we find the human on the other side of the phone, their identity will be reported to the cops, and they'll have no choice but to face the horrible consequences of their actions.

The comforting heat blowing from the vents helps settle me down. I hoped I'd be warm enough in my ivy-green sweatsuit, but the lack of sunlight is doing me no favors. Noticing my shiver, Dev twists a knob on the dash and increases the blow.

"I take it you slept as little as I did?" he asks, backing out of the driveway.

"Less, probably."

A breathy laugh escapes his lips. "That's quite the feat. I'm sorry you didn't sleep well."

I shrug. "I'm not sure any of us could expect to get a full eight hours after what happened."

He responds to this with a nod. A stale silence fills the warm air of the vehicle. I promise myself that after a quick conversation and some garlic knots, this awkwardness will be behind us, and we can be a proper team again.

Dev's gonna lose it when I tell him I'm playing along with this mysterious messenger.

The drive into town is only a few minutes. Unlike my sleepy start, the people of Hathaway are taking advantage of what will likely be one of our last Sundays without snow.

Downtown Hathaway is exactly two blocks of small businesses—most of which exist in buildings that haven't been updated since their construction in the late fifties. You either accept the charm of the old-school structures or you side-eye the lack of evolution.

The small lot behind Cheezy's Pizza is already full of

lunchtime patrons, so Dev's forced to find a spot off one of the tight side streets. A misty drizzle begins to speckle the windshield as soon as the truck is put into park.

"Crap, I don't have an umbrella," Dev mutters, frantically feeling under his seat.

"We won't melt."

"You're already cold. Let's drive closer and I'll drop you off out front."

"It's fine, Dev," I insist. "Let's just make a run for it."

He sighs, blinking at me apologetically. I shrug at him, trying to convey that a little rain is the least of our worries.

We step out into a biting air. I'll never admit it aloud, but an umbrella would've been handy. The mist is heavy enough to slice at our cheeks and leave dewdrops in our dark hair. It'll take a bit for my shoulder-length locks to dry. Dev's lucky that his mother made him trim his thick head of hair last week. He'll be warm and dry in no time.

Dev grabs my hand as we bolt down the alley for cover. For a moment, I allow myself to get lost in the bliss of holding my best friend's hand. For so long, I resisted him. I had no idea that giving us a chance would make my life so much brighter.

Our situation might feel dim now, but all we need is this conversation to go well, and we can get back to normal.

Cheezy's red-and-yellow awning provides a reprieve from the rain, which appears hellbent on growing heavier by the second. As soon as we step inside, we're blasted with a wave of warmth and the smell of herb-and-garlic-butter-brushed pizza crust. My stomach immediately rumbles. Only Cheezy's has the power to break through my anxiety-induced fast.

The pizza parlor is busier than normal, even for a weekend. Most of last night's Hauntland guests must've remained in town overnight. I wonder how many of them are lingering because they heard the news about Alice Crane. I've come to learn that where there is a scandal, there are people who are more than eager to recount how "they were there when it happened." Like it's something to brag about. There are those who simply can't help but find a way to make a tragedy about themselves. If you ask me, it's a pretty pathetic ploy to garner attention.

"You go find a table," Dev suggests after seeing the long line at the register. "I'll order."

"Look for me in the back."

There are two dining rooms in Cheezy's. The one with the pizza counter and ovens is full of locals who know it's the warmer of the two. I nod to some people from school who've wisely claimed the booth nearest the fountain beverages so they can sneak free refills.

Victor, the owner, loves any excuse to decorate his restaurant. The pizza parlor has been strung up with bat garlands and littered with plastic pumpkins since the first week of September. It clashes horribly with the classic red-and-white-checkered diner aesthetic he has going on, but I don't think he cares.

I head for the back room which, as expected, is full of out-of-towners. I don't recognize a single face. Most appear to be in their twenties. There's a group of friends wearing matching black-and-neon-green Hauntland hoodies and a couple with dark circles under their eyes eating in silence. One family has children far too young to be visiting Hauntland. Unfortunately, when it comes to decision making, I've come to expect the worst out of our guests.

Sliding into a red-vinyl booth in the corner, I settle into the seat with a full view of the joint. Nowadays, I feel safer in a crowded room when I can have eyes on everyone.

Although, I guess I should be more concerned by the familiar faces in the other room than any of these strangers.

You know me.

Dev slides into the chair across from me, expertly balancing two cups and a little plastic dish of ranch dressing for our pizza. He unloads it all on the table before grabbing the cup of water and taking a big gulp. "They said the pizza's going to be a minute. Just got slammed, I guess."

"Makes sense." Everyone wants a warm slice before holing up for the rest of the day.

He pushes the other cup, which is filled with something dark and fizzing, in my direction.

"Pop is all yours." When my eyebrows raise, he goes on to explain, "Because you didn't sleep well last night."

Despite the situation, I can't help the appreciative smile toying at my lips. This is what makes Dev so precious. He's endlessly thoughtful. Considerate beyond measure.

There's nothing I want more than to get on with our Sunday. Snuggle up and focus on solving the far more pressing problem at hand. But we can't do that without a little affirmation first.

"Did you see the news this morning?" I ask after taking a large swig of the drink, letting the bubbles dance down my throat. It's cherry cola, my favorite.

His boyish expression falters, but he must have known this conversation was coming.

"About Alice Crane? Yeah. It's everywhere."

Something about the way he says her name has my pulse quickening. Was there an ounce of familiarity in his tone? Or am I again looking for connections that aren't really there?

I don't dare blink when I say, "She was in her school orchestra."

Dev's nostrils flare. "How'd you hear that?"

"Valerie."

Those expressive eyebrows raise. "You talked to Valerie?"

I nod. "After you dropped me off and this morning."

"No wonder you didn't sleep well last night."

I scoff. "Yeah, that's totally why I couldn't rest easy. Definitely not the memory of Alice's body in the wave pool."

Or you standing over it with your ex.

He leans over the table suddenly. "Jeez, Gwen, keep your voice down."

Leaning back in my seat, my arms cross. "I'm really sorry for what I'm about to ask, Dev. Truly, I am. But I need to know."

He mimics my posture, though his movement is accompanied by a heavy sigh. "You're going to ask if I know her."

I guiltily nod again, hoping he understands that I don't want to pry, but for my sanity, I have no other choice. My brain won't let this go until I hear some reassurance leave his lips. "It's just a unique commonality between you, Jenna, and Alice."

"A lot of kids pick up a stringed instrument to satisfy their music credit."

"It's the last choice after choir and band," I point out. Let's not pretend orchestra is a popular class.

His jaw clicks. "Fine. Okay. I knew Alice. We met at this regional youth philharmonic showcase last spring break."

Breathing is suddenly impossible. As anxious as I was, I didn't expect him to *actually know her.*

"It's not like we knew each other well or anything," he continues, the explanation suddenly tumbling out of his mouth at rapid speed. "Just pleasant greetings in passing. She's a violinist, so we never sat anywhere near each other. I don't have her number or follow her on anything. I haven't even thought about her until we found her."

He left out Jenna's name, but I know she likely went to this philharmonic thing, too. If Alice was a violinist, Jenna definitely knew her. They might even have been stand partners.

"So you recognized Alice last night?" I whisper. We both know there's no going back once I hear the answer.

His expression grows strained. "I didn't get a great look at her..."

"But did you have an idea about who she was, Dev?" The question comes out firm and desperate.

There's nothing I despise more than feeling desperate.

It's his turn to respond with a terse nod.

And I thought breathing was hard a moment ago. My ears start ringing as I process this unexpected reality. Dev really lied to me. I point blank asked him at the wave pool if he knew who she was and *he lied*. He's no better than the rest of them.

What's worse is that I have this horrible feeling there's still something he isn't telling me.

Stop. Do not spiral. This is Dev, which means there must be a reasonable explanation.

"Did you withhold this from the cops, too?"

A different shade of guilt casts a shadow on his face. "No, I told them everything. Anything to help her get back to her family faster."

Tears begin to toy with the corners of my eyes. I shouldn't be surprised that Dev fessed up to the police. But why keep it from me? He knew Alice's name would come out eventually. Did he really think I'd never find out she was in the orchestra and connect the dots?

These questions must play on my face because he hurriedly says, "I wasn't trying to lie to you, Gwen. Please—you have to believe me."

"But you still did."

"I was trying to protect you from going through all this again. I know what last summer did to you. I didn't want you to worry."

"I'm even more worried now, Dev!" My chest heaves as I struggle to keep my voice down. I don't need to attract the attention of tourists pulling gooey slices from a communal pie onto their plates. "How am I supposed to believe anything you say when you lied about something this important? Last night, you promised that you and Jenna went to Wetlands based on a funny feeling. Now, I'm supposed to believe you just happened to stumble across the body of someone you two know?"

"We didn't do anything to Alice," he cuts in with narrowing eyes. "How could you even go there?"

"How could I not?" I hiss back.

"Because you're supposed to know me better than anyone!"

"I really want to believe you but—"

"Dev!" a voice calls from the other room, making us both jump. I'd completely forgotten that we ordered a cheese pizza to split. My appetite is completely shot.

All I want is to hide away in my covers until my head stops spinning.

"Be right back," he huffs, and I can tell he feels the same way. He stiffly rises from the table.

"Maybe ask if we can get it to go?"

His attention snaps to me, and I instantly feel guilty for the hurt glinting in his eyes.

No—I shouldn't feel guilty. He's the one who should be feeling this way. I'm not the liar.

And, right now, the last thing I have time for is liars.

"If that's what you want, Gwen." I hate how defeated he sounds, but I need some time to process this. To decide the weight of this lie. Is it heavy enough to drown our whole relationship?

He lumbers away, shoulders drooped with defeat. I don't want to make him feel this way, but after the anonymous message I received this morning, I'm not in a state to offer blind trust to anyone. Not even the boy who was rewriting everything I thought I wanted out of life.

Glancing around helplessly, I freeze when I find someone else's eyes trained on me.

The boy sits at a table by himself, ripping apart a garlic

knot into doughy pieces. Grated parmesan coats his fingertips while he works methodically to deconstruct the roll.

Looks like I'm not the only one without an appetite.

He appears about my age, with chestnut curls, pale skin, and a face dusted with a smattering of freckles. His eyes are such a violent blue that I'm instantly reminded of a hissing bolt of electricity. Everything about his appearance startles me. Most of all—he doesn't shamefully glance away after I make it clear that I've caught him staring. Rather, he boldly ducks his chin, nodding at me in greeting.

My eyebrows raise as I hastily search my memory for any recollection of who this boy may be. I draw a blank.

He's a perfect stranger, but it's abundantly clear he somehow recognizes me.

"Gwen, right?" he calls over. His voice is lower than expected, and there's a sorrowful tone behind the way he says my name.

How does he know my name?

A lot of people know your name now.

"Yeah?" I say, not hiding the edge in my voice. I'm not about to hash out the horrors of my life with a nosy stranger.

Before the boy can respond, Dev returns, a pizza box in hand. He blinks between us with confusion.

"Hey," he says after clearing his throat. "I'm Dev."

"I know." The stranger blinks to my boyfriend with amusement before standing to introduce himself. "I'm Asher Crane."

My lips part. "You're—"

"Alice's twin? Yeah."

"Oh my gosh, we're so sorry about what happened. It's horrible," Dev says hurriedly, and I know we're both guiltily wondering if Asher overheard our earlier conversation.

"You're here alone?" I ask, searching the pizza parlor for any sign of the boy's family. "Are you okay?"

Asher shrugs, and I guess I can't blame him for not

wanting to answer that question to complete strangers. "My mom and dad are at the station. Or maybe the morgue. They keep bouncing between the two." He takes a long slurp of his fountain drink. His fingertips leave oily parmesan prints on the plastic cup. "They wanted me to stay at the hotel, but I was going stir crazy. I thought I wanted to eat, but—"

He trails off, a tortured expression crossing his face.

"I understand," I hear myself offer. Grief has the power to sway even the best laid plans.

Immediately, I feel like a fool for freaking out over Dev's lie. It still matters. But this poor guy lost his sister while on vacation. I can't think of many things worse than that.

"Is it true what the cops said? That you were some of the people who found her?" Asher might ask the question to both of us, but his electric eyes don't leave mine.

Dev clears his throat uncomfortably before confirming, "Yeah, we did."

I watch helplessly as Asher's gaze glosses over.

"Did it," he begins, the words wobbling in this throat, "did it really look like she..."

He can't finish the question, but he doesn't need to. We both know what he's asking.

"It was really dark," Dev says apologetically. "But if you really want to know—"

"I do."

I'm starting to feel trapped in this booth with both boys looming at the end.

Dev's lips purse for a long while before he decides it's not his place to withhold any information from the mourning boy. "It looked like she acted alone."

A new kind of agony dances over Asher's face for a split second, then he masks the emotion with a stoic expression. It's one I know well.

He might be a stranger, but my heart can't help but ache for him. This is how I felt when I lost Valerie, and that all turned out to be a hoax. Asher's sister is really gone. There's no surprise reunion waiting for him in his bedroom.

Suddenly, his eyes snap back to me. "And what do you think?"

My brow furrows. "What do you mean?"

"Do you think she acted alone?" There's an intensity to the question that has an honest answer slipping off my tongue.

"I'm not sure."

Dev's head jerks to face me with surprise. "You're not?"

Asher squints while he studies me and my spine stiffens beneath the heat of his gaze. He almost appears satisfied with my answer. However, he must realize the concern this has caused my boyfriend, because Asher finally says, "Sorry, I shouldn't have pried. According to my parents, I need to stop needling people with questions and let your esteemed police department do their job."

He sounds far more bitter than apologetic.

"Sometimes, asking questions—even those with tough answers—is how we heal."

Asher seems to appreciate my response. "I think we'll be in town a little bit. My folks aren't going to leave until Alice's case is closed. Do you think I could get your numbers? It would be nice to have someone in town to talk to who isn't dodging my questions."

My stomach does a nervous flip. I don't like talking with strangers more than necessary.

But is Asher a stranger? I know his name. I saw his sister's body. That probably qualifies us as acquaintances, at the very least.

I had Dev, my family, and my guidance counselor to help me heal. Right now, Asher is here alone, for an unknown length of time. Who knows when he'll return to his full support system? Showing him an ounce of kindness might make up for the fact that I'm actively hiding my knowledge about this unknown messenger from the authorities.

Only for the time being, I remind myself. As soon as I have any idea as to Unknown's identity, I'm running straight to the cops.

I extend my hand for Asher to place his phone in it. "You can text me whenever."

He brightens, immediately passing me his cellphone for me to enter my number. Once I finish, I sneak a look at Dev out of the corner of my eye. He appears positively perplexed at my readiness to give this guy my number, but after a beat, he also inputs his contact information.

"Thanks, guys," Asher says, sliding his phone back into his pocket. "Maybe we could meet up sometime. There's so much I want to understand, but no one wants to tell me anything. My parents think they're protecting me from hearing the gory details, as if we didn't just pay to visit a living nightmare." He scoffs at the irony but quickly regains his composure with a stiff nod toward our pizza box. He backs up enough for me to finally slide out from the booth. "Sorry, I don't mean to hold you up now. Your pizza is probably getting cold."

"It's okay, man," Dev says, though a puzzled expression still creases his forehead. "Let us know if you need anything."

"I appreciate that." Asher says before glancing back toward me. "And thanks for finding my sister. I'm sure that couldn't have been easy."

"Of course." I can't think of anything better to say. I'm certainly not hitting this grieving boy with a *"you're welcome for discovering your twin sister's body."* Though, from the way his eyes are still boring into mine—like he's somehow capable of seeing these thoughts play through my mind—I wonder if he hoped for a meatier response.

"And don't worry," Asher goes on to say, "we're going to get to the bottom of this."

"What do you mean?" Dev asks at once.

Asher still doesn't break eye contact with me as he

answers. "I know my sister as well as I know myself. She would never hurt herself. Someone did this to her."

Someone who is toying with me now.

"Whoever it is, they're still out there—confident they got away with it."

So confident that they've challenged me to find them.

"But," Asher's gaze finally shifts over to Dev, "no one's getting away with anything."

CHAPTER
TEN

I EXPECTED Dev to have questions the instant we were back in his truck. What I did not expect was the fury in his tone.

"Okay, now it's my turn to ask. Do you know that Asher guy?"

"Uh, no?"

"Then why was he looking at you like he knows you better than I do?"

"He wasn't," I scoff. "I've never seen the guy before today. But can you blame him for being interested in the people who discovered his dead sister?"

"That's the thing, Gwen. He wasn't interested in me. I doubt he even cared to have my number. All his attention was on you."

And that's my fault?

Dev's not done. "Do you really think it's good for your mental health to be answering this guy's questions? I respect that he's old enough to set his own boundaries, but why are you letting yours down on account of him? You hate talking about anything that even reminds you of last summer."

"His sister is dead."

"Which is horrible, but that doesn't mean I have to like

the way he looked at you just now. You're sure you don't know him?"

"Babe," I say, attempting to keep my voice even, "whether you like it or not, this is my first time ever speaking with a Crane. Not everyone in this truck can say the same."

His nostrils flare. "I swear, Gwen. Alice and I only knew of each other in passing. I know how it looks, but these coincidences are just that. You have to believe me."

"I really want to."

"And yet you don't." His voice is starting to shake with desperation. "I thought you understood the kind of person I am, Gwen."

"I do."

"Are you sure about that?" His grip on the steering wheel tightens as we turn into our neighborhood. The pizza box is still warm in my lap, but I suspect neither of us will touch a single slice. "Because why do I get the feeling you are more inclined to believe a stranger's theory than your own boyfriend's side of the story?"

"Because another freaking lunatic is playing games with me!" I want to scream but bite my tongue. There's a pull at my gut to not trust Dev with this revelation just yet. Not until I know more about what happened the night Alice Crane died.

Pulling into my driveway, he frustratedly throws the vehicle into park. For a long moment, the only sound is the pattering of raindrops on the windshield.

"I don't know what else to tell you, Gwen. You either believe me or you don't."

"I—"

"Please don't answer right now. It's been a long twenty-four hours for the both of us. Let's try again when we have clearer heads."

Finally, something we can agree on. I'm sick of debating the truth. Every minute it continues, the more it hurts. All I want to do is crawl back in bed and forget any of this ever happened.

But I don't have that luxury.

I have a puzzle from a killer to solve.

That's when it hits me—I've been so concerned about the killer's identity that I haven't been focused on who might be their target. It could be anyone I know. Even the boy I care about most of all. Am I being foolish for not fully trusting him? Am I putting him at risk?

"The pizza is all yours," I say to him. "I'm not hungry anymore."

Dev's only response is a nod.

Once I climb out of the passenger seat, I turn back before closing the door. "Stay inside, okay?"

His lips pinch. "You, too, Gwen."

To his credit, he's not so angry that he doesn't wait for me to get inside before pulling away and driving back three houses to his own. I know that I've upset him. All I need is one concrete sliver of proof that Dev isn't lying to me, and then he can help me.

But until then, I'm on my own.

With that in mind, I spend the rest of the day making a list of suspects comprised of everyone I know. Fighting back the urge to vomit with guilt, the first names I write down are those of my family, boyfriend, and friends. If I learned one thing last summer, it's that everyone is a suspect until proven innocent. *Everyone.*

Then I jot down the name of every crew member I work with regularly. After that, I add anyone I interact with in town and school. The names become easier to add as I widen my net to include people I consider acquaintances.

After I write down the name of every single person I can think of, I sit back against my headboard and survey my handiwork.

Suspects

Mom, Dad, Gil, Dev

Work: Jenna, Valerie, Milly, Weston, Estelle, Wendy Thatcher, Hannah Flannigan

School: Jeremiah (government), Carmen (theatre tech), Samantha (environmental science), Kendra (environmental science), Greg (environmental science), Mrs. Lloyd (guidance counselor)

Hathaway: Ralph (gas station), Sue (library), Victor (Cheezy's), Mayor Dillard (I think he knows me?)

THE LIST IS EMBARRASSINGLY SHORT, but I generally keep to myself. I decided to not add any teachers, other than my guidance counselor, Mrs. Lloyd. I'm not sure I would classify my relationship with any of them as "someone I know." Besides, if the killer is someone I forgot to jot down, the chances of me identifying them are near impossible anyways.

Immediately, I start crossing out a few names. I know where Mom, Dad, and Gil were last night. They took Gil and his friends to the movies before dropping them off at a neighbor's house for a sleepover. From the abundance of pictures my mom texted me throughout the night, I have a solid log of where they were and when. I highly doubt my ten-year-old brother or uptight parents had anything to do with the murder of a teenage girl from Ohio.

I also cross out Jeremiah's name, because he documented his entire night online. One of Weston's teammates on the hockey team, Jeremiah has an alibi by way of a football game in Ann Arbor.

Suspects

~~Mom~~, ~~Dad~~, ~~Git~~, Dev

Work: Jenna, Valerie, Milly, Weston, Estelle, Wendy Thatcher, Hannah Flannigan

School: ~~Jeremiah (government)~~, Carmen (theatre tech), Samantha (environmental science), Kendra (environmental science), Greg (environmental science), Mrs. Lloyd (guidance counselor)

Hathaway: Ralph (gas station), Sue (library), Victor (Cheezy's), Mayor Dillard (I think he knows me?)

STARING AT MY LIST, the confusion only seems to grow worse. I can't imagine anyone I know having what it takes to be a killer.

Although, as Valerie pointed out last night, I guess one girl on this list already qualifies as one. It might appear that Jenna Thatcher returned to her good-girl ways, but it's awfully suspicious she was at the scene of the crime.

Suddenly, the scenario begins to appear in my head. One where Jenna lures fellow-violinist, Alice Crane, into Wetlands and kills her for a yet-to-be-determined reason. Then Jenna returns to Pineland, spins some tale about a security concern to Dev, and they go check out the water park together. They stumble across the body, and shortly after, we appear. It feels implausible, but if I've learned anything about Hathaway, no leap is too great.

But what about the person who visited both of us during work? Maybe they are simply a prankster who chose the wrong time to make a move.

Or they're her accomplice.

Another thing I learned after last summer is to never assume there's only one person behind all this. This could very well be a group project. If that's the case, I'll need to unravel the truth bit by bit.

How to go about that? I have no freaking clue.

Before I can think better of it, I pull out my phone.

GWEN GARDNER

It's not a very fun game if I can't play.

It takes a moment, but a response appears from a completely different number. A new burner phone, I suspect. They'll likely dispose of the original one now.

UNKNOWN

It sure looks like you're playing to me.

Before I can press for a clearer clue, another message pops up.

UNKNOWN

You're closer than you think, Gwen. What's
yet to be seen is if you're brave enough to
go all the way.

Whether they realized it or not, this is the greatest—and worst—clue I could've received. Everything makes sense. This is why they've opened themselves up to getting caught. It's not because they're trying to make headlines like Ride or Die, or even because they're some freak who wants to be found. No— this killer doesn't think I have what it takes to turn them in.

Whoever this is, they must believe that I care about them enough to not give them up to the police. Even though they committed murder.

But they're wrong.

I'm not a game piece or a safe gamble. Anyone who sees me as such receives no mercy from me. Not even those I love most.

Still, I must proceed with caution. Accusing the wrong suspect could ruin someone's life. I cannot report anyone to the authorities unless I am absolutely, without a shadow of a doubt certain they are the murderer.

I glance down at my list and reread the names of people I know best in this world.

At least one of them did this. All that's left to do is figure out who.

CHAPTER
ELEVEN

SUSSING out who of my loved ones is a murderer is a lot harder than one would think.

Pushing beyond the encompassing guilt, there's the actual act of determining who is capable of such atrocities. The answer I want to believe is "no one," but Unknown has made it incredibly clear they're someone in my life. Specifically, someone who thinks I'm a coward. Incapable of hunting them down and turning them in.

That's how I know this killer doesn't understand me the way they think they do. If they'd paid close attention to my relationship with Valerie after she betrayed me, it would be abundantly clear I have no loyalty to the people who hurt me. Valerie didn't even kill anyone, and I still came to the conclusion we can't be in each other's lives. Betrayal may come in many shades, but it all stings the same.

The only culprit who might completely ruin me is Dev. If he is the one behind all this, I'm not sure I'll ever recover. That betrayal will do more than sting. It'll destroy everything I ever thought I knew about the good in humanity.

I'm choosing to hope it's not him. That's the only thing getting me out of bed on this gloomy Monday morning and readying myself for school. After cramming the last of my notebooks and textbooks in my backpack, I carefully fold up my list of suspects and tuck it into the front zippered pocket.

I still have absolutely no idea how I'm going to start crossing off names. Is my best bet to interrogate people until they crack? Or rifle through their things to see if I find a burner phone?

All I know is I don't have time to waste here. It's Monday. Halloween is on Saturday. If I have no leads in the next day or two, I'll no choice but to loop in Detective Weegan. I'm not going to bear the sole responsibility for someone dying.

Seniors can drive themselves to school, a privilege Dev and I have been taking advantage of since the first day. I wasn't sure he'd want to give me a ride this morning, but sure enough, there he was, parked in my driveway at 6:45.

But something is still off.

He's not leaning against the hood of his truck, waiting to kiss me good morning and open the passenger door for me.

The message is loud and clear. He's still upset that I didn't immediately believe his account of what happened at Wetlands.

Whatever. That makes two of us. Even if he's not associated with my unknown messenger, I don't like that he initially hid his knowledge of Alice Crane's identity from me.

Still, I can't help but think he should be groveling a bit more. It's not like I'm the one who lied.

You're lying to him by not telling him the whole truth about Unknown.

My lie is a necessary safety precaution. As far as I know, Dev's was not.

After I struggle to climb into his passenger seat on my own, I pointedly slam the door shut after me. It's not until after I click my seatbelt into place that I dare look over at him.

I gulp when I find his eyes on me. Before I can even open my mouth, his lips quirk into an obnoxious smirk.

"Kind of annoying when we don't work together, huh?"

I huff out a laugh. "Is that the point you're trying to make?"

I should've known he'd never let me struggle because he was actually angry with me.

Dev innocently raises his dark eyebrows. "Did it work?"

"Are you sure you wouldn't rather work with Jenna?" I ask back, my voice sickly sweet.

His head drops back down to the steering wheel as he groans. "Babe—"

"I'd love to be a team, Dev," I say earnestly, "but it's you who has to gain back my trust right now. If you could just give me something to help me believe your account of Saturday night—"

"My word isn't enough?" He glances up at me helplessly.

My head shakes. "You understand me well enough to know it's not."

His lips pinch with frustration because, whether he likes it or not, he does know this.

"I don't have anything else I can tell you," he finally utters. "I haven't talked to Jenna since we were inside Wetlands. You can look through my phone and confirm that."

As tempting as it might be to snoop through Dev's texts, it feels like an insult to do so. No, I need to be on the lookout for a burner phone.

"I think it's just going to take some time," I whisper back at him. Before I can resist, my hand reaches across the center console so my fingers can comfortingly weave through his thick hair. I don't like upsetting him, and I sincerely believe time is precisely what we need. Time for someone else to incriminate themselves. Time for us to rebuild our trust in each other. We've done it before and can do it again.

All it takes is time.

Unfortunately, I don't have much of it. Saturday is going to be here before we know it.

Dev finally raises his head and meets my eyes. "I wish none of this was happening," he murmurs sadly. "We shouldn't be wasting away our last year in Hathaway."

Instantly, a new wave of guilt twists my gut. I may not care, but Dev's making a point to relish every last day of his life in the town he loves.

One of the negative aspects of starting to date someone during the senior year of high school is that you have to make some pretty big life decisions swiftly into your relationship. There's an abundance of questions you're forced to ask early on. How serious is this? Are we going to stay together after graduation? Are we going to keep each other in mind while diving into massive changes?

"We aren't," I promise him, and although those two words could be interpreted as a lie, they're not because I genuinely mean them.

With that sentiment in mind, I peck his forehead. "It's just a blip. Something we'll giggle about one day."

Unable to resist, he nudges his nose with mine. "Let's hope that day isn't years after graduation."

I highly suspect it will be, but I don't dare admit this to Dev. Even after last summer, he hasn't come to accept that Hathaway's horrors aren't merely a seasonal attraction. Disappointment and distrust are the status quo in Hathaway. I'm not going to be the one to burst Dev's bubble.

So instead, I jerk my head toward the road. "Unless you're not planning to graduate, we gotta go."

With an understanding nod, Dev shifts gears and backs out of my driveway. Like every other drive in this town, Hathaway High is only a few minutes away. It's just east of downtown, which makes stopping for a coffee convenient, even if we sleep in a little.

Unfortunately, we don't have time for a latte this morning because I'm supposed to meet with the guidance counselor before first period to discuss my plans for next year.

Mrs. Lloyd is gonna kill me when I show up without a narrowed-down list of schools deserving of an application. I did my homework and perused the websites of every single college and university in my family's budget, but not a single one jumped out at me. If I'm going to spend a boatload of money on tuition, I want to be abso-freaking-lutely positive the school will be worth it.

Not a single school I've toured with Mom and Dad has pulled at my heartstrings. There's always something wrong. They don't have my major (not that I'm even sure what I want to study anymore). They're out of my budget. They're within three hours of my hometown.

I feel like I'm already supposed to know where I'm going to land next fall. Most of my classmates do. But instead of excitedly showing my school pride by wearing a college t-shirt or applying early decision, I'm stuck feeling entirely apathetic about my future.

The only thing I'm sure about is how much I'm going to miss Dev's hand resting on my thigh while he drives us to school.

His parents are professors at Griswell University, a small private college in Ann Arbor, so Dev's guaranteed a massive discount on tuition. Unfortunately, Griswell is completely out of my budget, even with the Park Ranger scholarship Ms. Thatcher felt obligated to give me last summer.

We've always known we won't be going to the same college. Dev will be staying in Michigan, and I'll be—

Somewhere.

Not here.

After driving past a few miles of corn fields, Hathaway High appears. It's a modest, two-story brick building that hosts a thousand more horrors than Hauntland could ever dream of employing. Teenagers in scary costumes? That's mild compared to my peers without their masks.

Dev pulls into our usual parking spot at the back of the lot (perfect for a speedy exit) and instinctively moves for one last kiss before class (because there's no PDA allowed in school). An inch away from my lips, he pauses, as if remembering I might not be on-board with kissing him in our current state.

Before I can allow myself to spiral and overanalyze, I close the gap between us and pull him to me.

Immediately, Dev sighs with relief as he breathes me in. I swear, this boy still kisses me like he can't believe it's happening.

"A blip," he murmurs against my lips.

"A blip," I promise back.

My concerns are valid, but if I know Dev like I think I do, they won't remain that way for long.

Mrs. Lloyd waits outside her office with her arms crossed and an *it's-too-early-for-your-nonsense* expression. Her auburn hair is streaked with thick patches of gray, and it's pulled into its usual tight bun at the nape of her now-pale neck. Mrs. Lloyd is one of the few people I know who willingly relocated to Hathaway after her husband wanted to return to his hometown to care for his aging parents. Before moving into town last year, they used to live in Boca Raton, Florida. The only thing that faded faster than the woman's tan was her chipper personality. But a lack of sunlight will do that to you after a while.

Mrs. Lloyd's current situation is what I would consider my worst-case scenario. When I finally leave Hathaway, I have no intentions of returning.

If Dev and I wind up getting married, hopefully we can convince our parents to relocate to wherever we settle. I'm aware of how unbelievably selfish it sounds, but nothing good happens in Hathaway. The sooner we all accept that, the better.

"Hope your will and testament is up to date," Dev mutters as soon as he claps eyes on the woman.

I snort before approaching Mrs. Lloyd with my sweetest

smile. It's such an unnatural expression for me that the woman actually frowns.

"I take it you did *not* narrow down our list of prospective schools?" she asks with one eyebrow quirked in an accusatory fashion.

"I worked pretty late—" I begin before Dev cuts me off.

"It's my fault she didn't get it done," he excuses. "My laptop wasn't working and Gwen let me borrow hers so I could write an essay."

How easy the lies are coming to him these days.

This one's for you, I remind myself.

Mrs. Lloyd doesn't want to hear any more. She waves Dev off before grandly gesturing for me to enter her cramped office.

All I see before she closes the door after me is Dev's pitying expression.

I plop down into one of the cushioned wooden chairs in front of Mrs. Lloyd's cluttered desk as she gracefully slides into her own.

For a woman who only moved into this office a year ago, Mrs. Lloyd's already filled the space to the brim. The walls are plastered with letters from past students from her tenure in Florida. There are a thousand sticky notes of student names and a one-word reminder as to why she needs to hunt them down. I can only imagine what mine says. "Gwen G. - future???"

I glance up from my clasped hands to find the guidance counselor staring at me over her wire-rim glasses. "You know, Ms. Gardner, no one is going to force you to spend thousands of dollars on a higher education that you clearly do not want to pursue."

"I want to go to college!"

"Do you?" She laughs at this, which only makes me slink further into my seat. "Students in your situation—"

Broke.

"—typically show some initiative when it comes to taking control of their futures. You have everything in your arsenal to make that future a reality. Good parents who take time off work to tour colleges, highly qualified teachers who are more than willing to help you raise your grades, and to be frank, a very compelling personal story for your admissions essay."

Is it compelling or is it nightmare-inducing?

Mrs. Lloyd is convinced I need to write about last summer in my personal essay because "girl who got duped into thinking her best friend was kidnapped by a serial killer" will totally convince a college I'm smart enough to be admitted.

"I understand that it might seem like I'm not putting in a lot of effort—"

"—because you're not—"

"—but we both understand what's holding me back."

"Your inability to make a decision despite declaring you want nothing more than to pursue a life outside of Hathaway."

I blow out a breath. Mrs. Lloyd is the most honest person in this freaking town, I'll give her that. It's what inspires me to hit her back with a truth of my own.

"I don't want to waste money on the wrong decision."

Unable to watch the woman while she scrutinizes me for any semblance of an excuse, I focus my attention on fidgeting with my ring. On the other side of the door, I hear the rowdy hallway begin to settle down as students disperse to their classrooms.

Thank goodness. I won't have to endure this much longer.

After what feels like an eternity, Mrs. Lloyd finally says, "Then maybe now is not the time to force a decision."

My hands rise to rub down my face with frustration. "That isn't an option for me. If I don't decide, I'm stuck—"

"Here. We know. But would that really be so bad for an extra year or two?"

"Yes," I answer without hesitation. It's the only truth I've been confident about for my whole life. I'm not meant to live here. Bad things will continue to happen if I stay.

Mrs. Lloyd's brow creases with concern. "Is something happening at home that I should know about?"

My head shakes immediately. For once, everything is totally fine at home.

"What about here at school? Or work?"

Another shake. No one at either has been unkind to my face after my foolish actions over the summer. Behind my back, I'm sure they're judging the shit out of me. I would be.

"And how about online?"

Thoughts of my new anonymous friend pop into my head, shortly followed by Mrs. Lloyd's name on the suspect list currently stuffed into the bottom of my backpack. Until her name's crossed off, I'm admitting zilch.

"I deleted all my accounts, like you recommended."

The woman dips her chin once, but I don't miss how her lips purse before doing so. What? Did she think living life offline was going to cure me? Because these freaks are still finding ways to get into contact with me.

Freaks that I have no clue how to identify...

"And there's nothing else bothering you?"

My eyebrows raised. "Do I appear bothered?"

"Frankly, yes."

I swallow, careful to keep full control of my face, lest it betray me as I lie. "I'm still pretty tired from work this weekend."

This time, when Mrs. Lloyd scrutinizes my face for any sign I'm deceiving her, she does it quickly. Either she doesn't want me to know she knows I'm lying, or maybe I'm just that convincing. It could go both ways.

"I heard about what happened at Wetlands," she murmurs quietly. Her forehead creases with concern, but I've been on the receiving end of that look one too many times for it to leave an impression. "How are you feeling?"

I shrug. "Like I saw another dead body."

At my blasé response, her head cocks to the side as she attempts to discern how much I actually care. I refuse to remove my mask. I am not in the mood to relive the finer details of my latest waking nightmare. It's not even 7:15 am.

"It was quite the group. You and Mr. Vishwakarma, I expected, but I'll admit, I was surprised to hear you were with Valerie, Milly, and Jenna."

"Me too," I say, and this time, I mean every word.

"We don't have to get into it if you don't want to."

My lips purse. "Like I said, it was a long weekend."

"I understand completely." She sounds like she means it.

My list in mind, I take advantage of her pause and pivot. "Yours can't have been worse than mine. What did you do?"

Behind her glasses, her eyes narrow at my obvious subject change, but she recovers quickly with a small laugh. "No, yours was certainly worse. The highlight of mine was going on a date with my husband."

"Where to?"

"Does it matter?" she asks lightly. "I prefer to keep my life outside of school private."

Coming from anyone else, those words would shoot off alarm bells, but I know the woman means them. Other than attending after-school functions, Mrs. Lloyd is one of the few Hathaway residents who rarely shows her face around town. I've never once seen her in line at Pineland or grabbing a slice at Cheezy's. She does all her grocery shopping in the next town over.

Unfortunately, this doesn't cross her name off my list, either. Until I hear a shred of proof and a believable alibi, she remains an active suspect. Albeit an unlikely one. Mrs. Lloyd doesn't strike me as the type to murder an innocent teenager and then taunt me before striking again. You don't become a high school guidance counselor if you harbor that much hate in your heart.

But maybe I'm not the best judge of character.

We both blow out a breath when the bell rings. Hers sounds frustrated, while mine is relieved. The conversation of my hazy future is tabled for another day.

An innocent smile playing at my lips, I rise from the seat and sling my backpack over my shoulder. "It's been a delight, as always, Mrs. Lloyd."

"You can avoid this conversation as long as you want," she states back. "It's not my life being put on hold."

My tongue sticks to the roof of my mouth. "Maybe the clouds are about to part, and I'll find some clarity."

Her eyebrows raise doubtfully. "Your clouds will never part if you pretend the sky beyond them doesn't exist."

"I don't control the weather, Mrs. Lloyd."

"Don't you?" she questions, waving me out of her office.

With a sheepish shrug, I slink out the door and nearly smack into a boy on the other side. And it's not the one I expected. Where's my boyfriend now?

"Hey, Gardner," Weston greets me, his eyes downcast. Still, I don't miss the dark shadows that loom below them.

"Are you not feeling any better?"

His shoulders droop in response.

My brow furrows at the sight. Weston McCray—one of the most popular guys in school—is a boy who always has a reason to stand tall with his chin out. Now, his shaggy blond curls hang limp in his face, looking like they haven't been brushed since we clocked out of work on Saturday night.

What's wrong with him?

Other than the lingering troubles of last summer, of course.

But out of everyone, I'd say Weston survived with the least scars. Or so I surmised.

"Hey," he says again, lowering his voice so only I can hear, "can I talk to you later?"

I do not have time for this. I'm supposed to be unmasking a murderer. "I—"

"It's important, Gwen," he cuts me off.

His pale blue eyes bore into mine with such intensity that I cannot help but nod in agreement. I study him as his throat bobs with relief, like he was nervous I'd refuse.

"After school?" he proposes. "I'll drive you home."

I'd rather ride *Wolverine Racers* without the lap bar. Weston and I have remained cordial since the events of last summer, but it didn't turn us into friends. We both returned to our normal lives the best we could. And let's face it—outside of work, our lives don't intersect in the slightest.

But if he's wanting to talk to me now, something must be really wrong.

"Come in, Mr. McCray," Mrs. Lloyd calls from inside. "We don't want Ms. Gardner to be tardy for class."

Rolling my eyes, I slide out of Weston's way. Like I care about a tardy slip.

"After school," I whisper in agreement as he slips past me.

"It's a date."

There's the Weston I know. The boy would flirt with a brick wall.

"No, it's not," I snip back before closing the door after him.

Turning on my heel, I immediately search the hallway for the boy who is supposed to be waiting for me. Very few students still loiter in the harshly lit walkway. The threat of a tardy slip—and potentially detention—has most of my peers slamming shut their faded royal-blue lockers and scurrying into their first period classrooms.

Dev and I both start the day in mathematics—him in economics and me in statistics—so we always walk to the math wing together.

Except, he's nowhere to be found.

Maybe he decided to head over once the bell rang. Mr.

Palmer, the econ teacher, hands out tardy slips like Halloween candy. Anyone who dares knock on his classroom door after the final bell sounds might as well say "trick or treat" after he frustratedly flings it open. Where Mr. Palmer is concerned, it's *trick*, every time.

Hoping to catch up with Dev, I hurry toward the nearest staircase and speed walk past rows of lockers to the opposite side of the building, where all the math classes are conducted. The hallway is nearly empty now, and I prepare myself to not reach him before the final bell rings. There's nothing my well-behaved boyfriend hates more than being late for class. I'd be willing to bet pretty much anything that he's already sitting at his desk, feeling ridiculously bad for making the decision to ditch me for the second time in three days. At least he has a good excuse this time. I wouldn't want him to get in trouble on account of me.

I don't dare pull my phone out, unless I want my father to leave work early to pick it up at the front office. Maybe I should risk Mr. Palmer's wrath and give Dev a quick thumbs up through the window.

As I'm about to round the corner, I hear his voice echo down the empty hall.

"I have to," he says.

Heart pounding with relief at hearing my boyfriend's voice, I pick up the pace, until the sound of a higher tone stops me in my tracks.

"Don't you dare," Jenna Thatcher hisses.

My mouth goes dry. He ditched me because of her. Again.

Maybe he just ran into her, I attempt to naively convince myself. Jenna is in my statistics class, after all. Unfortunately, the pull in my gut tells me that's not the case.

Snooping is last thing I should be doing if I want to rebuild trust with my boyfriend, but I'm desperate to understand what's going on between these two.

And so, against my better judgement, I press myself closer

to the lockers around the corner. The swivel locks dig into my back uncomfortably, but I barely notice as I focus on listening.

"If I don't tell her everything, she's going to dump me." The desperation in Dev's voice has my throat bobbing. They're talking about me. "I'm not losing her because of your stupid decisions."

"It was your idea to enter the park, Dev. I was content to stay outside when we found the parking lot empty."

I startle when my phone vibrates in my pocket. My heart stops for a moment when I see it's a message from an unknown number before I realize it's Asher Crane.

MAYBE: ASHER CRANE

Hey, it's Asher. Are you free later today?

What is going on? I've never had so many people ask for a moment of my time in my life. Unfortunately, Asher Crane is going to have to get in line.

Shoving my phone away without responding, I return my full attention to the conversation between my boyfriend and his ex.

"Don't try to pin this on me," he bites back. "You were the one who wanted to drive to Wetlands in the first place. And it's a good thing I came with you. What if whoever hurt Alice was hanging around and decided to come after you?"

So, he does think someone killed Alice? Why would he insist otherwise to me?

Jenna laughs at him. "If you're expecting a *thank you*, don't hold your breath."

"Trust me, I know better."

A long silence ensues. Just when I was beginning to wonder if they finally dispersed into their respective class-rooms, Dev speaks again.

"I don't understand what's going on, Jenna, but it feels like someone is trying to set us up. That person who found you in the haunted house is the reason we thought to go to

Wetlands. Whatever they're up to, I want nothing to do with it, and neither should you."

"Agreed." Her voice is barely audible, but even I can hear the fear behind the one-word response.

"We need to keep our heads down until this blows over." And then after a long moment, Dev asks, "Why are you looking at me like that?"

"Because I don't trust you, Dev," Jenna responds bluntly.

"How come?" The hurt in Dev's voice makes my insides twinge with jealousy. I don't want him to care what she thinks about him.

"Do you really need me to spell it out?"

He huffs. "No."

Dev might not want to hear her reasoning, but I certainly do. Why can't Jenna trust him? What does she know that I don't?

Whatever it is, it causes Dev to storm into his classroom and roughly close the door after him. I hear Jenna sniff with disdain before slipping into our first period.

Before I can follow her inside, I desperately need to regain control of my erratic heartbeat, but the organ refuses to calm down. Can I blame it?

Dev is lying about something. Even Jenna thinks something's fishy with him.

By association, I guess that makes me the resident fool. Again.

CHAPTER
TWELVE

I CAN'T SAY I've ever been eager to drive anywhere with Weston McCray, but I guess there's a first for everything.

However, before I can hitch a ride with our school's most popular athlete, I have to explain why I'm doing so to my boyfriend.

"You're driving home with *who*?" Dev questions, his eyebrows rising high onto his forehead.

"Weston," I repeat myself.

"And why would you be catching a ride with him?"

I really don't want to reveal that I don't have any idea other than it's "important", so I leave it at, "Because he asked me to?"

Dev blinks at me like I'm growing a second head. "And you agreed?"

I shrug in response. The less detail I provide, the better. Dev knows me well enough to see right through most of my excuses.

Apparently, that understanding of the other doesn't go both ways. Nothing—absolutely nothing—can be good about something Jenna knows concerning Dev that I don't.

How does this keep happening? I continue to place my trust in people who inexplicably keep secrets from me.

There must be an explanation. If you just ask him for one, I'm sure he'll provide it.

With a shrug of his own, Dev tucks his car keys back into his pocket. "This oughta be interesting."

"What are you doing?"

He juts his chin out like it's obvious. "Driving home with Weston like you want. We'll have to walk back here afterwards and pick up my car but—"

It's all I can do to keep from running my hands down my face in frustration. Why is he making this so hard?

I struggle to find the right words that'll keep him here. "It's okay. You don't have to—"

"Make sure my girlfriend gets home safely?"

"—suffer through an afternoon with Weston."

Dev's eyes narrow when he realizes.

"You don't want me to come with you." He doesn't bother framing it as a question.

I clear my throat uncomfortably. "He only asked me to join."

"And when was this?"

"After I left Mrs. Lloyd's office. You weren't around to receive an invitation." The words come out harsher than intended, and my lips purse when I see Dev wince.

"I didn't want to be late for class."

Liar.

Stop calling him that.

And stop arguing with yourself!

Maybe it's time I start catching up with some lies of my own. "Weston asked to speak with me alone. You saw how skittish he was this weekend. I don't want to make him uncomfortable."

Dev huffs out a breath at the thought of someone as

popular and tough as Weston feeling any sort of discomfort in our high school.

"I'll catch you after he drops me off," I say, shutting my locker before he can argue.

"Gwen—"

But I'm already waving back at Dev as I head toward the parking lot reserved for student athletes. It's on the far side of the gymnasium, so no one really considers the lot "preferential treatment." It's a hike just to get there.

Feeling ridiculously guilty for ditching Dev, I allow the noisy hallway to fill my head. I can practically feel the warm confidence radiating off my peers. With it being Halloween week, everyone has something to discuss. Whether it be their costume, party plans, or which houses still entertain teenage trick-or-treaters.

Not even the Hauntland crew members who work on the holiday are missing out on the fun. Wendy Thatcher is throwing a party in the park after it closes to guests. I'm not sure who thought that was a good idea. The last time there was a crew-member-only party at Pineland, a crew member died.

Still, Dev thinks we should hang around for it. His philosophy is that it'll be good for us to make some better memories in the park, and before Alice's death, I was inclined to agree. Now I'm not sure the park is capable of providing positive memories. Perhaps Pineland is merely meant to be a paycheck and nothing more.

We were planning to use what we had in our closets and scrounge together an "emo couple" costume. His idea, not mine. With how this week is trending, I doubt either of us will be in the mood to party come Saturday, which is just as well to me.

The thought of recent events spurs my memory. I still owe Asher a response. Dev will think I've lost my mind if I meet up with Weston and Asher in one day, so I'll have to find a different time to speak with Alice's brother. Ideally, after I've made some progress in identifying Unknown.

Above all else, that must take priority. I can't let Weston deter me for long today.

Keeping my head down, I hurry through the gym, where the volleyball team is starting to warm up before practice. A thrumming beat blares from the weight room. I'm surprised to find most of the hockey team lifting inside. Why isn't Weston with them now? The question only makes me pick up the pace. Something must be seriously wrong if he is excused from a team workout.

As soon as I step outdoors, the October chill envelops me. I can't remember the last time the sun graced us with its presence. Stuffing my hands into the front pocket of my hoodie, I head toward the beat-up sedan everyone knows belongs to Weston. It's one of the few vehicles in the parking lot that's rumbling. The boy sits behind the wheel, and when he spies me, he jerks his head toward the passenger seat.

"You still want to drive me home?" I ask, opening the door.

"Sure, but we've got a pit stop along the way."

My eyebrows raise. "Where?"

In a bored voice, he challenges, "Get in and I'll show you."

And for some reason, I do.

In any other world, Weston would be the last guy I trust to drive me to an unspecified location. But right now, I need someone on my side. Someone who actually understands what I've endured—which means I can't exactly be picky here. So, Weston McCray it is.

I barely have time to buckle my seatbelt before Weston is backing out of his spot and pulling out of the parking lot.

"Don't you have hockey practice?"

His grip on the steering wheel tightens as he mutters, "Not on the team anymore."

"What?" I gasp, my attention snapping to the boy. "Since when?"

"Since I spiraled into a hot mess during tryouts a few weeks ago. Coach says if I keep playing, I'm only going to get myself or someone else hurt."

A painful pause follows this admission. I may not know Weston *that* well, but it's not difficult to imagine the loss this is for him. His entire life revolved around hockey.

It's shocking that I didn't hear this news through the Hathaway High grapevine. Although, after recently being raked through the rumor mill one too many times myself, I've pretty much tuned it out.

"I'm really sorry to hear that, Weston. I had no idea."

He shrugs, his face completely neutral. "Is what it is."

But that doesn't mean it's fair. After the events of last summer, Weston's life was altered. His best friend, Luca, wasn't just a liar—but an actual murderer, too. And what's worse, Weston was framed for Luca's death. It never went too far, but I can't imagine what that sort of accusation would do to a person.

It's a fear I know well. The kind of terror that takes control of your entire life. It's unfair to expect him to simply bounce back.

"What about your hockey scholarships?" I dare ask.

"Like I said," Weston murmurs, "it is what it is."

I immediately feel guilty. No wonder Weston is meeting with the guidance counselor. His entire future is up in the air, too. Everything he thought he had was yanked out from under him right before it was supposed to be his. Can he still afford college without a scholarship? Does he even know what he wants to do with his life outside of the sport?

Weston doesn't elaborate as he drives through town, nor does he play any music. All that fills the silence is the AC blasting through the vents. It does little to dissuade the salty odor that seems to cling to every inch of his car.

Desperate to change the subject, I remark, "Still have the AC on, huh?"

"You think it's cold out?" he questions in response.

"Uh, yes."

"Interesting," is all he says. The AC stays on.

Weston may feel like one of the few I can trust, but that doesn't mean he's considerate. I wish he'd tell me what he wanted to talk about already, but it's apparent he's not in the mood to speak on it yet.

Unfortunately for him, I'm not in the mood to follow his social cues. I don't have time to mess around. I need to find a murderer before they strike again.

"I figured you to be a rock music kind of guy."

"Can't listen to music anymore," he grunts as we whiz toward town. Cornfields stop abruptly, making room for modest buildings housing some of the less-touristy small businesses in Hathaway. A real estate firm, a few medical offices, and a dance studio.

My eyebrows raise. "Why not?"

"Gotta stay alert and be aware of my surroundings."

"Stay alert for what?"

His eyes briefly dart to me before rising to look out of the rearview mirror. "You never know who's out to get you, Gardner."

This shuts me right up, because regrettably, I know exactly what he's talking about. He has every right to be paranoid. We both do.

That's when it hits me. Maybe I'm not the only one receiving messages from unknown numbers, prompting me to play a deadly game without rules. I'm tempted to ask, but my own paranoia urges me to wait until he brings it up first. I don't want to show my hand and be wrong.

I frown when Weston drives through downtown Hathaway without stopping. I assumed this "pit stop" was a basic errand like picking up more protein powder or something.

"Where are we going?" I ask again.

"Where do you think?" he mutters as he starts speeding toward the last place I expected to visit on our day off.

I groan. "Why are we going to Pineland?"

"I got sent home early on Saturday," he says, as if this is a good enough reason to visit our place of work when it's closed.

"So?" I prompt, unable to hide the exasperation from my voice.

"So, I left my physics binder in my work locker."

"You're taking physics?"

"Don't think I'm smart enough for it?" he bites back, effectively silencing me again.

The car's wheels crunch as he drives down the gravel road to the crew member parking lot in the back of the park. As expected, only a few cars are in the lot, all belonging to the park's leadership team. They're the only people with ongoing projects when it's closed to the public.

I really don't like the idea of stopping by the park when only the important people are here. It's not like crew members aren't allowed to briefly pop by, but I make an effort to not visit the park when it's empty. Nothing good happens at Pineland after hours.

"You can wait in the car if you want," Weston offers, noticing my apprehension.

"And be a sitting duck who dies in the parking lot? I don't think so," I grumble, opening the door and climbing out.

"That's what I figured," he retorts, following me through the parking lot to Crew HQ.

During the school year, I keep my work ID and my student ID next to each other in my wallet. Fishing out the lime green badge, I scan it at the front door. These days, I make a point to always scan my badge before walking through any locked door because I want everyone to know where I was and when. There are too many eyes on the Pineland security team after last summer's access control log switcheroo for anyone to be messing with the records now.

I don't miss how Weston waits for the main door to close completely before he scans his ID, too. Neither of us are in the mood to take any chances.

The empty atrium doesn't look eerie in the middle of the afternoon. Just off. Like being in school in the middle of summer. We might be allowed to be here, but that doesn't mean our presence is necessarily welcome. Especially the presence of two teenagers directly involved with the park's recent scandals.

Weston makes his way toward the adjacent hallway that houses the locker rooms and wardrobe department. Wordlessly, he yanks open the door to the men's locker rooms before turning back to blink at me.

My mouth grows dry. "You want me to go in with you?"

Maybe this was a bad idea.

"I thought you didn't want to be a sitting duck," he responds dryly.

Swallowing nervously, I swiftly debate the lesser of two evils. The demon I know or the one I allegedly know but cannot yet identify.

I decide to take my chances. If this is it, at least they'll be able to put all the new security upgrades to good use and identify Weston as my murderer.

As expected, the men's locker room is identical to the women's. There are rows and rows of olive green lockers lit by fluorescent lights. A long mirror occupies the front of the room with a laminate counter and a few plastic chairs below it.

However, now that we're operating as Hauntland, the countertop is full of faceless mannequin heads that host gruesome masks and matted wigs. There're also a dozen squeeze bottles full of fake blood. As a result, little drops of scarlet liquid have dried everywhere. It's all over the countertop and the linoleum floor. Custodial gave up on mopping it up a long time ago, claiming they'll clean it at the end of the event's run. Until then, it feels like we're in the middle of a crime scene. Knowing Pineland, we probably are.

During my shifts, I'm normally fine with all the freaky accessories. I know it's fake. But when we're here alone, everything suddenly feels far more menacing and real.

"Weston, wait—" I say when it hits me. The hair on my arms stands on end. "The lights are already on."

"It's okay," he assures me, heading toward the farthest row of lockers. "They're supposed to be here."

A chill shoots up my spine. This was a mistake. I shouldn't have followed him in. My voice cracks when I ask, "*Who's supposed to be here?*"

My answer appears as soon as I round the locker bay. I frown at the sight of Valerie, Milly, and...

"Asher? What are you doing here?"

The boy looks entirely out of place backstage. Something about the ambitious glint in his eyes scream "I've never been on the verge of a mental breakdown back here." I still haven't texted him back, but it appears I didn't need to.

Immediately, I begin to question the diligence of those new security upgrades. There's no way a gathering involving four employees always at the scene of the crime and the brother of the latest victim would go unnoticed. Someone should've intervened by now.

Milly may no longer work in security, but I'd be willing to bet she bribed one of her former colleagues to accidentally turn off the cameras long enough for us to have a conversation.

Feeling ambushed, my arms cross when Weston joins their huddle. "What's this about?"

They all turn to Valerie, assuming she'll take control of the situation. This makes me huff out a sarcastic laugh.

Her head rolls to the side and I find myself bracing for

whatever explanation she's about to provide. "What do you think this is about? Homework? Asher's sister was murdered."

The boy bristles, earning a rare apology from Valerie.

"And why are you, Milly, and Weston involved with Asher's business?"

Valerie shrugs like it's obvious. "Because he asked us for help."

Apparently, I'm not the only person Asher reached out to. If I had known, I would have advised him to steer clear of these two girls.

Valerie Ross and Milly Dillard have spent the past few months employing every strategy under the sun to clean up their images. Volunteering for charity events, never skipping school, keeping their head down at work. Getting mixed up in Pineland's latest tragedy will do nothing but remind everyone of their original sins. Perhaps their aim is to be on the right side of the story this time.

"Help with what?" I lock eyes with Asher, and again, I'm startled by their bright shade of blue.

"It's like I told you earlier," he answers fiercely. "No one is getting away with killing my sister. But my spineless parents are listening to whatever story the cops are telling them. I don't know what else to do. Someone will pay for what they did to Alice."

The panic in his voice makes my pulse pick up. It's a kind of desperation I know all too well.

"The police still don't think another party was involved?" I was hoping they'd be on the same page as me when I revealed Unknown to them.

"Of course not," Weston answers for Asher. "Jenna's mom doesn't want her resort turning into another crime scene and there's nothing Hathaway Police Department loves more than quickly closing a case."

"Are they out of their minds?" My head shakes with disgust. "Have we learned nothing?"

"You aren't siding with HPD," Valerie remarks knowingly, scrutinizing my face. "Which means you believe Alice *was* murdered. What do you know that we don't?"

I falter, realizing I've flashed my hand.

"Nothing," I finally mumble.

Milly snips, "Now look Asher in the eyes and say it again."

"Take it easy," Valerie mutters under her breath, but this only frustrates me further. I don't want my former best friend looking out for me.

"There's been a development since we last spoke." Asher fishes in his pocket for a phone. After unlocking it, he passes the device to me. It's a newer model than the one he handed me yesterday, with an aqua case and beaded strap. "It was Alice's."

My brow furrows. "How do you have this?"

"Alice gave me her phone when we were at Hauntland on Saturday night."

"Why would she do that?"

"Because she didn't want our parents checking her location after she slipped away."

My pulse quickens. "Slipped away to do what?"

"Meet her secret boyfriend."

It's clear the others have heard this information already, because I'm the only one to react. "She went to Wetlands to meet some guy? Do you know who?"

Asher shakes his head once. "She never told me his name. All I know is he asked to meet at Wetlands."

"Did he have a way in?"

"Must have."

"Where'd she find a secret boyfriend?"

"That *Liarland* chat server online."

"The what?"

"You haven't heard of it?" Weston cuts in, and when I shake my head cluelessly, he continues. "It's an online chat room for people who are, um, *interested* in the Pineland deaths."

"That's putting it gently," Milly scoffs. "All they do is obsess over Luca and Val, all while rehashing last summer repeatedly. Freaks."

Clearly, Milly has heard of this server, too. In fact, judging by everyone's unfazed expressions, they all have.

So why haven't I?

When I say as much, Weston shrugs. "You must be better at protecting your peace than the rest of us."

Suddenly, I realize this is why Weston doesn't listen to music while he drives. He's spent too long scrolling through conversations of jerks who glorify our worst nightmare and is now convinced they're after him.

What was Alice doing on a server like that? *Falling in love?*

Jaw clenched, I glance back down at Alice's phone. "Why did you hand me this?"

Asher prompts, "Look at her most recent text conversation."

Wishing he'd just tell me the last piece of the puzzle instead of making me find it myself, I still do what he asks. Something about this boy—maybe it's the grief or the transparency—makes it easy to comply.

Alice Crane's last text was sent to a user saved in her phone as "Boyyy." Opening their messages, I find all the normal texts between a high school couple. They go back and forth about their day, Alice apologizes about ditching him for the weekend to visit Hathaway with her family, and then "Boyyy" says he hopes to find a way to still see her.

"Why aren't there any texts from the night Alice, um—"

"Was murdered?" Asher finishes for me. "Because this guy called her while we were at Hauntland. After she hung up, she asked me to keep her phone so she could 'slip away to the bathroom.'"

I open the call log and confirm a call occurred around 10:30 pm. It appears all communication stopped after this.

I glance up at Asher. "This guy doesn't seem too concerned that he hasn't heard from his girlfriend in a few days."

"Probably because he killed her."

"Why haven't you given this to the cops?"

Asher's dark eyebrows raise. "I have. We only got it back this afternoon."

"And they still didn't think this was any cause for suspicion that Alice was killed?"

Asher shrugs. "I can't say what they're thinking. All I know is her phone was returned to my family, but we have to stay in town in case they need it back or have any further questions."

As the air grows still, I look between the others. "I thought you all said they were closing Alice's case."

The seconds that follow are charged and tense in a way that only follows a lie.

Valerie caves first. "Okay, fine, we don't have proof they are closing the case, but we were hoping to see how you'd react to that sort of development."

"Enough with the lies already!" I groan, rubbing my hands down my face in frustration. "Come on! This is why no one believes us when we tell the truth."

"What is the truth?" Weston goads me, leaning against the row of olive lockers.

They all gape at me, waiting for me to speak. "I don't know what you all are expecting me to say. I've got nothing."

Except that's not the truth. I *know* Alice was murdered, and I also know whoever did it intends to strike again.

Again, it's Valerie who answers for the group. She carefully tucks a strand of her long raven hair behind her ear. I don't feel an ounce of nerves until she sets me with a pitying stare.

"Gwen," she begins cautiously, "we want to know if there's something you're not telling us."

They know.

I hear myself breathe out, "Are you all receiving messages again, too?"

Judging by the way their heads all rear back, this was not what they expected me to say.

Shit. I just showed the wrong hand.

Weston immediately whips his head to face Valerie. "I thought you shut down the Ride or Die account?"

"I did!"

I cut in with, "It isn't Ride or Die messaging me. It's someone who has my phone number."

"Who is it?"

I shrug helplessly. "Someone with plenty of burner phones."

Stop talking, I plead with myself. *Half of the people in this room are still on your suspect list. Stop. Talking.*

"Start talking," Weston demands.

For some reason, I find my gaze meeting Asher's. The brokenness displayed on his face makes my heart ache. This poor boy lost his sister. He just wants answers. I'd be a horrible person not to share what I know with him.

And so, I look Asher directly in the eyes when I say, "Someone's trying to rope me into some game."

I leave out the fact that I have technically already started playing. It seems so foolish now. Did *I* learn nothing after last summer? I'm not a freaking detective. It is not my job to run around and try to hunt down a murderer.

Time is ticking, and I still have absolutely no idea how to even start finding out who is on the other side of the phone.

"What game?" Asher asks, his voice barely louder than a whisper.

"You know me. You know who I'm going to kill next. Catch me if you can or enjoy the show," I recite the words that have plagued every one of my thoughts since I first received them.

The others become immobile with horror. Only Asher remains composed enough to speak.

"Do the cops know about this?" he demands.

I shake my head, feeling so guilty that I might combust on the spot. "This freak made it clear I have a choice. I can share this with the police, or I can save someone's life."

"Save someone?" Valerie cuts in. "How?"

"By identifying who's behind these messages before Halloween."

The locker room goes quiet again as we all process the impossible task ahead. Someone's life is at stake, and we barely have time to save them. We don't even have a clue where to start.

It's Valerie who shatters the silence. "They want to be found?"

"It doesn't make sense to me, either. Not yet at least."

"So, Alice's secret-boyfriend-murderer *is* from around here," Milly murmurs.

"We already suspected that?" I ask, waiting for someone to fill me in. My lips pinch when they all turn back to Valerie.

"Open up the photos on Alice's phone," the girl says guiltily. "You're going to have to scroll up a bit."

Despite my better judgment, I comply, because I need to know.

At first glance, I find exactly what I expect for a teenage girl's phone. There are lots of selfies, as well as pictures of friends, classroom whiteboards that list weekly homework assignments, and a few pictures of stray cats on the street. Nothing sticks out to me as out of the ordinary.

"Keep scrolling," Valerie prompts. "You'll know it when you see it."

The row of lockers seems to press in on me when I reach pictures from last spring.

There it is. All the evidence I need that my boyfriend has been lying to me. You don't take selfies with someone "you only know in passing."

And yet, here it is. Plain as day. A photo of Alice with my boyfriend, Dev Vishwakarma, and his ex-girlfriend, Jenna Thatcher.

The picture itself is sort of blurry. The kind of photo you would delete unless it meant something to you. They're all goofily grinning at the camera. Dev has his arm around Jenna, who in turn, is kissing Alice's cheek. They look like honest-to-goodness friends.

Now one of them is dead while the other two are acting highly suspicious.

Suddenly, I'm fuming so hard I can't see straight. Those *liars*.

"I'm sorry, Gwen," Valerie whispers, shattering what's left of my heart. They believe my boyfriend to be our culprit. Unknown. The murderer. Do I agree with them?

"He didn't do anything," I whisper as the world begins to spin. I'm not sure who I'm trying to convince. The others or myself.

Asher's bright eyes capture my attention, and with a few words, he rips my heart out. "Are you sure about that?"

CHAPTER
THIRTEEN

WESTON REITERATES Asher's question about a dozen times while driving me to my house.

"You're going to get yourself killed."

"Take a left here," I respond instead, guiding him into my neighborhood. We've officially hit the time of year where the sun starts its descent in the late afternoon, leaving an orange sky and a shadowy earth in its wake. There's nothing worse than eating dinner and doing my homework in the dark, but the season gives us little say in the matter.

Before we turn onto my street, Weston swiftly pulls over and throws his car into park. Man, this day is just never ending.

My hands raise helplessly. "I don't know what you want from me."

"I want you to dump your cheating killer boyfriend before he kills you or any of us!"

"My cheating killer boyfriend? Really?" I bark out a laugh. "You've known Dev since elementary school, Weston. He wouldn't hurt a fly."

"Okay but how confident are you about that?"

When I falter for a moment, Weston gestures to me as if to say, "See!"

I swiftly find my voice. "Breaking up with Dev is not part of the plan."

Not that we have much of a plan to begin with, but we couldn't leave the Pineland locker room without any idea of how we're going to identify Unknown before Halloween. I didn't bother showing the others the pathetic suspect list I made. It would only piss them off to see their names included. It's just as well. That scrap of paper wasn't getting me anywhere.

Our only real lead is the *Liarland* server. Alice met her boyfriend there. According to Asher, his twin sister never showed any signs of being a true crime fanatic obsessed with murderers, but I guess he's also learning how easily the people we know best can blindside us. With all of us joining the server, hopefully one of us will get lucky and discover this boy's identity.

Thankfully, Asher told the police all about Alice's secret boyfriend and how they met, which means the detectives should also be checking out the same lead. This also means there's a good chance the authorities have seen the photo of Dev, Jenna, and Alice. If Dev's been asked additional questions by HPD, he hasn't told me. The best case scenario is Weegan knowing something we don't, so he doesn't suspect Dev. Even better, perhaps the detective will identify Alice's mysterious boyfriend, realize he's the killer, and prevent anyone else from dying without our interference.

However, if by Friday, we have no leads, we've agreed to tell the cops everything we know. Maybe we're fools for waiting so long, but Unknown's been anything but predictable thus far. We don't want to set them off and trigger the death of someone we know—or one of us.

Unlike Ride or Die, Unknown has made little contact with me. But that's about to change.

"Fine," Weston retorts. "Take your chances. But here's an idea: text Unknown when you're with Dev and see if his pocket buzzes."

My eyes roll. "Unknown isn't Dev. He's also not Alice's secret boyfriend, so don't even go there."

Weston merely shrugs, which only makes my defensiveness for Dev grow.

"I thought you two were cool," I say accusingly. "How can you turn on him so fast?"

"Because sometimes the people you know best betray you," Weston snaps back, no doubt thinking of Luca.

My lips pinch. Weston and I aren't so different, really. Our view of the world was forced to change, and now nothing looks right.

"I'm going to reignite my conversation with Unknown," I promise Weston. "We're going to get to the bottom of this. No one's going to die."

"We better." Weston's baby blue eyes dart in my direction. "Maybe I'm spending too much time in that chat room and it's messing with my head, but—"

"But what?"

His throat bobs. "But I think it's going to be one of us."

"Who's masquerading as Unknown?"

"No. I think it's going to be one of us who dies."

This makes my mouth grow dry. I want to ask why he believes that, but before I can, he's throwing the car back into drive and steering onto my street. It isn't until he's pulling into my driveway that I realize he knew which house was mine without any directions.

"You know where I live?"

"Just in case," he answers with a shrug.

With that, I decide I've had enough of Weston for one day. He has a knack for making my pulse spike.

"Thanks again for the ride," I say, climbing out of his car. "And the help."

"It was sort of nice to be all back together, wasn't it?"

He must be missing his hockey team because the last thing I'd consider "nice" is having a secret meeting in a cursed theme park with my ex-best friend, her accomplice/girlfriend, a scapegoat for a murder, and the brother of a murder victim.

"I guess," is the best I can manage.

Seeing right through my fake response, Weston's lips quirk. "Whether you like it or not, we gotta keep an eye on each other, Gardner."

I can't decide if we're keeping an eye on each other because we're potential victims or possibly the villain, so with a singular nod, I close the car door. With a parting duck of his chin, Weston pulls away.

After shaking the ominous chills from my system and heading up the driveway, I can't help but glance over to Dev's house. His truck is parked out front. Did he see Weston drop me off so late? Does he wonder what we were doing? If the tables were turned, and Dev had taken the long way while driving a girl home from school, I know I'd be pissed.

But Dev has a lot to apologize for at the moment. It seems only fair that I rack up a few offenses of my own. Not my most mature approach, but I'm beyond the point of caring.

I let myself in the front door. Immediately, I'm hit by the fragrant smell of blistered tomatoes and oregano. Ever since my dad started making it a priority to be home from work in time for family dinner, my mom has started putting in a little more effort into our meals. She's still working with canned pasta sauce, but she's started sprucing it up with her own herbs and such.

Popping my head into the kitchen, I let Mom know I'm back.

"You're home late." It's not worded as a question, but I know it is one.

I lean against the doorway, shifting my backpack onto one shoulder before answering. "You remember Weston?"

From the stove, she looks over her shoulder to eye me suspiciously. "The hockey player?"

"Yeah." Before her mind can wander, I explain. "He's been having a tough time since this past summer for, well, obvious reasons. He asked to talk a bit after school, and so we did."

I don't need Mom to spare me another look to know she's unhappy. "Was Dev with you?"

"No, but he understood that Weston wanted to talk with me in private."

"Alone?" she asks sharply.

"It wasn't a bad situation, Mom. I promise."

After a long pause, my mother finally says, "I trust you're making the right decisions. Do what's right and what's right will be done by you."

"Yes, ma'am." I adjust the backpack strap on my shoulder. "I'm going to go get some homework done before dinner."

"Don't forget to look into Cranview University before our tour on Saturday."

My nose wrinkles. I'd completely forgotten we scheduled that tour for Cranview, which is a school about an hour away. It means I'll have a busy afternoon before working a full shift on the busiest night of the season.

"I'm still not sure that's going to be a great fit for me."

"You never know, honey! It's around our budget and they have an environmental science program!"

"Yeah, I guess."

This earns another glance over her shoulder. "You don't sound very enthusiastic."

I prickle with guilt. Even with the Park Ranger scholarship I earned last summer, we'll need to take out an intense student loan. It's the kind of investment that's going to take years to pay off. How can I expect anyone to help pay for my education if I can't even muster a basic level of eagerness? It's too costly to fake caring.

"Maybe I'll rediscover my zeal for education while we're touring Cranview!"

"Why don't you get on their website and try to get excited before your father takes off a Saturday afternoon to tour the campus with you?"

Point taken.

"Of course. I'm on it."

My backpack suddenly feels heavier as I lug it up the stairs and into my bedroom. I wish I could just flip a switch and start feeling hopeful about my future again. I thought I wanted to study environmental science, but now I'm not so sure. After last summer, when I realized just how bad some of the big players in that field can behave, I sort of lost my zest for it. I still care a lot about doing good for the environment. What I'm not so sure about is having to work alongside corporations that care more about their bottom line than making a difference.

Which leaves me at square one. I have absolutely no idea what I want to for the rest of my life. The thought of wasting money while I try to figure out my future feels like the most selfish thing I can do.

It's embarrassing to realize I don't feel passionate about anything. It makes me wonder if what I thought I cared for—the environment, theatre, exploring the world—were all things I was ever really excited about. What if I only liked those things because someone told me that's what mattered to me? Now that I don't have that directive bug in my ear, I'm clueless. I don't know which of my interests are actually mine.

Changing out of my school clothes into a pair of ratty sweats, I flop onto my bed and tug my school-provided laptop out of my bag. It's not supposed to be used to access websites that aren't for school, but no one ever actually checks the browsing history.

Homework and college research can wait. I want to familiarize myself with this chat room before I re-engage Unknown in a conversation.

Using the link Weston shared with me, a black web page appears, prompting me to set up a profile. A few clicks later, "KillaSquirrel" exists, fit with a red squirrel with X's for eyes as the profile picture.

It shouldn't be this easy to gain access to a chat room full of murder-obsessed freaks, but what do I know? Maybe welcoming anyone and everyone is their goal.

My eyes widen as the page reloads and opens the server.

"Oh my gosh," I breathe out. There are more people in here than I thought.

There's an active conversation going on right now. A few users are debating which ride is the deadliest.

sybilslayer: Most people would say Wolverine Racers but that ride didn't actually kill Sandy

PineBanned: it's still the most intense ride in the park

MartyParty: Incorrect. Not enough G-forces. Michigan Madness has a better drop.

PineBanned: luca picked wolverine for a reason... he knew that ride could mess a person up

At the mention of Luca's name, about a dozen accounts join the conversation to pay their respects and type "RIP."

My lips pinch. I knew there were people who worshipped Luca, but it's unnerving to witness just how many of them are out there.

PineBanned: back to wolverine racers...

MurderMod: Can we take this to a Park Chat channel and stop clogging up the general chat, please?

The moderator is obeyed in an instant and the general channel falls silent. There are other topic-based rooms for me to enter. They organize all sorts of conversations, from basic park tips to Hauntland excitement to far more sinister sounding rooms discussing the many deaths at the park.

Scrolling a bit, I'm surprised to see how kind and

supportive this group is to each other. Whenever a member mentions getting judged for their fascination with Pineland offline, the others are quick to console them. They're constantly validating their interest. To them, wanting to learn more about the Pineland murders isn't morbid, but only natural curiosity. Still, it's clear they've adapted an "us vs. them" mentality. As if they're the real victims in this scenario.

I start in the room called "Body Count" first. If my harasser is anywhere, I have a feeling I'll find them here.

This channel is concerningly active. I guess that checks out, considering the recency of Alice's death.

First, I scan the list of users in the channel. They all have ominous sounding profiles, but not a single one jumps out to me as an obvious culprit.

My phone buzzes, though my pulse only spikes for a moment before I see Weston's name as the sender.

WESTON MCCRAY

That you, Killa?

GWEN GARDNER

Yup

WESTON MCCRAY

Keep a low profile. Don't draw attention to yourself and they won't even notice you. I don't ever dare talk.

GWEN GARDNER

I'm just gonna lurk too

He answers me with a thumbs up. I think our side conversation is done before my phone buzzes again.

WESTON MCCRAY

You hit up Unknown yet?

WESTON MCCRAY

BTW we gotta come up with a better name
for them than that.

GWEN GARDNER

No

WESTON MCCRAY

You want to keep calling them a dumb
nickname like Unknown???

GWEN GARDNER

No, I haven't reached out to them yet! I
wouldn't get your hopes up for a response.
They could've already ditched their used
burner phones.

WESTON MCCRAY

Exactly. Clock's ticking, Gardner. Hop to
before they do.

GWEN GARDNER

What do you expect me to say?

WESTON MCCRAY

Ask them if they had a good day

GWEN GARDNER

You're kidding

WESTON MCCRAY

I don't joke about murderers, Gardner. What
kind of sicko do you think I am?

WESTON MCCRAY

Don't answer that

GWEN GARDNER

Fine we'll do it your way

Perhaps an afternoon with the school's cockiest guy has

influenced me. Switching over to my most recent conversation with Unknown, I type out the quick message.

GWEN GARDNER

Long time, no talk. You having a good day?

I pause for what feels like an eternity, but there's no response. Feeling gutsy, I type more.

GWEN GARDNER

I thought we were playing a game! Don't you want to play?

Still no response. I switch back to my conversation with Weston.

GWEN GARDNER

They didn't answer me. That phone's probably trashed.

WESTON MCCRAY

Or they're waiting for something before hitting you back up

GWEN GARDNER

Like what?

WESTON MCCRAY

That's up to us to find out

Our conversation falls silent as we both return our attention to the *Liarland* server, where they're eagerly going over the details of Alice's death for what I'm sure is the umpteenth time. Somehow, they know Dev and Jenna found the body, and that Valerie, Milly, and I appeared shortly after. Is someone at HPD leaking this information to them?

They speak about Alice with such pride. She was one of them, and now, she's infamous. Forever a part of the park's legacy.

I try not to bristle at how there are complete strangers having full-blown conversations about me in private chat rooms.

Ouch. Little do they know, Valerie was the reason I went to Wetlands that night, but not because we thought there was going to be a body. Valerie knows she's on thin ice. There's no way she'd get herself mixed up with another murder scandal willingly.

My eyes widen. Was this Thrill2Kill person watching me? And come on, I certainly was not batting my eyes at Asher. I try to remember who was at Cheezy's on Sunday that I'd recognize, but no one stands out to me. There was the young family and the couple giving each other the silent treatment. But I don't *know* any of them. The only person present I actually knew was Dev. I clamp down on the inside of my cheek, like the pain will make the horrible thought evaporate from my mind.

Thrill2Kill: That said, Gwen has a habit of placing her trust in all the wrong people.

Their username makes my nose wrinkle with disgust. Thrill2Kill. It's like some cheap imitation of Ride or Die. I guess that's more than likely their aim. Still, I can't help but find the parroting a tad pathetic.

It's hard not to try and picture the human on the other side of the screen. Someone lonely and miserable, no doubt. Are they Alice's boyfriend? Is that how they recognized Asher in the pizza place?

Thrill2Kill: She could be standing next to a dude waving a giant freaking knife and she'd still make some excuse as to why she believes in him.

I would not...

Not if I saw there was a knife...

But what if they had a good reason to be holding the knife?

"They don't know you," I remind myself, before feeling unbelievably pathetic for having to do so aloud.

The little voice in the back of my head reminds me that whoever killed Alice claims to know me. Which means someone I know well is lurking in the shadows of this chat room.

Thrill2Kill: Point is... if someone is toying with her, she's not playing right.

There's no way that word choice is a coincidence. I pick up my phone to text Weston, but I find he's beat me to it.

WESTON MCCRAY

Feel suspicious to you?

GWEN GARDNER

Yeah. I don't like that they're aware I know Asher

It's easy to understand how Weston got sucked into this rabbit hole. From the way these people are talking—like every one of their statements is a cold hard fact—it's easy to believe what you read. They're incredibly convincing because they sound so sure of themselves.

LastBreathBalloon: Luca should've taken Gwen out while he had the chance. She's such a boring heroine for this story.

I resist the urge to remind these losers that this is real life and not some scary movie they're watching. As if reading my mind, I receive a text from Weston.

I blink at my phone with surprise. That was oddly kind of him. Before I can respond with something clever, new messages in the chat room regain my attention. They're still on the topic of me, unfortunately.

PineBanned: i know right? she's not even good at her job. i went to hauntland a few weekends ago and i think my group scared her more than she scared us

LastBreathBalloon: That's because she's a pansy. Luca and Valerie were onto something when they picked Gwen to be their target. She'll roll over and do whatever anyone wants.

PineBanned: pretty bold of her to still work at pineland. she's just asking for trouble staying there.

RottenCoaster: Like I said… glutton for punishment

LastBreathBalloon: If you ask me, she didn't get enough punishment the first time around. Ride or Die took it easy on her.

RottenCoaster: Because Valerie is soft.

Thrill2Kill: I fear Luca and Valerie lacked the resources to be true showmen

crowsandprose: What would you have done differently?

Thrill2Kill: You'll have to wait and see ;)

This remark earns Thrill2Kill a shower of "exclamation point" and "thumbs up" reactions.

If I wasn't sure before, I certainly am now. This "Thrill2Kill" person is my unknown messenger. But can they actually be someone who knows me in real life? Or are they simply some stranger who's deluded themselves into thinking they know me?

If that's the case... I'll never be able to unearth their identity. I might as well give up now.

"What are you looking at?"

I startle at the voice behind me. Turning, I find Dev standing in my doorway. "You scared the crap out of me."

He rubs the back of his head sheepishly. "Sorry. Your mom let me in."

"And she let you come upstairs?"

His lips quirk. "So long as we keep the door open."

I let the ease in his voice settle my nerves. Sure, I definitely have some explaining to do, but at least he doesn't seem mad.

He plops down onto my bed beside me, also laying on his stomach to look at my laptop with a puzzled expression. "So, what's this?"

"A chat room Weston wanted to tell me about," I answer honestly before scrutinizing my boyfriend's face for any sign he might be familiar with the server.

Dev's face remains blank. "Why'd he want to show you this? Does he think Alice's killer is hanging out here?"

"That's exactly what he thinks."

"And why are you lurking about instead of calling the cops?"

"Pretty sure the cops are already in here," I say before closing my laptop. "I was just checking it out."

Dev frowns at me. "You know that's not good for your anxiety. You shouldn't be exposing yourself to these disgusting people. It's not healthy."

"I'm okay," I promise him, and when he offers me a skeptical look, I tack on, "I really am."

He blows out a breath, not taking his eyes off me. "Is that all Weston wanted? To talk to you about this chat room?"

"Not really. I think he just wanted to hear my perspective on Alice's death. He's been having a really hard time since summer."

"Why didn't he want to hear my perspective?"

I don't have a better answer than the truth. "Because he thinks it's weird that you found her."

Dev groans as his head falls over his arms on the bedspread. "Not him, too."

"Weston's been spending a lot of time on this server. It's kind of messed with his head. He thinks everyone is suspicious and out to get us."

"Us?" Dev notices my word choice immediately. "You two are an *us* now?"

"We both were targeted by Ride or Die last summer," I hurriedly explain. "That's all."

"So, he's not trying to trauma bond with you and ask you out or anything?"

I laugh, scratching the back of Dev's head. "No, nothing like that. Besides, everyone knows I'm far too invested in the boy I'm currently dating to be distracted by anyone else."

Dev finally raises his head. "You mean that?"

"Please," I pet his cheek, "it took ages for us to finally figure this out. I'm going to need a really good reason to give you up now."

"I promise not to give you one."

It's my turn to ask, "You mean that?"

"Cross my heart," he swears, leaning over to peck my lips. There's nothing I want more than to believe him.

Eager to reclaim any ounce of normalcy between us, I risk pulling him closer. After sneaking a peek at the doorway over my head, he happily responds.

The others are wrong to assume the worst, and so am I. My sweet Dev isn't mixed up with this.

"Kids!"

We fly apart at my mother's call from downstairs. Immediately, I pat down his hair while he wipes away some of my smudged lip gloss.

"Want to stay for dinner?" I ask him.

He breathes out a relieved laugh. "As long as you'll have me."

I let Dev take the lead as we depart my room. While he compliments my mother on how good the house smells, I slip out my phone and quickly type one last message to Unknown. Thrill2Kill. Whoever they are.

GWEN GARDNER

The only one who doesn't want to play right is you.

And to my horror, I see Dev's pocket light up.

CHAPTER
FOURTEEN

THE TEXT from a new number lights up my phone hours later, right as I'm crawling into bed. I try not to think about how Dev only left an hour ago to squeeze in some cello rehearsal before also retiring for the night. I received my 'good-night' text from him five minutes ago.

Has he really fallen asleep?

Stop putting those thoughts in your mind. I'm already hearing enough of it from Weston, who has completely convinced himself into believing Dev is actually a murderer.

Thinking of Weston reminds me that I should be responding to Thrill2Kill while I have their attention—especially if a clue to their identity is at stake.

Their reply comes in so swiftly that I realize they must've

had it already typed up. They knew I would be down before I even responded.

I sit up in my bed, staring at my screen in shock. It's nearly eleven o'clock at night. I'm not breaking into Pineland.

But what if this is my one chance to learn more? If I chicken out now, someone could die.

And so, despite my better judgement, I'm climbing out of bed and pulling on some black leggings and a matching hoodie. If I'm about to break into a freaking theme park, I might as well look the part.

But how on earth am I supposed to get in? The obvious answer pops into my head. And with my subconscious already on break, I'm reaching for my phone to make a call before considering the consequences.

She picks up on the third ring.

"Gwen? What's wrong?"

"Hey, Valerie," I breathe out, the gravity of what I'm about to ask suddenly sinking in. "I need your help."

Less than twenty minutes later, I'm slipping out of my house and jogging to Valerie's car, which is parked a street away. Spying Milly in the front seat, I quickly slide into the back. As I suspected, they were together when I reached out to my former friend. If we're going to have any hope of finding whatever clue Thrill2Kill left in the haunted house, we're going to need Milly's friends in security again.

"Thanks for this," I say to both of them as they study me from the front seats.

Valerie's eyes linger on my a little longer. "I'm glad you called."

As we drive through town, I explain my plan.

"Milly, you walk into security and tell them you're missing a ring light or something, and that you can't put off retrieving it any longer because you need it for work."

"You think Davis is going to buy that?" She laughs. "Actually, scratch that. He's probably so bored working the overnight shift that he'll take any excuse to talk with someone."

"Good. Keep him talking."

Only a few headlights pass us. It's too early in the week for tourists, so our fellow drivers are likely locals returning home after closing down their diner or gas station for the night. Hopefully none of them recognize us.

Yes, there's a decent chance we are caught on camera while sneaking into the park, but as long as Davis—who is meant to be monitoring the camera feeds—doesn't see us, we should be fine. If we're caught and arrested, so be it. I'll take it as a sign to quit playing games with a killer and let the cops take it from here.

"The hood makes you look like you're about to rob a bank," Valerie whispers to me once she parks her car in the lot. "You might as well carry a neon sign that says, 'I'm suspicious!'"

Rolling my eyes, I remove the black hood from over my head. If she weren't about to break the law for me, I'd remind her that she once ran around the park in the dead of night wearing a dark-and-mysterious hoodie of her own. Judging by the pinch of her lips, she knows exactly what I'm thinking.

"Yeah," Milly huff sarcastically, "can we please try our best not to get arrested tonight?"

"Babe, need I remind you that you have 'Mayor's Daughter' immunity?"

"Babe," Milly pointedly matches Valerie's tone, "that immunity only lasts if my dad wins his reelection."

"You better hope he does," Valerie kisses her cheek, "otherwise, you're mortal like the rest of us."

Milly can't fight off her grin. "Wouldn't you just love that."

There's no denying it. They make a pretty cute couple. I wonder what their plan is after graduation. Will they stick together? That doesn't seem like something Valerie would like —strings attaching her to the hometown she spent years hating. But maybe I'm not the only one whose perspective has changed. Surrounding yourself with different people will do that to you.

The parking lot gravel crunches under our feet as we reach the door to Crew HQ. Milly scans her ID into the front door while Valerie and I make a show of searching our pockets for our own IDs. When we come up empty-handed, we shrug and follow Milly inside. Hopefully, the guy watching the monitors will assume our trip to Pineland was not premeditated.

Though, I doubt showing up to the closed park twice in one day helps prove our case.

Before we make it four steps into the Crewmunity Hall, Davis appears. He's a tall, slender guy who graduated from Hathaway High about six years ago. Like many of his peers, he stayed close to town and took up a job at the park to put himself through college. But after he got his degree, he decided to keep working at the park.

I guess it's no longer my place to judge. I can't even muster up the energy to think about college.

He flicks his brunette bangs from his eyes to get a better look at us. "What are you three doing here so late?"

Immediately, Milly begins her spiel about the brand

campaign she had to stop shooting because her ring light died, and how she's confident she left a spare down in security.

"This couldn't wait until morning?"

"The content is due by then, and unless you want to be the reason I'm blacklisted for not submitting my deliverables in a timely manner—"

"Whatever, whatever." Davis raises his hands to cut her off. "Let's go get it."

Milly offers him a wide smile that only someone with "Mayor's Daughter Immunity" could get away with. "You're the best, Davy."

"Yeah, yeah. You two stay right here," he orders me and Valerie with a jab of his finger.

"Sure, after we go to the bathroom real quick," Valerie says.

Davis' eyes narrow skeptically, but what's he going to do? Tell us we can't use the restroom?

"Fine," he concedes. "But make it quick."

Valerie salutes him seriously. "Aye, aye."

We wait until they disappear down the stairwell to the security dungeon before hurrying out the back door and toward the park.

"Hood on," Valerie instructs.

I scoff with disbelief. "I thought we didn't want to look like bank robbers?"

She offers me a "girl, please be real" expression before tugging her hood over her dark hair.

I sigh, doing the same.

"Keep your head down and let's keep this quick."

We're quick to traverse into the dark park. With it being a Monday, there aren't any other signs of life. No overnight maintenance or crew members power washing the park. There aren't even fluorescent work lights on to illuminate the walkways or ride tracks. I can't remember the last time I saw the park in this state. Like it's been abandoned.

I can't help but wonder if that's the inevitable fate that awaits this cursed place. How many more scandals can it endure before someone steps in and closes it for good?

The *Play With Us* house is located near the main entrance turnstiles, so we veer in that direction. The creatives behind the haunted house were clever to build it inside the closed *Preying Plants* exhibit. No one is trying to learn about deadly plants—especially ones used to kill employees—so why not make use of the empty space?

"Did we ever stop and think that this could be a trap and Thrill2Kill is waiting inside to kidnap us?"

I freeze, feeling like a fool. Not once did this possibility cross my mind.

Reading this on my face, Valerie nods sarcastically. "Awesome. I always knew this stupid haunted house would be the death of me, but I'd hoped my cause of death would be being worked to the bone."

"Wait, let me tell Weston where we are," I say, whipping out my phone.

"Don't let him come. That boy isn't chill enough to play it cool."

I finish my text to Weston before saying, "I told him to call the cops if he doesn't hear from us in twenty-five minutes."

"Fantastic. Our fates rest in the hands of a boy who spends his free time taking checks to the head. What could go wrong?"

"I'm not answering that," I retort, cautiously approaching the plywood dollhouse facade. It looks perfectly charming and normal, aside from the bloody toy block letters that read the house's title.

"Can't believe I'm going to die here on my day off," Valerie grumbles as we cross the threshold.

"Which room are you in again?"

"I'm the dolly that dances on the bed with a knife."

"Fun."

"Super duper."

The only time I've walked through this haunted house was toward the beginning of the event's run. Dev and I chose to forgo resting on our break so we could see what else *Hauntland* had to offer. He might not like to admit it, but I'm pretty sure the boy is a closeted theme park nerd. Every time the park has something new to share, he's gotta be one of the first to see it. My complaints vanished as soon as he started holding my hand and protectively guided us through the house.

I can only hope we have many more opportunities to brave a haunted house together. All I want is for my suspicions to be totally off base. This clue could be exactly what I need to cross his name off my list.

Play With Us isn't terribly scary without the performers. The larger-than-life dollhouse is really just that without the killer dolls. I glance over the wooden furniture and loud wallpaper, looking for anything out of the ordinary.

That is, until I breathe in the smell.

My nose wrinkles at the rancid, but otherwise indescribable stench that seems to cling to every inch of the haunted house. All I know is I've never smelled anything this horrible in my whole life. "What on earth is that?"

"I heard a rumor they wanted to make our house more unsettling," Valerie says, pulling her sweatshirt over her nose. "Maybe they added a smell machine?"

I nearly gag at the odor. "And forgot to turn it off?"

"Remind me to call out of my next shift. This place is going to smell vile if they leave it running nonstop until then."

More motivated than ever to get this task over with, we pick up the pace, searching the dollhouse for any obvious clues as to Thrill2Kill's identity. There's colorful furniture in every room, and mannequins dressed up as plastic dolls strewn all over the place. As the story goes, the little girl who owned all these dolls never wanted to play with one for long before wanting a new plaything. Finally having enough, the abandoned dolls rebelled and now seek revenge on anyone who dares play in their dollhouse now.

"Nothing stands out to me," Valerie groans as we walk from room to room. The odor only seems to get worse the deeper we get. It's starting to make my eyes water.

Not wanting to miss anything, we run our hands over all the props, searching for anything that isn't glued down. But nothing budges. Not the pots or dishes in the kitchen, nor the toiletries in the bathroom.

Then we enter the bedroom, where Valerie is assigned to terrorize guests. If Thrill2Kill was going to hide a clue anywhere, this would be the most likely place.

Suddenly, my phone vibrates, making both of us jump.

"Tell Weston it hasn't even been ten minutes," Valerie grumbles, clutching her heaving chest.

"It's not Weston," I whisper, staring at my screen in shock.

Immediately, Valerie is at my side as we both read the message.

> UNKNOWN
>
> It appears you require another clue. You're looking for a bow.

"A bow?" I ask in disbelief. "Like a hair ribbon? How is that supposed to be a clue to their identity?"

"Maybe they wrote something on it? Or maybe we're about to discover Thrill2Kill is actually a Hathaway High cheerleader?"

"I don't know any cheerleaders!"

"Let's find the dumb bow first, and then we can decode its meaning."

She steers me through the closet door, which leads to a long hallway jam packed with racks of doll clothes. It's intentionally claustrophobic, and if I'm remembering correctly, performers dressed as furious dolls are staged behind the hanging clothes, ready to lunge out at unsuspecting guests.

My eyes widen when I realize long strands of hair bows hang in between the racks. A nuisance to get in the guest's face while they try to escape the dollhouse in one piece. There are dozens of them.

"Let's get to work," Valerie groans, picking the strand nearest her and inspecting every bow.

I do the same, standing on my tiptoes to reach the bows on the top of the string. "They all look perfectly ordinary!"

"I know." Valerie huffs with frustration.

But that doesn't stop us from searching every single bow. One by one, we inspect the pink-and-red ribbon tails. But nothing stands out. There aren't any secret messages or symbols written in sharpie. Hell, the bows are barely tattered or covered in blood.

When we reach the last few bows, our shoulders slump with defeat.

"Maybe there are other hair bows in the house?" I suggest, already feeling like we've lost. Was this just some test to see if we'd do exactly what Thrill2Kill wanted? Drop everything and obey their orders?

"There's only one room after this," Valerie reminds me. "And I highly doubt there are any bows decorating the playroom. Only toys."

She's right. The house's grand finale is a large toy room featuring every maniacal toy the dollies could want to enact their playtime revenge. Seesaws with chainsaw handlebars, rocking horse skeletons, and a ball pit full of grenades.

Out of habit, we run our hands over everything to see if anything moves. Toy blocks, colored pencils, and miniature knives. But nothing budges.

Helplessly, I glance around the room, looking for anything that might strike any sort of familiarity for me.

My mouth grows dry when my eyes land on it.

"They didn't mean *hair* bow," I whisper, staring at the

setup of musical instruments in the corner. There's a drum kit, trumpet, saxophone, and... a cello.

My lips pinching, I know the cello's bow will budge before I even reach for it. Still, as soon as I'm capable of lifting the bow from the stand, a cry rips through me.

"Gwen, are you sure?" Valerie's voice is a mile away.

This can't be real. It must be a cruel trick. Why would Dev leave this for me to find? Of course, I'd know the bow was his. I've seen it in his hand a thousand times.

When my phone vibrates, I feel close to puking. Are they watching? How do they know I've found it?

Why does *he* want me to know it's him?

UNKNOWN

It seems this exercise taught us both a lot about the other. All that's left to be seen is if you have the courage to do something with what you learned.

UNKNOWN

I know I do.

CHAPTER
FIFTEEN

Nearly forty-eight hours later, I still haven't heard anything else from Thrill2Kill, nor have I done anything with the bow. After sneaking it out of Pineland underneath my hoodie, I promptly stashed it in the darkest corner of my closet. As far as I was concerned, it could rot there alongside my other skeletons.

Unfortunately for me, the others seem to think differently.

"You have to confront him with it," Weston hisses during our private meeting in the school parking lot on Wednesday afternoon. "We're going to run out of time!"

We're loitering outside Milly's car in a tight huddle, as if that will rescue us from the abrasive October chill. The wind is determined to overhear our secrets, whether we want it to or not.

Only Asher is missing because his parents decided it would be best for them to attend a family counseling session together. I'm not sure how much longer they plan to stay in town. His parents have been delaying the funeral as long as possible. According to Asher, their hope is to put all of this to rest at once. Their daughter and her murder investigation, which is beginning to feel completely stagnant.

Aside from this "clue."

"That was Dev's bow, wasn't it?" Milly asks, sporting a no-nonsense look. As far as she's concerned, this situation is completely black and white. Thrill2Kill left us a crystal-clear clue. Now it's time to do something about it.

But I don't see the situation so clearly.

It's such an obvious clue. Too obvious. Why would Dev purposefully make his involvement with a murder case so apparent?

He wouldn't.

Which is why I'm so skeptical.

"You're all so desperate to catch a killer that you're not asking the right questions. Why play games when Dev could've just told me the truth himself?

"It was a test to see if you would do whatever Dev wanted of you, and you passed with flying colors."

I bark out a laugh. "Dev already knows I'd do anything for him! He doesn't need some creepy test to know that."

"Maybe he's secretly into some star-crossed criminal shit!" Weston throws his hands in the air, making it clear nothing is too outlandish to presume. "He needed to know if you were willing to break into Pineland for him before telling you the truth.

My eyes narrow with disbelief. "Are you listening to yourself? This isn't some criminal mastermind we're talking about. This is Dev!"

"Gwen," Weston's blue eyes lock onto mine, "when are you going to learn that people aren't always who they say they are?"

He not-so-covertly jerks his thumb in Valerie's direction.

"She gets it, asshole," Valerie says before grimacing at me. "But he kind of has a point, Gwen."

My shoulders slump. Not Valerie, too. She knows Dev nearly as well as I do. How can she turn on him so fast? It took me ages to start suspecting her last summer.

Am I still too trusting? My thoughts jump back to the *Liarland* server, where they all believe me to be the most gullible girl on the planet. Perhaps they have a point.

I didn't think that was possible. But judging by the looks on everyone's faces, I don't know anything at all.

They're all offering me the most pitying looks. Like I'm the saddest fool they've ever met.

My jaw clenches. "So what? You think I just march into Dev's house, waving his bow, and asking if he's a serial killer? Is that really what you think I should do?"

"More or less."

"And what if it's not him and I've just accused my boyfriend of being a murderer?"

Weston shrugs. "Then you beg for forgiveness."

"Have you forgiven Valerie and Jenna for framing you for murder last summer?" I ask point blank.

"I kind of feel like you all are acting like I'm not standing right here," Valerie grumbles.

"It's not our fault you're our best reference for a serial killer," Weston says unsympathetically.

"I didn't kill anyone!"

He shrugs at her again. "I forgave them. Sort of."

Valerie rolls her eyes. "I don't need your forgiveness. I was doing what had to be done and you didn't get arrested."

"That doesn't make it right," I remind her. Weston's newfound anxiety may have altered the course of his life forever. What if he can't afford college without a hockey scholarship?

Our classmates are racing out of their parking spots at a speed that would make our school resource officer hang his head. It seems like everyone has somewhere to be after school today.

Valerie exhales a watery breath. "I don't know how many more times you want me to apologize for last summer."

"You don't have to apologize anymore," Weston says, his

face surprisingly blank. "But you do have to accept that you've changed the way we think and make decisions."

"Val, you being on the, um, other side of this scenario," Milly interjects, clearly trying to insert some positivity into this conversation, "might actually be more helpful than you know. Do you think Dev could be mixed up in this?"

After studying her shoes for what feels like ages, Valerie meets my gaze. "I can't think of why Dev would ever want to take on the role of Ride or Die. As far as we know, he's a stand-up guy. Good grades, likes to follow the rules, strong moral compass. I highly doubt he's secretly harboring some blood-thirsty desires."

"Of course not," I scoff. The idea of my courteous and cautious boyfriend wanting to kill anyone is laughable.

"So," Valerie continues, after a shaky breath, "if Dev were to pick up that mantle, it would be because he thought he had no other choice. Which means it's not so great of a leap to assume someone or something is forcing him to do so."

This perks me up. "You think there's a puppet master pulling his strings?"

"I don't know what to think, Gwen, but I don't think we can leave anything off the table right now."

"Agreed," I nod my head, "which is why I don't think it's a good idea for me to walk into Dev's house and wave this bow in his face."

Weston tilts his chin skyward. "You're killing me, Gwen. There's a reason Thrill2Kill left it for you to find."

"Yeah, they want to see if I have the guts to bring it to Dev, or worse, the cops." I take a long moment to meet everyone's eyes. "They want me to play, but what if I'm playing right into their hands? I don't want to make any rash decisions and do something wrong. This is feeling more like a trap every day—one we're walking right into.

"So, no, I'm not going to show anyone the bow. It can stay

hidden in my closet until I'm ready to do something with it. Are we clear?"

There's a long pause, but one by one, they all concede with nods.

"Good," I sigh with relief. "We need to tackle this better than last time. We know everyone in this freaking town is a liar, so why are we dead set on believing everything they say?"

"Fair point," Valerie mutters under her breath.

"Hey, what are we all talking about?"

We all freeze at the sound of Dev's voice. I barely have the courage to look over my shoulder at him as he comes to stand behind me. But that doesn't stop me from being totally aware of his presence. I'm surprised I didn't sense him walking up. The sweet smell of his juniper-scented cologne and his innate ability to make my insides sizzle when he's close by.

Please let it not be him, I plead with the universe.

"Halloween plans for the party after work on Saturday!" Valerie's lie slips out easily because of course it does.

"What's there to plan?" Dev might ask the question casually, but I hear the tremor of suspicion in his voice.

"Just debating if we should carpool or not!" Milly chimes in.

When he looks at me with skepticism, the bow flashes in my mind. So, with my insides screaming, I play along with the lie and nod at him.

With guilt nipping at my heart, I watch as the cruel reality dawns on my boyfriend's face. He knows I'm lying.

Does that mean we're even?

CHAPTER
SIXTEEN

Since that moment, Dev's been walking on eggshells around me. He's careful with his choice of words and provides unnecessary details about his day. His candor doesn't make me feel any better because that evil voice in the back of my mind is convinced it's all strategy.

Or maybe I've been spending too much time with Weston.

Now it's Thursday, and there's still no word from Thril-l2Kill. What's worse, despite spending all my free time on the *Liarland* server, all I have to show for my efforts is a boatload of new fears for people who think they know me better than I know myself.

It's so tempting to call Thrill2Kill's bluff and loop in the authorities. I know they said if I did, someone would die, but I've heard that line before and it was a total lie. The thing is— what if they're not bluffing? I allegedly know their next target. One wrong move and blood could be on my hands.

It's this fear, combined with the insistence that I keep my mouth shut from Weston, Valerie, Milly, and Asher, that holds me back. All I can do is scrutinize everyone I come into contact with and hope for another clue.

If Dev truly is Thrill2Kill, then he's got a scary good poker face. Not once has he let on that I accused him of being a cold-blooded murderer.

Maybe he's not.

He's probably not.

But what if he is?

Unfortunately, I have the worst poker face known to man. I know Dev can tell something's bothering me. I keep coming up with excuses as to why we can't hang out after school for long. Whenever he touches me, I find myself bracing instead of leaning in.

I know the invisible barrier between us hurts him, but I'm not the only one who built it brick by brick. Lie by lie.

Still, during our drive to our Thursday evening shift at Hauntland, it's clear Dev's had enough.

"Is something wrong, Gwen?"

I feign ignorance. "What do you mean?"

He barks out a laugh. "What do I mean? My lifelong friend-turned-girlfriend can barely look at me, let alone speak to me. It's obvious something is bothering you, and if I had to guess, you're still not over the Alice stuff."

Maybe it's a curse for some people to know you so well.

My only defense is silence. I bear it like a shield over the center console as I keep my attention forward. It's juvenile of me, but I'm past the point of caring.

"Don't want to talk about it?" Dev calls me out. "That's fine. I can talk for the both of us."

My jaw clenches, but still, I say nothing.

"You're pissed at me for not being entirely honest about how well I knew Alice."

So well that she has a photo of you on her phone.

"I understand what that looks like, especially when you see things with your particular lens."

"What lens would that be?" I snap.

"The lens of a girl who's been betrayed by someone she loved and then mocked by the world for it," he says back. "You have every right to be skeptical. I knew this when we started dating, so I only have myself to blame. I should've told you everything from the start, but I can't change the past. I can only hope my actions from here on out will help re-solidify your trust in me so we can move forward."

After a long, agonizing pause, he finally asks, "Is that want you want? For us to move forward?"

I sigh, because finally, this is a question I can answer.

"Of course I do," I confess. "There's nothing I want more than to move on from all this, but I still think it's going to take some time."

It's the truth. I need time to confirm my fears are off base.

I sneak a peek over at him and find his face expressionless. Then, after he realizes I've been staring, he offers me a single jerk of his chin.

"Of course, babe. Whatever you need. You set the terms. I'm on your schedule."

"Thanks," I mutter, praying he isn't going to make me define those terms right now.

Mercifully, he does not, and we pull into the crew member parking lot in silence. That quiet continues as we hop out of his truck and trudge into Crew HQ.

I'm pretty sure the only people not eagerly anticipating Halloween weekend are the crew members. A few weeks into our run, we've all had our fill of the holiday. And unfortunately, the job only gets tougher this weekend. Crowds are expected to reach an all-time high. Halloween night was already destined to be packed before Wendy Thatcher announced her grand firework finale.

Instead of bustling around the Crewmunity Hall, happy we're nearly done with our run, the crew members are dragging their feet. This, combined with the ghoulish monster prosthetics and ragged costumes, makes us look deader than ever. The guests will be thrilled.

Dev waves goodbye to me as we disappear into our respective locker rooms, wishing me a good shift. I guess he heard my underlying request loud and clear. I need some space to figure things out.

After I don my witch's garb and stringy wig, I dodge the makeup chair. I'm not in the mood for a bunch of uncomfortable prosthetics to be glued onto my face. Hannah spends most event nights locked in her office, so hopefully she won't notice I'm missing my witchy nose and warts. Even if she does, I'm not sure I can bring it upon myself to care.

Thank goodness it's a short shift tonight. On school nights, the event is cheaper and concludes at 11:00 pm. The schedulers are usually pretty good about releasing the high school employees first, so we can get a decent night of sleep before school in the morning. Not that it will keep most of my classmates from still showing up tardy on Friday. It's an easy excuse to give the front office.

Unfortunately, my parents have forbidden me from using it. They might say they don't care what people in this town think of them, but I know my parents are still secretly concerned with their reputation. As such, a Gardner will not be tardy. Not to school, work, or anywhere else.

With this in mind, I return to the atrium to hop in the long line at the complimentary coffee station. Sweetener and cream rest next to the carafe, and it appears someone has donated a few containers of pumpkin spice creamer. Longing to feel any kind of excitement ahead of what I used to consider my favorite holiday, I add a glug of the creamer to my cup. I already know it'll turn my coffee too sweet, but at this point, I'll try anything.

After not hearing from Thrill2Kill for a few days, I'm starting to wonder if I imagined the entire ordeal.

But when Weston appears next to me, I realize I'm not so lucky. He's already dressed in his Michigan Dogman costume, which doesn't appear as terrifying under the fluorescent lights. The wiry sideburns and eyebrows glued onto his face don't seem as wild. It's easier to remember the blood on his shredded shirt is fake.

I take a slow sip of my coffee, immediately wincing at how sugary it tastes.

"Well don't you look thrilled to see me," Weston snorts as he follows me out of the atrium and through backstage to the park.

Normally, I'd wait for Dev so we could walk over to our haunted house together, but I can't have him overhearing whatever Weston is about to say. Pushing away the guilty pit in my stomach, I pass around the tall wall that hides the back of house from guest view and enter the park of my worst nightmares.

"What do you want now?"

"We're meeting during our breaks."

I don't have to ask who "we" refers to.

"How do we know our breaks will be at the same time?"

"They will be," Weston says with such confidence that my eyes roll. No doubt he sweet talked someone in scheduling.

The park isn't open to guests for another twenty minutes, so the only people around are crew members preparing for the night ahead. Those at snack stands prepare treats exclusive to the event—cinnamon doughnut holes on a skewer, candy apples with blood-red coating that glistens in the flashing park lights, and pumpkin spice-flavored popcorn, which actually isn't as bad as it sounds.

Loud music blares over the park speakers. It's an unnerving playlist of intense-sounding rock songs overlaid with swelling synths and piercing screams. Not that we'll need artificial cries soon. The park will be filled with them in due time.

"And where are we meeting?"

"Inside the Fake Oak."

I stop on my tracks. Weston keeps moving as I spare a look at the enormous tree on my left. The park's centerpiece is lit bright purple for the event. My nose wrinkles at the sight of it. A secret meeting where Luca died last summer? Seriously?

I was under the impression that they put a new lock on the door so only maintenance and security could access it. But I guess I can't put anything past Milly and her shady allies.

Apparently, Weston doesn't seem to think this location is insensitive or ironic. We're nearly to his assigned scare zone, *Lair of the Dogman*. Prop RVs and a campsite loom up ahead, waiting to be "ravaged" by Weston the Dogman all night long. That is, until his appointed break, in which case, another Dogman takes over.

"Why are we even meeting?" I grumble, catching up to him. "I haven't received a message from Thrill2Kill in days. I'm starting to think this is all some sort of prank—"

Weston moves to block my path so swiftly that I jump.

"You're walking right into their trap," he says, not bothering to hide his disgusted expression as he gazes down at me. "They want you to get comfortable."

"You're spending too much time online."

"And you're clearly not," Weston agrees with a casual shrug. "Which is exactly what we're meeting to discuss."

My eyes narrow. "Did you see something on *Liarland*?"

"Not here." He takes a step closer, as if that'll make me lower my voice.

My jaw clicks as I evaluate the boy in front of me. He's changed so much in the last few months. Long gone is the guy too cool for anything. I guess I shouldn't fault him for caring. But I fear his constant paranoia is only going to make mine worse.

"Fine," I mutter under my breath as I duck around Weston and head toward my post, which is deeper into the park.

"Have a super-scary-save-the-world night!" he calls after me.

I pick up the pace.

The facade for *Flytrap*, my haunted house, comes into view. The name is written in glowing green paint on a wooden board that is nailed to an actual tree. The first half of the house begins with a trek through the real forest on the outskirts of Pineland before evidence of the Witch's lair begins to appear.

I pass through the eerie forest, where larger-than-life vines snap at guests. Instead, my costumed colleagues sit against the prop trees and enjoy their last few minutes of rest before the park opens. I try not to think how Dev will soon be stationed here, wondering why I ditched him back in Crew HQ.

The facade for the Witch's house appears, and I swiftly duck inside. The house is vaguely Victorian (aka cluttered with whatever the set dressing department could find at local flea markets) and full of emerald houseplants. But if guests closely inspect the hanging ivy and eucalyptus plants, they'll find them to be anything but ordinary. Speakers hidden in the planters make it sound like they have growling stomachs.

I'm not sure where Wendy Thatcher found the budget for such a setup, but I'm not in the business of questioning my boss's spending habits so long as it's not bribing teenagers to create scandalous headlines to sell park tickets.

Without warning, the haunted house's background audio starts blaring, making me jump.

The sound of a thousand flies buzzing all around is meant to unnerve guests while simultaneously reminding them they are part of the swarm. The Witch's precious plant monster has long graduated from eating little insects and is ready for a much larger and more human meal.

Swallowing hard, I attempt to calm my racing heart as I head through the house, out onto the back porch, and into the garden shed.

The last time I was here, my world got turned upside down. Again. Maybe I should've called in sick. My parents were apprehensive to let me return to work, but I was too scared my cowardness would put them in danger. I don't want to do anything out of the ordinary if Thrill2Kill is watching me. Under no circumstance can I give them the impression I caved and ran to the cops.

"Hey Gwen," a voice titters behind me.

I turn to find Jenna, wearing an identical costume as mine. Her blonde pixie cut is covered by the same long, silver wig. She, however, is wearing all the assigned warts.

Facing her is almost as bad as Dev. But it was bound to happen. She's the Mad Witch in the next room, after all.

She gives me the once over before grinning at me knowingly. For a moment, I wonder if she'll tattle—and then I realize I don't care.

"How's it going?" I ask dryly.

"Great!" She bears the grin of a girl who didn't stumble across a body in her mother's water park a few days prior. "Just have to get through tonight and then school tomorrow before it's Halloweekend!"

"Big plans?"

"My boyfriend is coming into town to celebrate."

My eyebrows shoot up. "Boyfriend?"

I didn't know Jenna was seeing anyone. Is this why Dev was so confident she was completely over him? Did he know? Why not say anything and ease my nerves?

"Uh-huh," Jenna says with a pleased smirk. My dislike for the girl quickly returns. She's enjoying the fact that Dev didn't tell me. "He's from out-of-town, so we don't get to see each other often."

Immediately, I'm reminded of Alice, who also had an out-of-town boyfriend on the down low. "How'd you meet?"

"Online! He—"

Our house manager, Frankie, enters with a clipboard. He fights off a grimace when he sees Jenna not yet in her place, but no one's going to tell off the boss's daughter.

"House opens in five, ladies!"

"Thank you, five!" Jenna chirps back in a singsong voice

that makes me want to claw my eyes out. This girl really brings out the worst in me.

"Gwendolyn!" Frankie gasps. "You forgot your makeup!"

Fantastic. Just what I needed to happen in front of Jenna.

I feign ignorance, running my hands over my face. "Oh my gosh! I'm so sorry. Do you want me to run back to Crew HQ?"

"We don't have time for that now," he groans. "Just make sure you fix it during your break."

"Gotcha," I respond with a thumbs up.

"Accidents happen to the best of us," Jenna consoles me. "It's been a long run for everyone."

With a wave of her fingers, she disappears into the next room, taking Frankie with her. Jaw clenched, I watch them disappear from view.

Man, that girl can get under my skin and she knows it. What's worse—I'm more frustrated at myself than I am at her. I'm the one giving her this power over my emotions. It's ridiculous.

Before I have time to properly brace myself for a long shift of horror, the guests start milling through the haunted house. Their screams ricochet around the walls of the shed, almost drowning out the ominous synths pounding through the speakers. I pop out on cue, waving my trowel, and chasing the terrified groups into the next room.

A figure with a black hoodie walks through the room alone, but they look to be a different build from the one who spoke with me last Saturday. Besides, a black sweatshirt at a Halloween event isn't exactly out of the ordinary. Half of the guests in the park are wearing black.

I don't let my anxious thoughts distract me from my work. I'm not going to spiral tonight.

I hold myself to that until the person in the hoodie walks through again. They're still alone.

I hit them with my most menacing snarl, but they don't

flinch or even pick up the pace into the next room. Which begs the question—just how many times have they walked through our haunted house?

By their fourth appearance, I begin to lose control of reality. Am I seeing things? Why are they walking through the house nonstop?

I really picked the wrong night to skip out on my face-concealing prosthetics.

"Be gone!" I hiss at them, trying to drop a hint while staying in character.

They say nothing back as they easily stroll by. In fact, they don't even glance my way. Have they ever? Not once have I caught a glimpse of their face. Their hood is always pulled too far over their head for me to make out any distinguishable features.

So what's going on?

Maybe I'm in too deep and searching for signs that aren't there. This could have nothing to do with me. There's a good chance this guest simply likes our house. Isn't that a good thing? Why does my anxious brain have to twist everything into some malicious, horrible scheme?

When they come through a fifth time, I'm starting to wonder just how long our line is and if we really should be open on a school night. If this guest can pass through so frequently, something's up. Or maybe they know the crew member working out front and they're hopping the line.

Whatever it is, I'm starting to completely lose my composure.

"What do you want?" I demand. "Go do something else already!"

Again, they say nothing as they stride into the next room.

I don't even bother popping out for their sixth and seventh trips through the house. Instead, I peek out of my hiding spot like I'm the one in the situation who's supposed to be cowering in fear. It's pathetic, but it's the only thing keeping me from absolutely losing my mind.

By their eighth pass through of the house, I've stopped popping at every single group that comes through. I'm beginning to wonder if I should report them to a manager. I am permitted to abandon my post if I feel uncomfortable in any way.

But technically, the guest isn't doing anything wrong. They're not saying anything to me. Hell, they're not even looking at me when they pass. I don't think they care one bit that I haven't popped out and scared them.

Get a grip and do your job.

If I don't want to feel like a victim in every situation, I need to stop acting like one when I'm not.

And so, despite the warning sirens going off inside my head, I muster my best snarl and prepare to give them the meanest scare of their life the next time they pass through. I don't have to wait long. I only hear a single set of footsteps approaching.

Just as I move to pop out of my hiding spot, I find the room empty. Then, movement to my right startles me upright. When I shriek, strong arms from behind me wrap around my middle, and despite my thrashing, they pull me into the dark hole.

"Let go of me!"

"Gwen," his voice is warm in my ears, "babe, it's just me."

Immediately, I sink back against Dev and let him cradle me close to his chest. Anxious tears blur my vision, making me feel like a fool. I worked myself into the most ridiculous state and over what? A stranger at a theme park? That shouldn't scare me.

And yet, I'm positively petrified. I'd go as far as to assume I'm the most terrified person at this theme park haunt.

"You're shaking. Gwen, tell me what happened."

"Someone was coming through the house nonstop.

They're wearing a black hoodie like the person from last week-end." Every few words are punctuated by a sharp breath as I fight to regain control of my breathing.

Instantly, Dev turns me around to face him. His dark eyebrows crease with concern as he searches me for any sign of harm. "Are you hurt?"

I blink away the tears clouding my vision as I cling to him. "No. They didn't do anything to me."

"But you think it was them?"

My breathing spikes as I confess, "I think *everyone* is them."

Dev sucks in a breath when he realizes what I mean. I brace myself for his retort, but instead, he takes my face into his hands as his lips crash onto mine.

I freeze in his arms, but only for a moment. I used up whatever resistance I had for this boy last year. Now, I'm incapable of doing anything but kissing him back.

Wrapping my arms around him, I kiss him deeper and allow the way my best friend tastes to flood my head. I wash away every thought of danger until there's only him.

"It's not me," Dev insists against my lips. "I swear it."

"I know," I say, despite not knowing anything.

As if sensing my apprehension, he kisses me harder. Only when I'm completely out of breath, does he pull back to say, "I know you, Gwen. I know how that head of yours operates. It's spinning round and round, trying to make sense of what's a lie and what's real. Give it a moment to rest."

And so, I do. Rising to capture his mouth with mine, I let my mind shut off for anything that isn't Dev. I allow my fingers to weave into his hair so I can tug him closer. He immediately complies, carefully walking me until my back is pressed against the plywood wall. His hands tight at my waist, I let Dev kiss me until I'm utterly breathless again.

"This is real, Gwen. You and me. We're real." Dev's thumb gently rubs against my bottom lip, ensuring my brain commits the way he kisses to memory. "You don't have to believe me now. Take as long as you want to find the truth. I'll still be here when you sort it all out."

"What if I take too long?" I whisper.

"I waited years for you, Gwen. I can be patient a little longer." His midnight eyes still manage to glisten in the dark. "Take your time and find the truth you need. It'll only make us stronger after you do."

"Thank you." The words crack in my throat as I swell with relief.

I watch him swallow before he asks, "Are you okay to finish your set? Or do you want me to get you out of here?"

I want nothing more than for the latter to occur, but I know I need to prove to myself that I'm capable of doing this job without crumbling. If I don't get into college or figure out what I want to do with the rest of my life, this place might be all I have.

"I can finish this set," I insist.

"See you at our break then," he says with a smile that only falters when he sees me wince. "What is it?"

"Weston wants to speak with me during break. Privately."

Dev's eyes harden. "Again?"

"He's helping me find the truth," is all I can manage. The guilt is making my tongue go dry in my mouth.

It's Dev's turn to wince. "And you trust him?"

"I'm doing the best I can."

His throat bobs again before he uses a finger to lift my chin, locking my eyes with his. "Tell Weston I'm driving you home. If that's what you want."

I raise on my toes to press my lips against his in answer. Soon, Weston and the others are going to try to further convince me of Dev's involvement with Thrill2Kill. This kiss is going to keep my head screwed on right. Dev would never betray me. I have to believe that to be true.

A loud group of guests passing on the other side of the thin wall has us remembering where we are.

"I'll see you after work," I promise.

Dev straightens my wig before pecking my forehead. "Already counting down to it."

And with that, he leaves me to finish pulling myself together in peace. The others are wrong about him. My Dev is too good to take part in such hideous deeds.

After ensuring my costume is hanging properly, I sneak a peek at my phone to see how much longer I have until break. I don't even register the time because a new text message claims my entire attention. My pulse spikes again as I read it.

UNKNOWN

I missed you, too.

CHAPTER
SEVENTEEN

I FIND Asher waiting for me outside of the haunted house. My pulse still hasn't settled since Thrill2Kill confirmed their presence at the event, but the sight of a familiar face brings me some ease.

"Hey," I say, walking up to him. "I didn't know you'd be at the park tonight."

I keep my hooded cloak wrapped tightly around my costume. Hopefully, no one will recognize me. I don't want one of these *Liarland* weirdos spotting me with Asher Crane.

"My parents are a lot to handle right now," he explains. "I know that's an awful thing to say given our circumstances, but I need a break from the wallowing. All they want to do is sit around, crying and feeling helpless."

I wince when a fake scream rings out over the park's speakers. "And this is better?"

"I don't want to waste away in a hotel room and think about how my sister is never coming back. I want to do something to avenge her." The fierce determination in his voice could drive anyone into battle. "Besides, Weston told me everyone is meeting up to discuss a new development."

Those bright blue eyes cut to something over my shoulder.

When a familiar shadow looms over me, I don't have to look over to know Dev has joined the conversation.

"Asher, right?" my boyfriend asks. "How are you doing with everything?

"About as good as you'd expect for a guy whose sister was murdered."

Dev and I both wince at Asher's harsh response. Unlike me, it's clear the boy has no problem icing Dev out until he's proven innocent. He believes Dev to be his sister's secret boyfriend, and subsequently, her killer.

"Have the detectives found any new leads?" Dev asks diplomatically.

"Not yet."

"I'm sorry to hear that, man."

"Uh-huh."

This is getting painful. Before I can attempt any sort of mediation between the boys, another shadow joins the conversation.

Glancing up, my lips part when I find the shadow attached to Detective Weegan.

Shit.

He's the last person I should be seen conversing with in public. What if Thrill2Kill notices and thinks I've given up the game? I highly doubt they're far off. They could be watching me right now.

As if on cue, the hairs on the back of my neck stand on end. It's all I can do to keep myself from glancing around guiltily.

"I wondered if that was you under that getup, Gwendolyn," the detective says breezily. "May I have a moment."

"I—uh," I stammer awkwardly. Neither of the boys jump to my rescue. "I don't have that long of a break."

"It'll only be a moment."

"Shouldn't my parents be present?"

"This isn't an official conversation whatsoever. Just a casual hello and catch up."

This feels anything but casual, but who am I to blow off the Hathaway Police Department?

Both Dev and Asher offer me looks of concern for entirely different reasons. Dev's nervous I might be in trouble, while Asher doesn't want me to overshare and put anyone else at risk. I give them a look that I hope implies everything is going to be okay. I'm going to walk this tightrope the best I can. All I can hope is that a net is strung up underneath.

After sharing a last suspicious glance at one another, the boys depart in opposite directions. His face expressionless, Detective Weegan blinks after them before steering me toward a nearby bench. Thankfully, it's a little out of the guests' normal walking path, as there's not a scare zone or snack cart nearby. Most people are walking to the queue for *Flytrap* or away from it. Hopefully no one will see me talking with the man.

We may be off the beaten path, but that doesn't stop me from glancing around to see if I spy a hooded figure lurking in the shadows. Somehow, Thrill2Kill feels everywhere and nowhere, only appearing when I least expect it and never on my terms.

I fear it's their way of reminding me who's in control.

"I don't want to take up much of your time," he begins, voice low and husky. "I know your breaks aren't nearly long enough."

"Do you?"

"Back when I was your age, I had a cousin who worked at Pineland. We'd visit him in the summer, and he'd complain all about the hours."

This piques my interest. "Does he still work here?"

"No." Weegan clears his throat. "But the point is that I'm going to get right into it."

"I thought this was a friendly catch up?"

"Did you, KillaSquirrel?"

I stiffen under his knowing stare. "How did you—"

His thick mustache quirks. "I know a lot more than I let on, Gwendolyn Gardner."

It takes me a moment to recover enough to say, "I guess that's probably a good thing."

"I suppose so." He pauses for a moment before asking, "What about you? Do you know more than you let on?"

"I told you everything I knew the night we found Alice's body."

"And how about since then?"

I attempt to harness whatever acting skills I picked up from Valerie and offer the detective a puzzled expression.

"A girl who's avoided any and all discussion of herself on the internet doesn't randomly join an online server centered around that very subject."

"How *do* you know I joined that server?"

"I wouldn't be a very good detective if I didn't take notice of any new members, and trust me, fresh faces are few and far between. All it took was a quick check of your IP address to confirm what I already deduced. So, now I must ask, what made you join?"

"I'm trying to get over my fear of people talking about me online."

"By throwing yourself straight into the inferno?"

Unable to outright explain why I joined, I decide my best way forward is to drop breadcrumbs. Hopefully, the detective is clever enough to follow them straight to Thrill2Kill.

"Some interesting people on there, don't you think?"

He studies me. "Incredibly. They're a bloodthirsty lot, who take pride in outdoing each other in terms of their grue-someness."

"Do you think any of them are actually capable of following through with what they say online?"

"Few are," he responds easily. "It would take a real

showman to transcend the online chatter and delude themselves into actually taking action."

The way he says this—with such confidence—gives me pause. It makes me wonder just how far into the mind of a murderer Detective Weegan has burrowed to solve his cases.

A chilling breeze dances past our bench, making me shiver. I'm beginning to wish we weren't so out of the way from guest traffic. Thrill2Kill might not notice me back here, but no one else will, either.

I decide to pivot our conversation. "How's the Alice investigation going?"

His eyes cut to me. "I'm sitting here and talking to you. How do you think it's going?"

I nod. "That's what I figured. If it makes you feel any better, you're as stumped as I am."

"Surprisingly, that doesn't make me feel good at all. Why are you digging your nose into this?"

"I can assure you, it's not willingly."

The detective sighs. "Gwen, I'm going to come outright and ask. Is Ride or Die back?"

I hold his gaze when I say meaningfully, "Ride or Die is not back, Detective, but you know as well as I that there are many dangerous people in this world."

"You know something."

"No more than you," I insist. "Not really."

"Please don't make me bring you in, Ms. Gardner."

"It won't help either of us."

His face grows expressionless again as he ponders my words. "What will?"

"Gwen!"

My heart pounds with relief at the sound of Asher's voice.

"I got you some!" he calls, waving a bag full of lime-green cotton candy.

"I'm gonna go," I whisper to the detective, "and enjoy what's left of my break."

"I thought you were seeing the Vishwakarma boy?" Weegan asks pointedly.

"I am."

The detective blinks after Asher before shaking his head like he doesn't care.

"Dev trusts me," I assure Weegan, though I'm not sure why I'm defending myself. I've done nothing wrong.

"Of course," the detective nods. "But I can't help but ask —do you trust him?"

"Why wouldn't I?"

"From my short tenure in Hathaway, I've come to learn it's hard to fully trust just about anyone in this town."

I breathe out a low laugh. "Ain't that the truth."

He examines me once more, his fingers tapping rhythmically on his knee as he does so. "This isn't some game to me. It's real life, which means there are real consequences. So, I'm keeping an eye on you, Gwendolyn Gardner."

"I'm counting on it, Detective." My gut twists in the same way it does when I've ridden too many roller coasters on an empty stomach.

I'm not lying, I try to tell myself. *I'm just dancing around the truth.*

But what if it's that very dance that gets someone killed?

As I jog to join Asher, the back of my neck continues to prickle. I don't dare glance around to try to find whose eyes are on me, but that doesn't stop me from shivering at the intensity of their hidden gaze.

Thrill2Kill is watching. Of that, I am sure.

All I can hope is that I passed their test.

CHAPTER
EIGHTEEN

THE LAST PLACE I want to be at night is inside the Fake Oak, but I'm learning that when it comes to this theme park, my wants are not taken into consideration.

Asher and I are the last to slip through the small utility door hidden at the base of the trunk. Weston, Valerie, and Milly stand in a tight circle in the rounded room, waiting for us.

Behind them, a stairwell winds up to the top of the cement tree. I try not to remember that one of our classmates died here a few months ago.

"Did we really have to meet in here?" I cross my arms to squash the chill shooting up my spine.

Asher's eyes are as big as saucers as he takes in the unsettling space. I watch his grip tighten around the bag of cotton candy, like it's a stuffed rabbit cuddled for comfort during a storm. "I'm gonna agree with Gwen. We can't think of anywhere better?"

Weston drawls, "Would you rather we meet at the Old Wheel?"

"No," Valerie and I say in unison. Our eyes cut to each other before we both turn away.

I'd pick a meeting at the center of the park over a decrepit, out-of-order Ferris Wheel on the outskirts of the property any day. Nothing good happens at the Old Wheel. *Nothing*.

"What took you two so long?" Milly demands, her eyes suspiciously darting between Asher and me.

Having just explained my conversation with Weegan to Asher, I sigh and restart the tale.

"Detective Weegan wanted to speak with me. He knows about the *Liarland* chat room... and he knows there's something I'm not telling him."

I feel the air leave the cramped space. "You didn't divulge the threat you received?"

"No," I admit to relieved sighs, "and hopefully, he can reach his own conclusions. But I'm worried our conversation is going to make Thrill2Kill unhappy."

"How would they know?" With one look at my face, Valerie presses further. "What happened?"

My lips pinch helplessly. "Someone wearing a hoodie kept coming through the house. I'm pretty sure it was Thrill2Kill."

The others gasp. "Did they say something to you?"

"No, but I finally got a text back from Thrill2Kill afterwards." I pull out my phone and read the message aloud to them. "I missed you, too."

Everyone frowns with confusion at the vague message.

Valerie finds her voice first. "But they didn't make contact with you before this?"

"No. I kind of freaked out when they kept coming through the house and Dev came to comfort me." I catch the others sharing a look over my head and immediately cross my arms with frustration. "Seriously? Come on! Can we finally move on from this theory that Dev is Thrill2Kill? My boyfriend is not a murderer!"

No one has the guts to meet my eyes.

"Why will none of you try to give him the benefit of the doubt!"

"Because I sure as hell didn't deserve one!" Valerie laughs dryly. "Good people can do bad things, Gwen. I figured you'd know that by now."

My head tilts skyward. Their insistence that Dev is involved only makes me want to prove them wrong even more. The more time that passes, the surer I become that someone is trying to set Dev up. Every single clue pointing to him is starting to feel more suspicious than the clues themselves.

Observing my agony, Weston graciously moves the conversation forward. "Did Weegan mention the gathering the *Liarland* people are planning?"

"What gathering?" I frown at him. "I didn't see them talk about that in *Liarland*."

"Because it was in a private, invite-only chat room," Asher explains, earning surprised looks from the rest of us. He shrugs. "If my sister's killer is lurking on there, you bet I'm finding a way into every dark corner of that server."

"You're in this private room, too?" I ask Weston.

He nods. "It's where the most, um, *eager* members converse."

"Is anyone else we know a member?"

"Thrill2Kill's on the list, if that's what you're asking. They all have tickets to come to the event tomorrow night and are planning to hit up every spot where someone died."

I can't keep the disgust from my face. Those vile, heartless *monsters*. There's no way my sweet Dev could be one of them. Not in a million years.

"Do we think they're going to try to hurt someone tomorrow? Bring one of their plans to life?"

"Who's to say?" Asher responds, "Which is why you're going to join in."

"Excuse me?" I gape at him. "We can't go anywhere near them. They'll recognize most—if not all—of us."

He tugs at a strand of my wig. "You're not so easy to spot in this."

"Thrill2Kill doesn't seem to be having a hard time finding me in the *Flytrap* house," I retort.

"That's why we are going to switch roles tomorrow," Milly says with a sly grin.

I slowly blink at the girl, not believing what I'm hearing. "Milly, you *hate* wearing monster makeup."

When Wendy Thatcher first announced Hauntland and asked crew members what roles they may be interested in, Milly made it widely known she wouldn't accept a seasonal role in entertainment.

"That makeup is horrible for your skin," I recall her loudly proclaiming. "All my skincare brand partnerships will drop me!"

Wendy Thatcher wasn't returning the girl to security, so that's how Milly Dillard wound up working in the wardrobe department. It was one of the few roles that kept the social media starlet backstage. Besides, Nathaniel Jones, the wardrobe manager, needed all the help he could get maintaining our brand new costumes. Though, none of them look all that new, considering they're shredded to pieces and drenched in blood.

"Nathaniel is going to know we've switched."

"Ye of little faith." Her head cocks to the side as she appraises me like I'm a clueless fool. "He always sneaks back home after dressing everyone at the start of the event before returning at the end of the evening. He won't be around to notice!"

"I still don't get why I'm the one going," I huff.

Weston replies, "You're the only one who's seen Thrill2Kill."

"Not really!" I can't keep the exasperation from my voice. Their idea of finding a killer is sending me into a party full of them? Absolutely not.

"But you've seen their build. Their walk. You're our best shot at identifying them."

"I'm supposed to know them in real life!" I argue back. "If I haven't recognized them yet…"

"You weren't on your game then," Valerie reminds me, her voice drenched with a patience I didn't know she possessed. "When Thrill2Kill stalked you during your shift, you were focused on scaring the shit out of people, not scrutinizing a potential murder suspect."

"Besides," Asher chimes in, "how confident are we that you do know this person? For all we know, Thrill2Kill could have just deluded themselves into thinking they know you after all their obsessing."

"If you're right, we might as well go straight to Weegan and tell him what little we know."

"He might not know it yet, but you're Weegan's only lead at finding this guy!"

My head is so messed up that I can't help but agree with Asher.

Still, this just might be our dumbest idea yet, but if it's my only way to clear Dev's name, what other choice do I have?

"If I die," I concede, "I'm going to be so pissed."

"No one's going to hurt you in the middle of operating hours," Weston promises. "You don't even have to stay long. Just enough to sus out our bad guy."

When our break ends, it becomes apparent that Asher is escorting me back to my post. I appreciate that he's looking out for me, but I fear being near each other is only going to cause more problems.

The park music wails all around us, but for some reason, I'm too busy internally screaming to pay much attention to the faux ones blaring through the speakers.

"You're sure you don't want to call out for the rest of tonight?" Asher asks me. "We could get away from all this nonsense and grab a bite to eat or something."

"I can't leave Dev."

Asher takes a bite of cotton candy, pondering his next

words before speaking with an electric-green tongue. "You really believe in that guy, don't you?"

"Of course, I do. He's my best friend and my boyfriend. I lo—"

The words get caught in my throat. Dev and I have yet to express our feelings for each other using the L-word. It feels too great of a declaration to just throw out without some kind of fanfare. And with how things are going, I can't help but worry we might never have the opportunity to say it to each other.

I fear when it comes to this matter, he's waiting for me to make the first move. It's only fair for me to admit it first after he was the one to initially profess his feelings for me.

But I definitely can't tell him until I have the truth in my grasp.

"Well, I think you're noble to still trust him," Asher says after a long moment. "I know it would be hard for me to do so after all the ways he's been, um, involved."

My lips pinch at what he's implying.

"Something does feel off," I say, which makes Asher's head jerk in my direction, so I hastily add, "but not with Dev."

"What then?"

"These messages I've been receiving. Thrill2Kill talks a big game but, as much as I hate to speak it aloud, why aren't they doing more?"

Asher barks out a shocked laugh. "*More?*"

"I know it sounds ridiculous, and I really don't want to jinx it, but why does it feel like they're all talk?"

"Did my sister's death feel like 'all talk' to you?"

"No!" I hurriedly insist, wishing I would just shut up already. But, of course, that would be far less embarrassing, so I don't. "Alice's death was horrendous. But I didn't start receiving messages until afterward, and since then, there's been a handful of ominous texts but nothing else."

"You just said they found you in the house and walked through repeatedly!"

"They walked by and then sent a creepy text... but that was it!"

"Do you *want* more than that?"

"No, of course, not!" I glance around the park helplessly, but no brilliant explanation comes to me. "But don't you think someone capable of killing a human would be, I don't know, far more dangerous than a few texts and a couple of laps around a haunted house?"

One nervous glance at Asher tells me we are not on the same page, which only makes me feel dumber. I don't want to be insensitive to his situation.

"What more are you expecting here?"

"I don't know! Ride or Die was leaving me all sorts of physical threats and having me complete tasks. This new guy is just kind of... nonexistent."

"Do you *want* to be helping them?"

"No!" I exclaim. "I'm sorry, I feel like I'm saying this all wrong. I'm not upset that they're not as involved as Ride or Die, but at least with them, I always knew what was going on. With Thrill2Kill, I feel so in the dark. It's hard to anticipate their next move or hunt them down with so little contact with them."

"Then maybe you need to prod them into action."

"We've tried and they've never taken the bait."

"So we give up?" Asher responds, and suddenly, I feel less bad. "Maybe another nudge is what we need to find them!"

It's my turn to glance at him skeptically. "Poking the beast doesn't seem like the wisest idea. Not anymore."

"Why not? We're running out of time, Gwen. We can't let someone else get hurt. Alice would want the senseless killing to stop with her."

I look up to find a determined glint in Asher's eyes. It's his confidence that convinces me to pull out my phone and open my recent conversation with them.

GWEN GARDNER

Do you want to have a play date?

It takes a few minutes, but eventually, I receive a response from a different number.

UNKNOWN

I do not have time for you right now.

Of course, they don't.

"See?" I say, holding out my phone for Asher to read. My eyes can't help but roll. "What is it with this person? Are the stakes high or not?"

"I see what you mean about mixed messaging," Asher agrees begrudgingly. "Do they want you to play or not?"

"For some reason, I don't think they care."

"Then tell them that!" Asher's eyes flash when I begin to protest. He steps in front of me, grabbing either side of my arms as he makes his case. "They want you to lose, Gwen. If you let them stick to their schedule, you certainly will."

My pulse quickening, I wonder if I dare.

Calling out a murderer can only have disastrous consequences. But how else am I supposed to find them if they won't make any moves? My mind made up, I type out a new message.

GWEN GARDNER

Let me know if you decide to actually do something. Otherwise, stop wasting my time.

CHAPTER
NINETEEN

As I READ the message again, the pit in my stomach grows.

Shit.

That can't precede anything good.

It took a while for them to answer me. As embarrassing as it is to admit, I eagerly checked for their response nearly every time I ducked back behind the plywood wall after finishing a scare. I almost got caught a few times. Wendy Thatcher usually comes through the house at least once a night to see her daughter in action, but during the last hour of my set, she walked through numerous times. On each trip through, she was accompanied by more people. Entertainment managers, park leadership, members of the security team. I even saw Detective Weegan join her, not once, but twice. Clearly, Ms. Thatcher was in the mood to show off her daughter.

It's a miracle none of them caught me checking my phone. I would've been in so much trouble. It would've been for nothing, too. My phone didn't illuminate with a notification until after the event closed for the night and I was departing the house.

Pulling my black cloak tighter around myself, I look around the front entrance for Dev. Most everyone else is already starting the long hike back to Crew HQ on the other side of the park. But there's no Dev to be found.

Did he seriously leave me again? I know we didn't spend our break together, but I thought we had an understanding.

Trying to keep my frustration at bay, I remind myself I have bigger problems to figure out. Namely, whatever fire I just lit under Thrill2Kill.

I guess I should've anticipated the challenge. It's what I asked for.

Use it, I remind myself. *You need to figure out who they are.*

Hands trembling, I type out a response.

GWEN GARDNER

Yes. Ride or Die was a hell of a lot better at this. If you're trying to measure up to them, you're doing an embarrassing job.

Their response—from a new number—comes faster than expected. Did they take so long to respond before because they were busy working in the park? Surely, someone so obsessed with last summer's murders couldn't be a crew member, right?

UNKNOWN

Then welcome to Act 2.

GWEN GARDNER

Act 2?

My eyes remain glued to my phone as I hurry through the empty park. Thankfully, the horrendous background music has been turned off for the night. As creepy as it is to walk through a silent theme park late, I much prefer it over the echoing soundtrack of fake screams and crunching bones.

Glancing around, I'm surprised to find my colleagues matching my pace. Some are even running. I'm eager to clock out, too, but it's not worth breaking into a sweat to be the first to do so.

"Hurry!" a man calls to his buddy as they sprint past me.

"This place is cursed," the crew member laments while trying to match his friend's pace.

Curious, I frown after them for a beat before returning my thoughts to whatever show Thrill2Kill has in store.

They still haven't responded by the time I cross backstage. I huff with frustration. This is getting ridiculous. Why am I wasting so much energy on this troll? They're all talk, just like the others who came before them. These weirdos want to believe they can live up to the standard Ride or Die set last summer and reach the same level of infamy, but they're all wrong. None of them have the guts to pull it off.

Annoyed, my thumbs swiftly type out another message.

GWEN GARDNER

That's what I thought. Shows over, and so is this conversation.

Stuffing my phone into the pocket sewn inside my costume, I trudge toward Crew HQ.

What awaits me inside the bright space has me halting in my tracks.

Nearly every single crew member is loitering on the outskirts of the room. Most of them are still in their monster makeup and attire, but the concerned expressions on each face is the most chilling sight to behold.

A woman is hysterically crying toward the center of the room.

All too quickly, my mind flashes back to that fateful day last June. The one where we all gathered around the Great Oak and witnessed the discovery of Luca's death.

Only, this time, it's not Valerie sobbing.

It's Wendy Thatcher.

Hysterical, she's wildly pacing around the center of the room, wailing at retreating members of the security team. She waves her phone in everyone's faces before they retreat, frantically pointing at something on the screen. "Find my daughter and find him!"

Find her daughter… where did Jenna go? Surely, Thril-l2Kill didn't do anything to her, right? But can the timing be coincidental?

With his hands raised before him, Weegan approaches her like she's a wild animal. Wendy doesn't acknowledge his closeness, swiveling madly around the room, searching for someone.

"Sit back and enjoy the show" rings in my ears, making me grow dizzy. This can't be my fault. I may have my issues with Jenna, but I don't want anything bad to happen to her!

My mouth grows dry when my phone vibrates.

But it's not a text from an unknown number. It's a message from my boyfriend.

Opening it, my eyes widen with horror at the sight of Jenna Thatcher holding a copy of the Hathaway Herald with today's date. A purple bruise mars one of her cheeks and there's a fierce gash on her jawline.

I can't tell where she is. But I know who kidnapped her.

I sense his approach from behind me before I see him. The familiar shadow of the boy I grew up with. The once-comforting scent of the one who has his hand wrapped around my heart. Before I can react, my boyfriend protectively wraps an arm around my waist and tugs me against his chest. He knows this scene will trigger one of my worst memories.

And yet, he also knows he's just given me a far worse one.

My ears ringing, I shove away from Dev.

"You forgot to use one of your burner phones."

His head jerks back with mock confusion. "Excuse me?"

I wave my phone in his face, watching as his eyes widen at what he sees.

"Gwen, wait, I didn't—"

"He's here!" I hear myself shriek.

All heads swivel in our direction. Dev's mouth drops open as his eyes gloss over with fear. "Gwen, I didn't do this!"

My head shakes with disgust. "You're a piss poor liar, Dev Vishwakarma."

Before he can respond, Weegan grabs Dev's elbow and yanks him through the atrium. Other officers appear to assist, but Dev isn't putting up a fight. All he is doing is looking over his shoulder at me.

"I didn't do this, Gwen," he insists. "It wasn't me!"

I go to respond, but the words get lost on their way out of my dry mouth. My head is spinning like I'm on an out-of-control carousel. There's nothing merry as the room turns round and round. My feet carry me after him, but every step feels sporadic and heavy. The judgmental whispers from my colleagues are bullets into my back. Every remark slows me down.

The open air of the parking lot does little to aid my light-headedness. Growing so dizzy that I fall to my knees, I watch helplessly as handcuffs are locked around my boyfriend's wrists, he's shoved into a squad car, and a cyclone of sirens carry him away.

The sharp sound snaps me back to my senses. Did I just fall for another trick? How quickly I gave up on the boy I'm supposed to care for most.

Suddenly overcome with nausea, I realize the deepest act of betrayal wasn't committed by my boyfriend. No—the knife to the back was thrown by me.

CHAPTER
TWENTY

WESTON MIGHT BE the one to grant my request for a ride to the station, but that doesn't stop him from bargaining with me the whole way there.

"You can't tell them," he insists.

"Jenna is missing!"

"Do you want them to find her alive or dead?"

"Obviously alive!" I anxiously fiddle with my ring. "Face it. All our ideas were terrible. We weren't making any headway on our own."

"The cops are holding nearly all the same cards as us, and they weren't making any big moves of their own, either. Aside from *arresting your boyfriend*."

This jolts my memory. "Jenna's dating some guy she met online! Maybe he had something to do with this."

"You want to blame another 'secret boyfriend' instead of accepting the truth right in front of us?"

I ignore what he's implying. "What if they can track Thrill2Kill—"

Weston cuts me off with a scoff. "Track a bunch of burner phones? Be real, Gwen. You said that picture came from Dev's cell."

"Someone is framing him!" I bellow. "And I fell for it! They want the cops and me distracted with Dev while they continue to work covertly."

"You have got to stop making excuses for him!" Not taking his eyes off the road, Weston shakes his head with disbelief. "Some people aren't who they say they are, Gwen. It's a cruel fact of life you're going to have to accept sooner or later."

I cross my arms in the passenger seat. Now more than ever, I'm convinced someone is setting Dev up. The look of pure confusion on his face told me everything I needed to know. Dev's not *that* good of an actor. He didn't hurt Jenna.

But who wants me to believe he did? And why?

If I had confessed everything I knew to Weegan earlier, Dev wouldn't be handcuffed right now. I could have protected him from this. Guilt manifests itself as nausea, and I start to worry I'm going to make a mess of Weston's front seat.

I thought our murderer was out for glory. Now, I'm starting to think their aim is merely chaos.

Out of the corner of my eye, I catch Weston sneaking glances at me, clearly waiting to see if I've come to my senses. He's not going to like that I still trust Dev, but I'm not abandoning my boyfriend when he needs me most.

I elect to pivot. "Last summer, I screwed up by not going to the cops immediately. What kind of person would I be if I make the exact same mistake again?"

"The kind of person who doesn't want her boyfriend to kill Jenna Thatcher!"

I fist my hair with frustration. "Dev didn't do this!"

"How can you defend a guy in handcuffs?"

"Because I lo—*know* him!"

"If you take his side," Weston warns me, "there's no telling what will happen."

"Dev would never hurt me—or anyone, for that matter."

"And what if you're wrong! This could be a huge mistake, Gwen."

I argue, "Since when is the truth a mistake?"

"I guess we'll see," Weston snaps back, signaling our arrival.

I don't allow myself to look back when I hear his car engine rumble as he drives away from the lot. I guess I shouldn't have expected him to wait for me. Not when he made it abundantly clear he disagrees with what I'm about to do.

Refusing to let his departure phase me, I shoot a quick text to my parents.

GWEN GARDNER

I'm safe, but I'm at HPD. They brought in Dev for something he didn't do. I have a feeling his parents are already on the way.

JONAH GARDNER

I'm coming too

Thank goodness my parents have a habit of not retiring for bed until after I return home. Mom will want to come, too, but I suspect she'll stay with Gil, who is likely already asleep. They might have left him home alone before our lives were thrust into the scandalous spotlight, but not now.

With the confidence that I have someone on my side, I march into the police station with my head high.

"You can't be here," an officer behind the counter greets me.

I hold up my phone, displaying the photo of Jenna.

The officer blinks at it once before picking up the phone on her desk. "Gwen Gardner is here. You're going to want to see her."

Detective Weegan appears a moment late, looking grim. "This is getting out of hand, Miss Gardner."

"I couldn't agree more, Detective."

He shows me into one of the interrogation rooms. I

assume Dev is in the other one, but the blinds are drawn so I can't catch a glimpse of him.

I can only hope he senses my presence and knows he isn't alone. Weston is wrong about him. Dev would never kidnap Jenna and then return to Pineland like nothing happened. A real killer would not accidentally send a message from the wrong phone.

Someone is setting Dev up—and now it's up to the detectives to discover who.

The interrogation room isn't fancy looking. It's a tight, rectangular space with cinderblock walls. On the wall shared with the hallway is a large window, also with closed blinds. The metal table bolted to the floor at the center of the room has a chair on either side. There's a spot for restraints to be chained to the table, and I can only hope Dev isn't experiencing that treatment next door. I bet Captain Nora Pierce is with him now.

Weegan gestures for me to take a seat after closing the door behind him. "Let's keep this quick. I've got a girl to find."

"You're not going to find her in Dev's basement."

"You're right—we didn't."

I wince, though I guess I shouldn't be surprised. They gotta rule out the obvious places first.

Detective Weegan sets me with a stern look. "Do you know where she is, Gwen?"

"Of course not. And neither does Dev." I unlock my phone and slide it across the table. "Someone is setting him up."

Weegan glances down at the image. "I received the same one. It was also sent from Dev's device."

My brow furrows. "Have you received any other strange messages?"

The detective shakes his head, staring at me inquisitively. "Only this one from Mr. Vishwakarma."

"And did Dev have his device when you brought him in?"

The man's jaw clenches. It's flecked with brown stubble that's graying far too quickly for his age. Spending too much time in Hathaway will do that to a person.

And yet, I can't seem to rekindle my motivation to actually pick somewhere else to live after high school. I used to long to escape this town, but now, the idea of submitting myself to the devil I don't know seems far more terrifying. However, this is not the time for those confusing thoughts.

"He did not."

"Let me guess," I lean back in my seat, crossing my arms. "Dev told you he realized his phone was missing at the end of his shift and went looking for it before returning to Crew HQ empty-handed."

Somehow, the man's jaw clenches even harder. He might not confirm my assumption, but it's enough for me to press further.

"Someone is framing Dev for this."

"Who would that be?"

"It could be anyone. Did you know Jenna has a secret boyfriend she met online? Which is interesting because Alice Crane did, too. Someone she met on that *Liarland* server."

"How do you know—"

"I'm really sorry for not showing you this earlier, but I hope you'll understand why I couldn't." Pressing my phone screen, I swipe away from my messages with Dev and jab my finger at the various chats with unknown numbers.

Wordlessly, Weegan picks up the phone and scans the different conversations.

"Why didn't you tell me about this when we spoke a few hours ago?"

"You read what they said. If I told you, someone was going to die."

His bushy eyebrows raise. "You fell for that again?"

I bite the inside of my cheek with frustration. "Their

threats seem pretty legit now, don't they? They kidnapped their next victim!"

The man sighs, pinching the bridge of his nose. "I'm growing tired of the antics that occur inside that theme park."

"Antics is putting it lightly."

Unamused, his dark eyes meet mine. "You should've told me immediately instead of waiting until someone disappeared. You're supposed to trust me, Gwen."

I point at the phone. "They claim to be someone I know, which means they could be anyone, including you."

"It's not me."

"How am I supposed to know that?"

"Because I have a badge and an alibi, Gwen!" He sighs deeply, frustratedly shaking his head. "I'm the one working this case. Not you."

"What case? You all think Alice's death was an accident or self-inflicted. As far as you're concerned, that case is closed."

He scoffs. "Is that what you think?"

I shrug. "I don't know what I'm supposed to think."

"Because you're not on the force, kid! You're not paid to think about this. Your only job as a civilian *and a minor* is to report what you know to the people who are paid to solve these cases—which by the way—are anything but closed. It's awful enough Mr. and Mrs. Crane are busy planning their daughter's funeral. I refuse to let Ms. Thatcher to do the same, but I can't solve anything if I'm not working with all the pieces to the puzzle."

I slump back in my seat, hating that he's right. I have no business running around and playing cop with my peers. "I'm sorry about not telling you sooner."

"You know, the older you get, the less 'I'm sorry' is going to cut it."

My lips purse guiltily. "Understood."

"So, you're convinced this unknown messenger—"

"Thrill2Kill," I interject. "We call them Thrill2Kill."

"Sounds a lot like store-brand Ride or Die. And who's we?"

Mentally apologizing to the others, I rattle off their names. "Weston McCray, Valerie Ross, Milly Dillard, and Asher Crane."

Detective Weegan frowns at me over the metal table. "Asher Crane?"

"He wants to find whoever killed his sister and is harassing me." Before Weegan can remind me we are anything but professionals, I hold up my hands. "Which I now recognize was a totally inappropriate and foolish thing to do."

Weegan studies me, his mustache twitching. Under his stern gaze, the walls of the small room seem to press in even further. "I understand how hard it is to feel helpless. Doing something—even if it's the wrong thing—can be comforting."

"The others don't agree with me because they're falling for Thrill2Kill's ruse, but I know Dev isn't the one who kidnapped Jenna."

"How can you be so certain?"

"You've read the *Liarland* chat room. They believe Ride or Die made far too many mistakes to deserve infamy. There are people who want to try to outdo Ride or Die."

"Thrill2Kill."

"Precisely."

"And you don't think your boyfriend is capable of outdoing Ride or Die?"

"Dev doesn't want to be famous. Hell, I can barely convince him to audition for a solo. He's content to simply be a member of the orchestra. Part of a larger team."

"Not having the courage to go out for a solo doesn't exactly disprove all the evidence pointing in Dev's direction."

"I know. And there's a lot of evidence, isn't there? But Dev can't tell you where Jenna is because he doesn't know. So you can either waste your precious time getting nowhere while questioning him or you can find who really did this."

"I'm obligated to follow all leads, including ones texted to me."

"I'd hope so. Follow every avenue, but acting as if Dev is your lead suspect is a waste of time. I used to think he was acting strangely, too, but I'm starting to understand it's because someone's gone to great lengths to raise my suspicion. They want me distracted so they can continue to enact whatever awful plans they have in store."

It's Weegan's turn to lean back in his seat as he ponders me. "And how do you suppose I go about finding another suspect?"

My eyebrows raise. "I thought I wasn't the professional."

"You're not," he says firmly. "But right now, it feels like you know a hell of a lot more than I do. Like I said, I'm obligated to follow all leads, especially when a kid's life is at stake."

Detective Weegan moves to clasp his hands on his desk. "So, Ms. Gardner, tell me what you and your little friends were going to do to catch this killer."

I grimace. "You're not going to like what we had in mind."

CHAPTER
TWENTY-ONE

It's well after midnight when I spy headlights turning down our street. I breathe out a sigh of relief.

They released Dev.

And I thought Dad and I were at the station late.

After about thirty minutes of speaking with Weegan, my dad, Captain Pierce—and then Weegan, my dad, *and* Captain Pierce all together—the Gardeners were released to return home for the night. Then we repeated the entire conversation for my mother, who had all the same reactions, but inevitably reached the same conclusion.

None of the adults liked the idea I proposed to Detective Weegan, but in the end, no one could deny it was the right thing to do with Jenna's life at stake and Dev at risk for taking the fall. My parents agreed so long as I remained under HPD's dutiful watch for all hours of the day—which is why we have a squad car stationed out front of our driveway now.

I wonder if the officer out front will catch me sneaking out. I should probably hope that they do, but I'm so desperate to speak with Dev, I'm going to risk the officer's frustration. The only truly terrifying consequence that comes from getting caught is the wrath from my parents.

Let's hope Dev still has some semblance of immunity in their eyes.

Not wanting to interrupt whatever family conversation the Vishwakarmas are likely having, I wait another thirty minutes before slipping out of my room and down the stairs. My parents have shut themselves in their bedroom. Their television is playing at a low enough volume that I know it's only on to mask what they're discussing.

It appears tonight is one full of hushed conversations.

I'm careful to avoid the step that squeaks before padding across the house to the back door. Hoping the officer on patrol isn't taking a lap around the house, I carefully unlock the door and slip into the frigid evening air.

At once, I'm thankful that I nabbed a hoodie before stepping outside. It's one I nicked from Dev, so it's oversized and cozy.

Crossing through the backyards, I'm careful not to trigger any of my neighbors' automatic lights. The trick is to stick to the shadowy tree line on the outskirts of everyone's property.

Reaching Dev's backyard three doors down, I'm relieved to find two rooms with lights on. Mr. and Mrs. Vishwakarma are likely in their upstairs bedroom, while Dev is ideally alone in his.

Dev sleeps in the basement, which makes it incredibly easy to slip into his domain unnoticed. All I have to do is hope he left the small window at the top of his bedroom unlocked for me.

Checking the latch, my stomach plummets. It's locked.

Maybe he's afraid of unwanted company. Or he didn't expect me to sneak over. Or he doesn't want to see me.

Don't spiral.

Hesitantly, I knock once on the window. Then I wait for an uncomfortably long while for him to appear.

Maybe he really doesn't want to speak with me.

He *has* to speak with me. I can't be confident that Weegan told him our plan to find another suspect.

Dev needs to know someone is on his side. He doesn't have his phone, so this is the only way I can tell him.

I go to knock again, only to startle when Dev's face appears on the other side of the glass. He must be standing at the top of the couch below to see out the window.

His face remains expressionless, but after what feels like an eternity, he finally unlatches the window and slides the glass away.

"Hi," I breathe out.

"Hey."

"Can I come in?"

Dev shrugs but moves to help me crawl through the window and onto the waiting couch below. It's a maneuver we've attempted countless times over the years. We'd perfected sneaking me in long before we ever started dating, but it comes in handy now more than ever.

Soon, the window is closed and locked after me, and we're both sitting on the couch awkwardly.

Dev's bedroom is pretty basic—though I suppose most rooms belonging to teenage boys likely are. Across from the couch is a decently sized television with a gaming console. His bed is on the far wall, covered in a navy-blue duvet and soft gray sheets. There's a small bathroom near the stairwell, which leads up to the first floor of the house.

The walls are littered with posters from concerts—some classical, some rock. His cello rests on a stand in a corner with a music stand in front of it. And next to the instrument is his—

"Your bow," I breathe out when I see it.

Not expecting me to start with this, Dev glances between his bow and me, an accusatory expression on his face. "What about it?"

"I thought yours was missing!"

"I heard about that."

"I—"

Before leaving the station, I detailed every single clue I received from Thrill2Kill. Of course, the authorities were going to interrogate Dev about them. Which means my boyfriend knows how long I've feared he was a murderer.

My pulse pounding mercilessly in my ears, the overwhelming sense of foolishness makes me feel like I'm going to pass out. Thrill2Kill tried time and time again to convince me they were Dev. I resisted for so long, but when it mattered most, I fell for it.

I helplessly slump onto the couch. Of course, it wasn't Dev's bow stashed in the haunted house. How could I have deluded myself into thinking it was his? This is what happens when I let my fears take control of the reins. I hear nothing but complete and utter lies.

Dev releases a heavy breath, but otherwise says nothing, which only makes me feel worse. I'm supposed to be the person who believes in him. The one who knows him inside and out.

And I failed him.

Remaining a few feet away from me on the couch, Dev rubs his wrists, not taking his eyes off his shoes.

"Did they hurt?" I whisper, realizing he's rubbing where the handcuffs were locked in place.

"They weren't comfortable by any means. Not that they're supposed to be."

"No," I agree with a shake of my head, "of course not."

The silence wins again. I can't remember the last time we fell victim to such an uncomfortable quiet. This isn't like us.

But I caused us to be this way. I fell for the most obvious setup in the world, and now I have to face the consequences.

All I can hope is that Dev will forgive me. "I know you didn't do it."

Dev huffs out a wry laugh. "You didn't look so confident back at the park."

"A lot was happening and that text took me by surprise."

"But you believed it." His voice is so hollow that my insides wither with guilt.

And what's worse—I can't deny a thing. The best I can do is more silence. We sit in it for what feels like an eternity. My head hisses like a kettle as the panic sets in.

I gave up on him when he needed me most. How can I still deserve to be his friend, let alone his girlfriend?

Finally, after an agonizing stretch of time, Dev looks over at me. His eyes glisten with disappointment. "You really think I'm capable of hurting someone in that way?

"I—"

"Maybe it was only for a moment," he continues, "but that moment still happened. You genuinely believed I had it in me to kidnap and abuse someone. And what's worse is, apparently, it wasn't the first clue you received to paint me as some kind of monster."

I cannot lie to him. But uttering any confirmation aloud makes me want to be sick, so like a coward, all I can do is nod.

"If you had just asked me, I would've told you my bow has been in here the entire time. Whatever bow you think you have isn't mine. I've never once been on that *Liarland* chat room, and the cops now have my laptop, so they'll be able to confirm that. Oh, and that picture of me on Alice's phone? It's just some random selfie, Gwen. She was friends with Jenna —who I happened to be dating at the time. That's all."

The three-and-a-half feet between us on the couch might as well be a canyon. He's never felt further away, but he has every right to be furious with me. Of course, there are reasonable explanations for everything.

"I overheard you and Jenna talking at school," I whisper.

"Detective Weegan told me," Dev replies pointedly.

"What didn't she want you to tell me?"

Dev actually laughs at this, and it only makes me feel worse. "You know what's funny? Jenna didn't want me to tell you that the reason we went to Wetlands was because someone came and found her in the house. She was worried that if it got out that someone nefarious was stalking her at the park, her mother would have to shut the place down."

"But you had already told me the same guy who found me went on to scare her."

"Exactly! I wasn't hiding anything from you, Gwen. I was lying to her! With everything going on, the last thing I needed was her freaking out on me. She's a lot scarier than you, Gwen."

"Jenna said she didn't trust you."

"For good reason! I'm guilty of being an awful liar, but not a murderer!" Dev stands up suddenly, raking his hands through his hair while fighting to keep his voice down, "And Jenna doesn't trust me because I spent our entire relationship trying to get over you! Which, I agree, is a pretty shitty thing to do, but it's not criminal, Gwen."

Blinking back tears, I find myself wishing that I could just disappear. How could I have been so wrong? If I had just been upfront to Dev about everything in the first place, we wouldn't be here.

"You're supposed to be the person who knows me best," he whispers, looking down at me with such sadness that my shoulders begin to curl in on themselves. "You're the one who's supposed to believe me when I say I didn't do it. But instead, you spend a week running around with people you barely tolerate to decipher if I'm a murderer, while there's a real one on the loose."

When he puts it that way, I feel like the most foolish person in the world. What was I thinking?

He takes a desperate step forward, towering over me. "I recognize the shit you've gone through and how it's rewired the way you think. When we started dating, I accepted you were going to have a hard time trusting anyone fully. But I also thought you knew me well enough to trust I would never—could never—hurt you or anyone else."

"I do!" I insist.

"Do you? Because from the looks of it, you bailed on me real fast. You've been having secret meetings with Weston, Asher, Valerie, Milly, and the police." He counts on his fingers with each name he sarcastically rattles off. "Those are the people you decided to trust over me."

Dev kneels in front of me. "Why didn't you just tell me you were receiving messages again? I would've helped you, Gwen! I could've helped you keep a clear head. We're supposed to be a team!"

The frustrated tears in his devastated gaze completely shatter my heart.

My eyes squeeze shut as I swallow hard. It sounds so awful when he says it aloud. How could I have ever deluded myself so deeply?

Because you're messed up now. Last summer ruined you.

"I'm sorry," is all I can whisper. "I got so lost in my head, but that's no excuse. You deserve better."

"I do," he agrees, and what's left of my heart crumbles away.

The silence that follows speaks volumes. It's an agonizing quiet. I almost wish he would start yelling again.

Unable to sit in it any longer, I finally murmur, "I should go."

His face unreadable, Dev nods once, and with that single gesture, I find it impossible to breathe. He doesn't want me to stay.

Why would he?

Shakily, I rise from the couch. Lifting my chin to eye the small window at the top of the wall, my lips pinch at the height. It's going to be a stretch, but I won't risk walking out the front door and getting the both of us in more trouble.

Climbing up on the back of the couch, I extend my fingers as far as they'll reach in the direction of the window. I'm still six inches away.

A pair of hands wrap around my waist, strong and steadying. I hadn't even realized he moved closer to help me. It takes all my willpower to not turn around and pull him into my arms.

Still, I'm not above freezing at his warm contact. I shamelessly linger long enough for my returning pulse to steady before nodding that I'm ready to be lifted up.

He raises me with ease, and sooner than I want to be, I'm crawling out the window. Kneeling on the damp grass, I finally brave one last look at Dev. I've never seen him so defeated in my life.

"Despite the odds," I hear myself promise when he moves to close the window. "If it's really supposed to be us, despite all the horrible odds thrown our way, I know it'll be worth the wait."

Dev's throat bobs, but he doesn't say a word.

That's okay. It's my turn to fight for him. It's what he deserves.

"It's a blip," I assure him, and in a way, myself. "Albeit, a big blip, but hopefully one day, it won't feel so enormous."

Still, nothing from Dev.

"And in the meantime, I'm going to do everything in my power to make this right."

His eyes glint with understanding before the bridge of his nose creases. My heart skips a beat. He's concerned for me.

Finally, he speaks, his voice hoarse and low. "Gwen, I need you to stay safe."

I offer him a nod. He must sense it's a lie because he tilts his head to the side with concern. "Please, Gwen."

"We're going to be okay," I promise before closing the window for him.

I hope it's the truth.

CHAPTER
TWENTY-TWO

The next day, Dev doesn't offer me a ride to work—not that I expected him to do so. However, I'd be lying if I didn't admit I was secretly hoping. But maybe he's planning to call out of his shift after skipping school.

Unfortunately, I don't have the same luxury because I'm on Detective Weegan's schedule tonight. It should feel freeing to relinquish this case over to the professionals, but it doesn't absolve me from my anxieties. Not with Jenna missing and Dev being framed for it. In fact, I'm feeling more guiltier than ever for my failure to unmask Thrill2Kill. What's worse—I fear the authorities have no idea what they're doing, either.

Dad is still at the laundromat, and Mom had already left to drive Gil to soccer practice. Meaning, unless I wanted to walk all the way to Pineland, I'm going to have to bum a ride from someone else.

Which is how I wind up in Valerie's beat up car.

In the short time she's had the vehicle, she's truly made it her own. There's a pineapple-scented air freshener stuck in her vents. The seats sport hot pink covers that she claims to have found at a thrift store. What surprises me most is that the mix CD I bought for her at the same thrift shop is in the player. It was my gift to her after she successfully passed her driver's test. She might not have had a car to play it in yet, but I wanted her to be ready when she did.

I can't believe she kept it.

Valerie doesn't take her eyes off the road when she asks, "Are you sure you want to do this?"

It's just us in the car. Milly decided to go into work early to make sure everything in costuming is all squared away before she spends the night covering my shift for me.

So I can go introduce myself to a bunch of *Liarland* fanatics.

Much to my surprise, Detective Weegan didn't loathe our plan when he first heard it—though he told me not to bother attempting to hide my identity. He seemed to think it was a decent idea to engage with these people offline and see how they respond to me. I took it as a sign that he was seriously struggling to find Jenna on his own.

Still, it was his confidence—and repeated promises to keep me safe—that convinced my parents to sign off on the idea. They wanted to come to the park, but Weegan insisted they go about their weekly routine as normal. Anything out of the ordinary might tip Thrill2Kill off that something was up.

I don't think my parents realized when they hugged me goodbye that Dev wouldn't be the one to stay by my side all night long.

It's going to be Valerie.

"I could ask you the same thing," I say back. "These people are a lot more obsessed with you than they are with me."

"Never thought the first autographs I'd sign would be to a throng of murder freaks, but here we are."

I scoff. "No one is asking you for an autograph tonight."

She glances over at me, one eyebrow raised. "You don't think?"

"Just the thought makes me want to be sick."

"You better brace yourself for the same treatment. You're wrong to think these people are more obsessed with me than they are with you. In their eyes, I'm the one who failed."

"And you don't think I did?"

She shakes her head. "No. I think they see you as their little heroine. It's why you're the one receiving the creepy text messages."

"I don't think they see me as the hero of this story," I disagree, remembering how they loathed the fact that I was this case's 'final girl.' "They're too busy rooting for the villain."

"Maybe, but I think they're equally fascinated by the both of you."

My lips pinch when I consider that. I guess you can't have a villain without someone for them to terrorize.

"And this villain," Valerie continues, turning to drive down the dusty gravel road that leads to the park, "isn't anyone they can pinpoint. Maybe some of them like to pretend it's Luca. Or Marty Boone. And yeah, I'm sure there are a few who believe it to be me. But I think they're more obsessed with the idea of 'Ride or Die' than they are the actual humans behind the account."

"And here we are, giving them more of a story to obsessively consume."

Valerie clicks her tongue. "Yep."

"But we have no other choice. We can't let anyone hurt Jenna."

"Or frame Dev," she says in agreement, not taking her eyes off the road. "We're not letting them write this story for us, Gwen. The pen is in our hands now."

I release a shaky breath before nodding. I need nothing more than for that to be true.

I'm so tired of other people controlling how I think or the decisions I make. It's such a consuming distraction that I'm not able to figure out what *I* want. I'm supposed to be touring colleges and deciding my future, not spending my Friday night wearing a police wire.

Valerie pulls into a parking spot but doesn't immediately open her car door. Neither of us is ready to finish this conversation just yet. Especially not in public.

"Listen, Gwen," she says, finally turning to look me in the eye over the center console. "I know there's not much I can say that will ever erase what I did to you. And I'm never going to ask you to forget."

"I'm not sure I could if I tried," I admit with a whisper.

She nods, her dark eyes glossy. "I know. Because I know you. I'm never going to be able to forget the friendship we had. I think that's just how it's going to be."

"Yeah, I get that."

Valerie Ross used to be the person I turned to for everything. So much so that I handed her the reins to my entire life. I'm not sure how good of a job I've done now that they're back in my control. I haven't metaphorically traveled anywhere, really. In fact, I feel more stagnant than ever. But is that so bad as long as it's my decision?

Is it fair for me to fault Valerie when I was the one who relinquished the reins in the first place? I can't deny that I'm responsible for taking myself out of the driver's seat.

No, the only thing I can stay mad at Valerie about is how she roped me into her mistakes last summer. Any additional resentment is more of a commentary on myself than her.

"I'm not going to ask you to move on or give me a second chance. I think you're doing better now than when I was in your life."

"That's not true. You and I had a lot of fun together."

She laughs softly. "Not more fun than you and Dev are having now, I'm sure." I shrug sheepishly before she continues. "It's great to watch you thrive, Gwen. I'm so proud of you, even though I have absolutely no right to feel that way."

"Will you stop ragging on yourself?" I scold her. "I know

you feel bad. I know you know that you messed up. But you deserve to thrive, too."

Her throat bobs as she studies me. "You think?"

"We're not even eighteen yet. One mistake you made as a teenager isn't going to define your entire life. Not unless you let it."

"Just like the Pineland murders shouldn't define yours. It can be a part of your story, but it's not the beginning, middle, and end, okay? Not unless *you* let it be."

I release a shaky breath, my eyes suddenly watering. When I finally have the courage to meet her gaze, I find tears in hers, too.

"Damn it," I laugh, "not you, too."

She groans, pulling down the sun visor and checking her appearance in the mirror. "My eyeliner was literally perfect today."

"Maybe some smudged eye makeup will help you live up to the narrative these freaks have written about you in their creepy little chat room."

She nods seriously. "Anything for the fans."

This makes my laugh turn into a cackle, and soon after, Valerie joins in. As tears leak down our cheeks, we giggle hysterically, letting our fears, frustrations, and messy history tumble out of us until all that's left are soft hiccups and gasps for breath.

Catching a tear as it slips to my chin, Valerie gives me a nod.

"We can do this."

"Yeah," I agree, because for the first time in a while, I believe her. "We can."

With an encouraging nod, Valerie opens her car door, and I do the same. We may not ever be the best of friends again, but I think whatever this is will suffice.

CHAPTER
TWENTY-THREE

Because we still have such a large suspect list and live in a town full of a bunch of big mouths, Weegan kept our plan as under wraps as possible. I'm not even confident Wendy Thatcher knows all the details of how Valerie and I will be skipping our shifts to surprise the throng of murder-obsessed guests during their gathering. I'm surprised she even agreed to let the freaks in her park—even if they are paying guests.

"Have you noticed that people seem to care a bit more that Jenna Thatcher is missing than when it was me?" Valerie loudly calls over to me while an officer helps her hide a wire in her sweatshirt.

"Had you been kidnapped?" Weegan drawls from the corner of the conference room Wendy Thatcher assigned to us for the evening. He should know better than to take her bait. When Valerie gets in the mood to cause a fuss, it's hard to diffuse her.

"I just don't recall any covert operations to pinpoint my whereabouts!" she responds innocently. "That's all!"

"We didn't have to pinpoint your whereabouts because we had security feeds of you running around the park!"

The detective's face is to the wall while his female

colleague finishes assisting the pair of us with our wires before she situates her own. Officer Sarah Mulligan, my neighbor and former babysitter, is currently dressed in a black Hauntland t-shirt and jeans. She's been tasked with going undercover to keep an eye on us.

I'm pretty sure her presence is a big part of the reason my parents and Valerie's dad signed off on us partaking in this plan in the first place.

"Clear," Sarah says to Weegan, who whirls around to face us.

"I'm sure I don't have to remind you two to stick to the script." His beady eyes dart between Valerie and me. "You're in public. Keep it that way. If you can't see Officer Mulligan, you've wandered too far. If someone says anything remotely threatening to you, give Sarah a look and walk away. And no matter what—"

"We stick together," we finish for him.

If you had told me a week ago that Valerie Ross and I would be working together to help Hathaway Police Department rescue Jenna Thatcher, I would've asked if you needed to visit first aid.

"No risks," Weegan insists. "These people idolize you two. They'll likely blabber in an attempt to impress you. You're there to listen. That's it."

"Understood," Valerie says.

Weegan fiercely eyes me until I also nod in agreement.

After a long pause, he finally mutters, "Good luck, girls. And thank you."

My mouth grows dry when I realize it's time to enter the park. I know this was our plan in the first place—and that the support and supervision of the authorities only makes it better —but there's a part of me that can't believe we're actually going through with it. I'm finally about to face the people who have spent the last few months ruthlessly tormenting me. They're the people who've made me fear the world outside

Hathaway. At least within the city limits, it's the evil I know. Out there is an entirely different ball game.

And I'm getting real sick of games.

As soon as we step foot onstage, we find the park to be packed. Every ride, haunted house, and food stand has a line that stretches far beyond the designated queues. I guess it's to be expected for Halloween weekend, but I can't remember the last time I saw Pineland so full.

I think most expected Wendy Thatcher to cancel the last two event dates with her daughter still unaccounted for, but HPD insisted it may be easier to find Jenna with business continuing as usual. Still, I can't help but wonder if the park president would've kept up operations either way. If she's returned home safely, I bet Jenna spends the rest of her life wondering where she falls on her mother's priority list. Poor girl. If last summer didn't mess her up, this experience certainly will. I never thought I'd come to pity Jenna Thatcher.

After spending the day combing through every inch of the park, HPD deduced Jenna was not on the premises. The blank white background of the photo provided nothing discernible. I know they would never admit it, but the cops are completely stumped. Why else would they be using teenagers to infiltrate a gathering of chronically online weirdos?

Sarah's going undercover as Weegan's online persona, *twistedtracks83*. One of the few perks of attending the first in-person gathering is that the *Liarland* members will only recognize each other by their handles. No one uses their actual face as their profile picture, and their handles are even less descriptive. It's the reason we might actually pull this off. Especially if any of them feel like they have something to prove to Valerie.

As we pass through the *Lair of the Dogman* scare zone, Weston jogs up to us in his half-man-half-dog getup.

"Y'all good to go?" he growls at us in character.

Valerie arches an eyebrow at him. "Do you think we would be out here if we weren't?"

His paws—hands?—raise innocently. "Just checking in on you two. No need to be a bi—"

"You do not want to finish that sentence."

"She's just stressed about what we're about to do," I excuse her, which feels alarmingly like old times.

"I guess," Weston responds coolly. "Well, good luck. I think it was a good move to go as yourselves... and together. But don't let them get under your skin so easily."

"We won't," I assure him before Valerie can do so less politely. It's not like her to be so uptight, but I guess I can't blame her considering the circumstances. Weston doesn't know the reason our plan shifted was because the authorities got involved. All we told him was I wouldn't be going in alone.

Weston's light eyes meet mine, and I'm startled to find a glint of concern in them. "You've got this. They're just a bunch of nerds. Don't forget that."

"Thanks," I whisper to him. I never expected to be so relieved to have a guy like Weston in my corner, but that seems to be the norm lately. My circle has shifted a lot the last few months, and it's clearly not done yet.

He spares me a long, scrutinizing look, followed by an encouraging nod. I attempt to offer him a smile in return, but I can tell by his amused expression that it comes off as more of a grimace than a confidence-instilling grin.

As soon as Weston is out of earshot, I check in with my partner. "Are you okay?"

"Please tell me I'm not the only one who feels like they might puke," Valerie whispers in my ear, interlocking our arms. The gesture is so familiar that I almost forget we haven't been walking this way together for months.

"Now, now," I fight to keep my voice even, "since when do you get stage fright?"

"Believe it or not, I think I've had enough attention for a lifetime."

This takes me by surprise. For as long as I've known her, Valerie has always embraced stardom. She's been prepping her entire life to be a famous actress. I figured her newfound popularity would only assist with jump starting her career.

"I hate to be the one to remind you, but I'm pretty sure that's like a job requirement of being a successful actress."

"Who says I still want to be an actress?"

My head jerks in her direction. "Excuse me?"

She doesn't meet my eyes as she says, "I got a taste of what it's like to have the public paint a picture of you. They tell whatever story they want, and no one stops to wonder if it's true."

"So, studying acting in California?"

"What BFA program is going to accept a villain like me?"

"You're not a villain, Valerie."

She breathes out a laugh. "Aren't I?"

"No," I say firmly. "Making a mistake doesn't label you as a villain. No matter what the internet says about you, the people who know you—Milly, your dad, and me—know the truth. Don't let them take your dream from you."

Her lips pinch, and it isn't until we pass the rowdy carousel with menacing clowns riding with guests that she finally says, "I'm not sure it's my dream anymore."

"And that's okay," I remind her. "You get to live your life however you want. No one gets to decide what it looks like but you."

When she looks at me, her eyes are glistening again. "Since when did you become the life coach out of the two of us?"

I squeeze her arm tighter. "Since I had to try and figure out my own life myself."

"Seriously, my eyeliner does not stand a chance if we keep this up." Wiping her eyes with her free hand, Valerie groans, "We have got to stop being so sappy."

"I think it's out of our system now."

She nods with understanding. "I think so, too."

"Now let's catch this asshole."

The *Liarland* gathering is planned to start at *Wolverine Racers* promptly at 8:15 pm. Their aim is a crawl through the park, stopping at every location where someone died, which is beyond disgusting, but to each their own.

"That's putting it mildly," Valerie scoffs.

"Didn't realize I said that last part out loud," I grumble back as we approach the scene of Sandy's death. Our poor old teacher. She didn't deserve to die because Chase couldn't bother to study. That's the only reason Luca picked her as his headline-making human sacrifice.

I wonder if these sick people will plan to *honor* Luca's death by gathering around the Fake Oak. Hopefully, we don't have to hang around long enough to find out.

As we near the coaster, I find a throng of fifteen or so people, all dressed in black, congregating off to the side of the wait time sign. Surprisingly, very few of them appear to be lacking general hygiene skills. In fact, I'd say they look like a fairly average group of twenty-and-thirty-something individuals. They're mostly male, but I count four girls, who are all standing off to the side together. Sarah, who clearly didn't take her time traversing the park, is already among them.

I'm frustrated to realize I don't immediately recognize one of them as the hooded figure who kept walking through my haunted house.

Still, my heart pounds at the sight of the group. The person harassing me—a dangerous murderer and kidnapper— could be standing just up ahead. What will my presence do to them? Will they engage with me or wait until I'm gone to text me a new threat?

I'll know soon. Only a few more moments before the group will recognize us. Then, I have to look them in the eyes and pretend I don't loathe every last one of them.

You're doing this for Dev.

He deserves someone fighting for him.

Valerie and I share one final look, silently asking the other if they want to back out. When neither of us shows any signs of protesting, we forge ahead and join the group.

It takes less than thirty seconds for someone to notice us.

"Oh my gosh?" one of the girls breathes out. "It's them."

"Surprise!" Valerie chirps. For a girl who swore she was close to throwing up, she sure sounds calm and collected now. She might no longer desire the fame that comes with a career as a starlet, but that doesn't mean she lost her ability to perform.

The group stares at us, dumbfounded. I only spy a handful of neckbeards, which has me reexamining everything I thought to be true. Why are these people so normal looking?

I don't recognize anyone, though I'm not sure I expected to. Thrill2Kill may claim to know me, but I've spent enough time in this chat room to realize these people *think* they have a strong understanding of me. They haven't a clue, of course.

"We heard you all were meeting up, and thought it might be fun to pop by," I chime in.

The pause that follows lasts for what can only be described as a painful span of time. The *Liarland* crew gape at us, in total shock of our presence.

"Or," Valerie slowly continues, her voice drenched with amusement, "we can go if you don't want us crashing."

This sparks some life into the group.

A man in his early thirties steps forward. The others look to him with such respect that I deduce he must be one of the more popular members of the forum. Could this be Thrill2Kill?

I guess I was expecting them to be someone closer to my age. Not a balding man with a surprisingly thick mustache and beer belly. But perhaps I'm a fool for not expecting a complete stranger to craft this game for me.

"No, no," the man says, his hands up. "We just weren't expecting such distinguished guests to show up, that's all. I'm Bobby—"

What a regular sounding name. There's no way someone named "Bobby" is the evil mastermind behind Thrill2Kill, right?

"But you'll probably hear people call me Pine."

My insides deflate. This guy must be "PineBanned," not our target.

Did you really expect Thrill2Kill to out themselves so easily?

If this person truly is trying to replicate Ride or Die, that means their identity is likely convoluted.

The others go around and introduce themselves. Only a few of them also share their server handles, but none of them claim to be Thrill2Kill.

Even so, I do my best to remember every one of their names, but they all float from my brain almost immediately. Thank goodness for the wire.

The man clasps his hands behind his back as he studies us with interest. "How did you two hear about our little gathering?"

"The same way as everyone else, I suppose," Valerie says coyly.

"You're in our server?" a college-aged girl gasps from the group.

Valerie simply answers that with a wink.

It's my turn to study their response. Are they ashamed by what they write about us online now that they can assume we were present to read every single word?

To my disgust, most of them seem thrilled by the prospect of our presence. Like it gives what they're doing an ounce of validation.

Vile, heartless freaks.

"Aren't you two supposed to be working?" I can't find the owner of the voice.

Anyone who truly knows Valerie would hear the tightness in her seemingly casual laugh. "Now how would you know that?"

There's some awkward laughing amongst the group. It appears no one is bold enough to answer her.

"Well, we didn't take off work to stand outside a bunch of rides," Valerie prompts them. The quicker we can get them back into their routine, the sooner one of them will say something of use.

Mercifully, they take the hint. After a final few awestruck looks in our direction, the crew begins to lumber into the *Wolverine Racers* queue.

"Valerie, do you want to ride with me?" one of the younger guys asks cautiously.

My stomach clenches, because I want nothing more than for her to say no, but of course, she doesn't. Valerie Ross is the bravest girl I know. She doesn't shirk away at the first sign of danger. Hell, the girl would skip right toward it.

"We'll see how things shake out when we reach the station," she responds with a friendly grin.

I don't know how she does it. Unlike her, I feel stiff as a board. Valerie must sense this because she gives our interlocked arms a squeeze before releasing me. The wordless reminder is loud and clear. Chill the hell out or this will be a pointless risk.

"Wait for me!"

We all turn to observe the guy jogging in our direction.

"Asher?" I hear myself say, earning another collection of gasps from the crew behind me.

They really hit the jackpot. Valerie, myself, and Alice's brother.

He bears the grin of a guy who knows he's intruding on a plan that most certainly does *not* involve him. I get that he's desperate to learn what happened to his sister, but this is a terrible idea. He's too close to be on his A-game.

"Am I too late for *Wolverine Racers*?" he breathes out.

"You're just in time, dude," says Bobby/Pine. "I was wondering if you were going to make it!"

My lips part with shock. I knew Asher was present in the chat room, but I was not aware that he made his identity known to some of the users. Why would he ever want the people obsessing over his sister's death to knowingly engage with him?

It takes all my willpower not to shoot daggers in Asher's direction. Secrets are dangerous at a time like this. How can he expect us to trust him if he can't be bothered to give us the same courtesy?

"The line's not getting any shorter!" Valerie regales the group with a sharp smile at Asher. "Glad you could make it!"

"You two know each other?" Bobby/Pine asks, his beady eyes darting between the three of us.

"It's to be expected in times like these, don't you think?" Asher responds far too easily for my liking. Exactly how good of a liar *is* he? My only solace is that anything else he says will be thoroughly analyzed by Detective Weegan and his team. The only people who know Valerie and I are wired are Valerie, myself, our parents, and the cops. As far as Asher, Weston, and Milly are concerned, we're simply following through with our initial plan to infiltrate the *Liarland* gathering with a few basic modifications.

But Asher's presence was distinctly *not* part of the plan.

So why the hell is he here? Is it because he doesn't trust us? Or far more concerning, because he wants to be here?

I try to remind myself that this boy's sister just died and we were the ones to find her. Asher has every right to want to take matters into his own hands. When someone you love has been hurt, there can be nothing more painful than sitting on the sidelines while other people do something about it.

"Glad you could make it," I mutter under my breath to him as the group finally enters the queue that snakes back and forth to the station. Somewhere ahead, I hear a crew member pleading with guests to stop leaning on the metal chains that separate the rows.

Valerie pulls away from me to insert herself into the front of the group. I wish she was sticking by my side, but she's doing exactly what Weegan requested we do. Stay close but capture a variety of conversations.

"Sorry," Asher responds in a hushed voice, "but I can't just sit on the sidelines. Not when it comes to my sister."

Because we're bringing up the rear of the group, I shoot him a pained look to remind him we had a plan.

"If it were your brother," he whispers in my ear, "you wouldn't be able to sit at home and hope your new friends didn't miss any clues."

I can't argue with this. If the tables were turned, I wouldn't trust people who were perfect strangers a week ago with something so important.

With a determined nod, Asher slinks through the line to strike up a conversation with Bobby/Pine.

I can feel Sarah keeping tabs on us out of the corner of her eye. She doesn't seem fazed when Asher joined the group, but I guess that's kind of a job requirement of going undercover.

Keeping toward the back of the group, I find eyes on me. The college-aged girl from before. She's staring at me like she can't believe I'm real. I guess if you spend enough time online, it's easy to forget that I am, in fact, an actual human.

Trying not to resent her for that, I force a small smile onto my face.

She beams back at me. "It's nice to finally meet you, Gwen."

"Yeah, you too," I say awkwardly. Poor Weegan is probably rolling his eyes at me back in Crew HQ. I clear my throat. "Will you remind me of your name?"

"It's Tiff."

Tiff's stringy hair is a shocking shade of sapphire blue,

which seems to glow against her porcelain skin. She's wearing a few pimple patches which means we're likely close in age. I can't decide if that's more astonishing or concerning. Why is this girl wasting her time obsessing over a bunch of murders online? Shouldn't she be studying, or partying, or both?

I nod with faux gratitude. "Where are you from?"

"Lester," she says the name of a suburb about thirty minutes away. "So I'm practically from Hathaway."

My eyebrows raise. Does her proximity to my hometown give her street cred in the chat room?

It would appear so, because a guy in line ahead of us turns around to interject. "You're so lucky that you can come here whenever you want."

"You really need to get an annual pass, Steve," she says back to him. "It pays for itself if you come like four times."

"It's the drive that kills me," Steve responds glumly. "I'm like four hours away."

"I thought you were looking into moving closer?"

"Yeah, the bank I work at is looking at building a branch in Hathaway, and I'm at the top of the list to transfer over."

I blink slowly. This dude is a freaking banker, and he's obsessing over a teenage killer? Am I out of my mind or is that a little ridiculous?

I feel a bit like a fool for bearing witness to this totally normal conversation. I don't know why I expected them to only talk about death and whatnot. Maybe they're conducting seemingly normal conversations in private chat rooms that I'm not a part of.

Why do they have to be so regular? I'd almost prefer them to all be a bunch of mouth-breathing freaks who still live in their parents' basements.

Luca seemed normal, too, I remind myself.

That's what makes these people so dangerous. They're perfectly regular people who decided to become entirely fascinated by the wrong thing.

"So, Gwen," Steve the Banker says to me, "what's your favorite house this year?"

My eyebrows might become permanently stuck at the top of my forehead. It's all so painfully normal.

We travel a few paces forward in the line.

"Um, I don't know." I try to think of what Weegan would want me to say. He'd probably want to see if mentioning Thrill2Kill's clue yields any interesting results. And so I say, "I think *Play With Us*."

Tiff and Steve both nod, as if this answer is acceptable to them.

"That's my favorite, too! I've been through it at least a dozen times." Tiff pauses, clearly waiting for me to display how impressed I am by this factoid.

"Wow!" I remark a beat too late. "That's definitely more than me."

"That makes sense, though," Tiff says, "because you're always working."

So not creepy.

Use it.

"How many times have you been through my house?"

"Wow," the girl shakes her head as she blows out a breath, "too many to keep track of at this point. It's so cool to see you and Jenna in action." At the mention of Jenna Thatcher, the girl's face darkens. "It's terrible they still haven't found her."

We move another few steps closer to the station. "You think so?"

Tiff nods sincerely. "I know some of these guys talk a big game, and sometimes they take things too far, but I don't think anybody ever actually wants someone to get hurt. Most of us are only *Liarland* members because we're obsessed with true crime and theme parks."

Taking one look at my face, she cocks her head to the side and tacks on, "Clearly, you don't agree with me."

"I've read some pretty, um, aggressive things about my classmates and myself on there."

"And yet look how you and Valerie are being treated now," Tiff points out, leaning against one of the wooden posts along the queue. "Seems like you have more fans than foes."

"Maybe to our faces."

"One would have to be face-to-face in order to be kidnapped, don't you think?"

"I guess."

She squints at me. "Is that why you, Valerie, and Asher dropped by? To try and sus out if one of us kidnapped Jenna Thatcher? Or murdered Alice Crane?"

For some inexplicable reason, I decide not to lie to her. "Yeah, kind of."

Hopefully, Weegan won't be too mad at me.

"I can't say I blame you, but if you ask me, the killer isn't one of us. We're consumers of the scandals, not the creators."

"You don't think someone on the *Liarland* server decided to try their hand at writing their own horror story?"

She shakes her head. "If you want my opinion, you should be keeping a closer eye on the people in your inner circle."

Her eyes dart up to where Valerie and Asher talk with members toward the front of the line.

"You think one of my friends is to blame?"

"I think your friends are the ones who started this narrative."

"Someone forced them to start it," I remind her.

Tiff's shoulders casually rise and fall again. "Bad things happen everywhere, Gwen. I can't think of a single theme park that hasn't been the home to some tragedy. But what makes Pineland's murders so salacious is that the culprit is always someone in-house. And usually, there's more than one of them."

If Tiff's assumptions are correct, that would mean Thrill2Kill *is* someone I actually know. Like Valerie, Asher, or Dev. Or all of them.

You've ruled Dev out, I remind myself. *We are not going down that spiraling road again because of this girl's theory.*

Still, the longer I'm with the group, the more I wonder if Tiff has a point. Sure, their activity is wildly insensitive and morbid, but they all seem harmless. As we traverse the park, they spend more time talking about attraction mechanics and operations than they ever do about Ride or Die.

It's not until we start to approach the park's new Ferris Wheel—a placeholder for the Old Wheel, where Chase's body was found—that I decide I've had enough. The last ride I'm going on is a Ferris Wheel. Just the sight of one makes my skin crawl.

Sensing my discomfort, Valerie whispers in my ear, "Let's get out of here."

"Are you sure?"

She nods. "We've got better places to be."

I catch her meaning. We're getting nothing useful out of this crew. She doesn't think our culprit is here, either.

Without bothering to say goodbye, Valerie begins to pull me away from the group. Officer Sarah spares us a sole glance that conveys her understanding. It appears she intends to stay and see the night through. Other than that, only Asher seems to notice our departure as the others lumber toward the line.

"You two dipping?"

"Yeah, I think we've had enough," I say to him quietly.

"Really?" He blinks at me with surprise. "But there's barely been any talk about Alice or Jenna yet."

"That's kind of our main reason for leaving," Valerie cuts in. "No point in hanging with a bunch of losers if they aren't going to be useful."

"Do all people you keep in your company have to serve some purpose?" Asher snaps back.

Valerie's eyes narrow. "No? I just don't want to hang out with strangers who think I'm some reformed vixen."

"Aren't you?"

Val roars, "Excuse you?"

"Whoa, whoa." I step in between the two. "What is happening right now? We're supposed to be a team."

"A team that does what exactly?" Asher's voice rises. "Pretend to care that my sister is dead and Jenna is missing? Act like we are making strides toward finding out who's behind this? We've literally gotten nowhere, while my sister is about to be buried and Jenna is about to follow suit."

"Keep your voice down," I urge him, but Asher is already storming back toward the group.

"If you two want to give up, be my guest," he calls over his shoulder. "You're the one who will have to live with regret, not me!"

CHAPTER
TWENTY-FOUR

Halloween morning arrives with an overwhelming sense of dread. I failed, and because of it, Jenna is going to die.

I wish I could prod Thrill2Kill into saying something, but Weegan's confiscated my phone. I guess I can't blame him for not trusting me to immediately alert him of any messages from Thrill2Kill. In the meantime, I'm working with a burner phone of my own that Dad picked up for me.

I should feel relieved that I've entirely handed over the reins to this nightmare. I don't have to solely bear the weight of what could happen if Thrill2Kill isn't identified before the clock strikes midnight.

All I can do is hope Weegan knows what he's doing.

I figured the detective would be disappointed with last night's failure, but when Valerie and I met up with him to return our wires, he seemed in good spirits.

"Did you not think tonight was a total bust?" I asked him.

"I heard exactly what I needed to hear."

Valerie raised her eyebrows. "And do you intend on sharing what that was?"

"Not with a bunch of teenagers, I do not."

"A bunch of teenagers who just went undercover for you."

"You went into a highly populated and heavily secured theme park wearing wires," he reminds us. "Not exactly the front lines, but I do appreciate your cooperation."

With that, Weegan had one of the officers drive us home. He might not consider Pineland to be a war zone, but he certainly didn't want us lingering around the park until the end of the event, either.

My mother was thrilled I was home early for two reasons. The first being that she only considers me to be truly safe if I'm inside the house. The second is that she and my father refuse to cancel the college tour we scheduled for this morning. I pleaded with them to shift the date until after Thril-l2Kill is apprehended, but my father insisted.

"We're not going to let them steal your normal life, Gwen," is his new favorite phrase.

I never thought I'd see the day when my parents were my greatest advocates. I guess I can't knock them for trying to be supportive now. They used to roll their eyes at my dreams of escaping Hathaway, but I've come to realize it's because they knew I was chasing Valerie's pipe dream. These days, I'm pretty sure they now want me as far away from Hathaway as we can afford.

Which is why we're in the car to visit Cranview University, a private school about an hour away. Never mind that it's completely out of our budget. Mom likes to remind us that private schools typically provide a plethora of scholarships to students.

A college tour should be far from our minds, but I think my parents would rather pretend the authorities have everything under control. And if not, they probably think being out of town isn't such a bad idea.

"We really should be visiting out here more often," my mother remarks, taking note of the department stores out the window. A thriving college town, Cranview is about triple the size of Hathaway. "Maybe we can stick around town after the tour and see what we can get into!"

"I have a shift at the park, remember?" I remind her from the backseat.

Gil, who is fiddling on his tablet beside me, is suddenly at full alert. "We can't stay here! It's Halloween, and I'm supposed to go trick-or-treating!"

Huffing, Mom glances over at Dad, waiting for him to back her up. Focused on navigating, it takes him a moment to realize, but eventually, he pipes up.

"Don't you think it could be a good idea to call out tonight and stay home?"

"And let whoever is trying to frame Dev get away with it?"

"Your job is to jump out at people in a scary costume, Gwendolyn. Not run around and chase murderers," he reminds me. "And I thought you and the Vishwakarma boy broke up?"

I offer Dad an eye roll when he meets my stare in the rearview mirror. Despite knowing Dev for nearly all his life, my father's resorted to calling him "the Vishwakarma boy" ever since Dev found Alice's body at the water park.

"We haven't broken up," I grumble. "We're just giving each other some space."

"That sounds a lot like a breakup to me."

His suggestion makes me flinch. I know it may seem like we're headed down that bleak path, but unless that's what Dev truly wants, I'm going to do everything in my power to ensure it doesn't occur. Boys like Dev are one in a million. Thoughtful, loyal, and clever. Other than my family, he's the only person who makes me feel safe.

I am *not* losing him.

"Cool it, honey," my mother warns him under her breath.

Grateful for the out, I say, "And what if chasing murderers is the right thing to do?"

Even if the authorities no longer seem to think my

boyfriend is their prime suspect, it doesn't feel right to completely wash my hands of this. Not when Jenna is still missing and Thrill2Kill only seems set on engaging with me... even if it's been a few days since they've done so.

"Then you can do so after earning a degree in criminology."

"You will *not* earn any such degree!" My mother gives my father a pinch. "Do not encourage her! You don't want to study such a horrible thing, right, sweetie?"

I nearly laugh at the desperation in her voice. "I don't think so, but I have no clue what I want to study anymore."

"What happened to saving the planet?"

"I still care about that," I say, "but sometimes, I worry that was a major I latched onto simply to have one. I wanted a direction and purpose like Valerie. But a degree is too expensive of an investment to not be 100% certain about what I'm studying."

Every time my parents hear me make this point, they go quiet. This time is no different. I can't decide if they are relieved I'm not planning to spend money on a future I'm not entirely set on, or if they're disappointed I have no idea what I want to do with my life.

"But maybe something will pop out at me while we tour Cranview!" I hurriedly tack on.

No one responds as the view outside the window captures all our attention. My eyes widen as I take in the sprawling campus. Simply put, Cranview is stunning. Ivy-clad brick buildings and winding walkways rest beneath looming trees. A few stubborn autumn leaves still cling to the branches in patches of orange and plum. All it would take is one good gust of wind to send them flying down to earth. I didn't think schools like this existed in the middle-of-nowhere.

"It's beautiful," I breathe out.

Maybe a few years here wouldn't be so bad. I wouldn't be more than an hour and a half away from Dev. We could see each other whenever we wanted, while still giving each other some space to embrace our independence.

What if this is where I start over?

I'm awakened from my blissful state as soon as we pull into a parking lot. All the other cars are models that belong on posters or on displays at the front of dealerships.

Even with a boatload of scholarships, there's no way my family can afford a school like this. One look at the manicured campus should've told me that.

I spy my parents sharing an apprehensive glance over the center console.

"But I bet the professors are as old and stuffy as these buildings," I surmise. I don't want my parents worrying I'm falling in love with a school that's out of our budget. "The student population, too."

"They do all seem a little preppy," Mom observes, her eyes lingering on the well-dressed families climbing out of the nearby cars. It must be a popular day for a tour. "But let's see what they have to offer before we pass judgement."

With that, we pile out of the car and head toward the student services office, where tours are assigned to check-in. The towering building is near the heart of the sprawling campus. Glancing up, I find a bell tower at the steeple— because of course they have a dramatic bell tower. This school feels straight out of a movie.

"Gwendolyn Gardner and family," my father introduces us to the woman sitting behind the check-in desk.

Glancing at her laptop, she nods once before passing me a folder and name tag. "Welcome, Gardners! We hope you adore our campus as much as we do," she says before lowering her voice. "After your tour, I have you marked down for a meeting with an advisor from our financial aid office."

Dad clears his throat. "That would be great. Thank you."

The woman smiles at us warmly. "One of the many perks

of our school is that we're able to accommodate many of our students."

"That's wonderful to hear," my mother says appreciatively while I focus on not melting on the spot. I knew we'd need support to send me to college, but how can I put that burden on my parents when I'm not even confident this is where I'm supposed to be?

I would feel much less guilty if I knew the price tag was worth it.

But something about Cranview feels different. Who knows—maybe this tour will be exactly the spark I need.

Trying to stay open-minded, I leave my family to mingle with the other parents and join the group of other Cranview hopefuls. No one's really talking to each other, but I do share a small smile with the girl nearest me.

Before the silence gets too awkward, a chipper boy with blond hair and hazel eyes joins our group. To the dismay of the entire admissions office, he's wearing a full-blown circus ring-master costume, top hat and all. "Nice! A full tour on Halloween!"

Still, despite the getup, the firm authority in his voice silences the rest of us.

"I'm Sean, a sophomore poli-sci major here at Cran," he says while tipping his hat. "Let's go around and say names again, shall we? Name, hometown, and what you think you might want to study."

A tall boy with an impossibly deep voice and semblance of a beard speaks up first. "I'm Brian from Grand Rapids. I'm hoping to play tennis here in the fall. Oh, and I want to study biology."

"Nice to meet you Brian from Grand Rapids who wants to play tennis and study biology!" Sean says in one breath.

That's going to get old fast.

The introductions continue around the circle while our parents look on. Most everyone else is from Michigan, with a few others from nearby states. Only a few make a point to share which boarding school they're currently attending, so I assume the rest are public school kids like me.

See—not everyone here is absolutely loaded. I bet a lot of us have meetings with financial aid afterward.

The girl next to me is Winona, and to my relief, she's undecided on her major. At least I'm not the only one who doesn't have a clue what they want to do with the rest of their lives.

As soon as Sean finishes saying, "Welcome Winona from Lester who is undeclared but maybe wants to study education," he turns to me.

"Um, hi," I begin, "I'm Gwen, and I'm from Hathaway. I'm also undecided."

There's a long pause as everyone gapes at me, as if they're just now seeing me for the first time. My stomach drops when I realize.

They recognize me. I'm the girl who made the news for thinking her best friend was kidnapped when she really wasn't and then proceeded to find a body at the top of a rundown Ferris Wheel. The whole story was dredged back up this past week with Alice's death.

Clearing his throat, a fascinated smile stretches across Sean's face as he mercifully breaks the spell. "Lovely to meet you Gwen from Hathaway who is also undeclared! Many Cran students start similarly, but we have some excellent academic advisors who will help you determine which major is right for you."

I feel the eyes of a few students still lingering on me as we follow Sean out into the open air, but soon, the campus captures everyone's attention. Sean diligently walks backward throughout the entire tour, using his top hat to point out the various academic buildings and dormitories. When we reach a display dorm room, he encourages each of us to take a seat on the bed and try to envision ourselves falling asleep here every night. It's cheesy as hell, but when it's my turn to sit, I find my mother proudly dabbing the corners of her eyes.

"You don't have to leave me here today," I remind her as we head back down the hall.

"Just the idea of it." She shakes her head with a sniff while Dad pats her arm.

The tour continues with a visit to the library, athletic facilities, and modest stadium. Sean is a decent guide, who's clearly trying to personalize the canned tour as much as he can. He makes a point to highlight anything that might be of relevant interest to those in our group, all while being hounded with questions from the parents. He patiently answers at least half a dozen from my mother.

We conclude with a trip to the dining hall, which is on the second floor of the student union. The whole place is decorated for Halloween, and surprisingly, I find myself taken with the charm of it all. I try to think of what it would be like to independently roam this building. I'd probably stop by the campus coffee shop before meeting some classmates for a study session at the library. If my roommate was cool, maybe we could eat dinner here a few times a week.

The longer I think about it, the more I think it might be possible.

Sean passes out little flutes of cranberry juice for each of us to sip on as we explore the various food offerings available.

"The dining hall is prepared to accommodate any and all dietary needs," Sean is saying when I feel a tap on my shoulder.

"Gwen?"

Whirling around, my eyes widen when I find a blue-haired girl gaping at me.

"Oh my gosh," she squeals. "It is you!"

My lips part with shock. "Tiff?"

My ears begin to ring as the future I was just envisioning whistles out of the station.

She's here. The seemingly normal girl who is secretly obsessed with the murders of my peers is here.

The girl breaks into a wide grin when I remember her name. "Two days in a row! How lucky am I?"

Not sure how to respond to that, I hear myself say, "You go to school here?"

She nods happily. "I'm a commuting freshman! Are you applying? That would be so cool. You'll love it here! It's a short drive to the park!"

"I—"

Blinking rapidly, I struggle to find what to say or even catch my breath as the harsh reality sets in. Everywhere I go, there will be people who know what happened to me. How many of them are secretly obsessed with the murders like Tiff? Do any of them also think it's a shame I'm still alive? What if, one day, they decide to do something about that?

"Honey?" I hear my mother say as she comes up behind me.

"We need to go," I say to no one in particular. My feet carry me from the dining hall as I fail to keep my emotions in check.

No matter where I go, near or far, I'm never going to be able to trust the people around me. Any hope of starting over and becoming someone new is futile. I'm always going to be Gwen Gardner, the most pathetic horror movie ingenue who ever graced the genre.

"Gwendolyn!" My father jogs to catch up with me, but I don't stop walking until I'm outside "What's wrong? What happened?"

"This isn't the right school for me," I say firmly.

He takes one look at my tear-streaked face and nods. Taking the glass of scarlet juice from my hand and placing it on the nearest ledge, he waves for my mother and brother to catch up.

"Let's pack it up, Gardners."

"What happened?" my mother asks him, but she's answered with a shake of his head.

"This school was far too stuffy for our little Gwen, anyways."

It's anything but the truth, but I'm appreciative of him saying it.

"Let's go home."

"We'll always have home," my mother agrees.

CHAPTER
TWENTY-FIVE

My heart skips an embarrassing number of beats when I hear the doorbell ring.

I know it's Halloween, and doorbell-ringing is to be expected, but to keep children from running about all night long, Hathaway has designated times for trick-or-treating. Kids aren't supposed to be appearing on our doorstep for at least another hour, which can only mean one thing...

Dev's here to drive me to work. Everything's going to be okay between us.

"I got it, I got it!" I holler, running through the house to be the first to yank the door open.

My head jerks back with surprise when I don't find my boyfriend waiting on the front step, but Asher Crane.

"Oh, hi."

A grin at my obvious shock tugs at the corners of his lips. "Weston gave me your address."

"Why?"

"Because I wanted to clear the air about last night. I tried to text you, but you didn't answer."

"The detectives still have my phone."

"It's just as well." Asher shrugs. "Call me old fashioned,

but I think some conversations are meant to happen face-to-face."

"Uh, yeah, okay. But I have to leave for my shift in a few minutes. Pretty big night."

"It is. Happy Halloween, by the way!"

"Back 'atcha, I guess."

There's nothing "happy" about it. Celebrating feels like the last thing we should be doing, especially when we're one of the few with the knowledge that we're hours away from a disaster.

It's a wonder Wendy Thatcher still hasn't closed the park, but Weegan must've convinced her it was best to keep daily life operating as normal. From what I hear, the woman's been camping out at the station, hysterically demanding the authorities locate her daughter. But I fear they're nowhere closer than they were last night.

Search parties have scoured every inch of Hathaway and the park. I heard HPD barged into every room at the Hathaway Hotel. Volunteers have been combing through the forest that surrounds our sleepy town for days. Neighboring cities have been alerted, but we all know the longer Jenna's missing, the worse her chances of survival become.

"Is that Dev?" Mom asks, coming up behind me. Upon seeing Asher, her voice raises an octave. "Oh, hi there, honey. How are you doing?"

Asher shrugs. "As good as I can be."

"Do you like hot apple cider? I was just making some for Gwen's brother to warm him up before trick-or-treating starts. How about you come in?"

"I actually love apple cider."

I shoot my mother a pleading look to remind her I'm supposed to be leaving for work, but I'm met with a stern *do-not-be-rude-to-the-grieving-boy-on-our-doorstep* expression.

With no other choice, I side-step out of the doorway so Asher can enter.

I'm not sure I'll ever be able to figure this boy out. He says he doesn't want to be around his sensitive parents, but mine are okay? Should I warn him to run before Mom breaks out the tissues?

Is Asher even the type to cry? I haven't seen him shed a single tear about his sister since we met. Last summer, I was a blubbering mess, and I didn't even come close to the kind of loss he is experiencing.

Asher offers my brother a warm grin while settling into the chair across from him at the kitchen table. Gil, who is already dressed for the evening's festivities, gapes at him.

My brother and his gang of ten-year-old buddies are all dressing up as infected zombies. He and my mother argued for days about him wanting to tear up one of his nice shirts for the costume. It wasn't until Gil played the "This could be my last year wearing a costume because I'm growing up" card that Mom caved and gave him one of my father's flannels to muck up. She must've felt pretty bad because she even splurged and bought lime green paint to dab all over his face so he looks truly diseased.

I didn't even bother trying to pull a costume together this year. Dressing up without Dev feels like a bad omen about the direction of our relationship. Besides, the staff Halloween party was swiftly canceled as soon as Jenna went missing.

"Do you want a cup, Gwen?" Mom asks while reaching to pull mugs from a cabinet.

"No thanks. Don't want to get too hot before my shift." It may be freezing outside, but scare acting is a workout.

Asher's head jerks in my direction. "You're still planning to go in tonight?"

"Why wouldn't I?"

"Uh, because unless the cops find whoever took Jenna, it's bound to be a traumatizing night? Are you sure you can handle another one of those?"

It's bold of him to assume what I can and cannot handle. We only met a week ago.

Before I can assure him that I'd rather be at work than sitting around the house and worrying, my mother chimes in from the counter while pouring cider into mugs.

"He has a point, hun. If there was ever a night to stay home, it would be tonight. You could help me pass out candy or walk around with your dad and Gil!"

I appreciate my parents not flexing their authority and making me call out, but it's clear they think I'm making a huge mistake by going in.

"Trust me, my anxiety will be far worse if I'm left to sit at home and wonder what's going on."

"No one says you have to sit at home," Asher says, blowing on his steaming mug before taking a gentle sip. "We could go get a slice of pizza, or see a movie or something."

"Aw," Mom coos like a traitor, "that would be so lovely! You both deserve a little break from the world."

"We can take as long of a break as we want, but that still won't make the bad things go away."

"Of course not," Asher says to me, "but stepping away makes it easier to handle the bad things as they come. And you and I know better than anyone that once they start, they never stop."

"Mrs. Vishwakarma told me Dev wouldn't be going in," Mom adds, landing the final blow.

"He's not?" I ask, disappointed that I didn't hear this update from the source myself. How long is Dev planning on icing me out? Sure, we've given each other space before, but that was when we were just friends. How long of a silence can our relationship endure before we don't have one to come back to?

Stop thinking about things like that.

Maybe I do need a break from everything...

"Okay, fine," I crack, meeting Asher's eyes. "Pizza. That's it. I can't sit through a movie right now."

"Fair," Asher agrees, breaking into a grin. "To Cheezy's we go."

I glance at my mother, waiting to see if she'll disapprove, but find her nodding at me encouragingly. Knowing her, she probably thinks Asher and I can help each other heal in our different ways.

Maybe we can.

Before I can change my mind, I borrow Mom's phone to send a text to my manager and let them know I won't be coming in. Thank goodness she has Hannah's number saved in her cell, because I don't have it in my temporary one. The team will probably be pissed that I'm leaving them hanging on the busiest night of the year, but it is what it is. They're too short staffed to fire me for it.

"You have your new phone?" Mom asks as soon as we drain our mugs and head out the front door. The sun has nearly set, leaving a cool-blue twilight in its wake.

Digging the hunk of plastic out of my pocket, I wave it at her. It has exactly three numbers saved in it. Mom, Dad, and Dev. Unless I'm dialing 911, they're the only people I can truly trust. The rest can find some other way to reach me if they need to.

"I want check-ins every thirty minutes."

"We're just going for pizza, Mom."

"Exactly. So, you should be home in less than an hour and a half. You can help me keep the candy bowl stocked. Asher, you're more than welcome to join in."

"That's sweet of you to offer, Mrs. Gardner, but I probably shouldn't be away from my folks for too long. They worry. Thankfully, it sounds like we're going home soon."

This makes my mother's eyes water. "Then you better check-in with them, too. We parents have a lot to fret about these days," she says, giving me a quick hug as we head out the door. She looks at the costumed kiddos already beginning to mill around our street with empty plastic pumpkins. "I swear, these kids start earlier and earlier every year."

My mother is full of it. There are few holidays she loves more than Halloween. Perhaps her fondness for the affair has dampened due to recent events, but she adores any chance to sit in the driveway, passing out candy and gossiping with the neighbors.

"Mom," Gil calls from the kitchen, "I gotta go!"

"Your father is on his way back from work!"

"I'm gonna be late!" Gil shrieks.

I tug Asher away from the house before the shrapnel starts flying.

"Sorry, he gets—"

"Don't be," Asher cuts me off as we climb into his family's van. "Family will be family. Just don't take him for granted."

My lips pinch at this reminder. Asher no longer has a sibling whose yells will echo around the house. He wanted nothing more than to put his sister's killer behind bars before they hurt anyone else, and we failed.

"I'm sorry, Asher," I hear myself whisper.

I give him the dignity of pretending like I don't notice him rubbing his eyes. "It's not our fault."

"It's not."

Clearing his throat, Asher starts the engine, effectively ending this discussion.

His parents must not have anywhere to be tonight. I still don't fully understand why they remained in town so long, but Weegan probably wants them nearby for some reason. That, or they're staying on their own accord. Maybe they only want to return home when they know their daughter's case is officially closed.

Still, it must be awful to have to hang around where your daughter died for a full week. I don't blame Asher for looking for a reason to get out of their hotel room. If he's anything like me, sitting in grief is far more agonizing than keeping busy.

Asher cautiously backs out of my driveway. Mom's right —the kids are after candy early this year.

He drives slowly down our street, careful of any children who might run into the road. When we pass the Vishwakarma house a few doors down, my mouth grows dry when I realize Dev is out front with his mom.

To my horror, we lock eyes through the car window. It takes him a moment to register it's me and whose car I'm in. Then he squints and rolls his head to the side, making his thoughts loud and clear.

"Maybe we should—" I start to say before the van picks up speed.

"I'm starving," Asher says over me, pulling out of my neighborhood. "Think Cheezy's is doing a Halloween special?"

So much for inviting Dev.

He's the one who asked for space, I remind myself.

The first thing I did when I got my new phone was text Dev the number. He responded that he 'got it' and nothing else. If he wanted to talk, he would.

Frustrated, I slump back against my seat. I knew what I was getting myself into with dating my best friend. I ignored all the warning signs and caution tape. And yet, I never thought things could get this messy.

But what did I expect? After developing severe trust issues, I walked right into every trap Thrill2Kill laid out. I should've never started dating Dev in my current state. I was only going to wind up hurting him in the end.

As the last of the sunlight disappears from the horizon, we hurtle through Hathaway. Asher must no longer be afraid of a brazen child darting into the road. It's green lights all the way through town, so there's nothing to slow him down.

I sit up straight when we drive right past Cheezy's.

"Sorry, I should've warned you. That was the turn back there."

"I know," Asher says. "I just realized I forgot my wallet back in the room."

"Gotcha." I slump back in my seat. Maybe I'm a bad person for not wanting to look Asher's parents in the eyes, but I'm not sure if I'm mentally prepared to do so.

The Hathaway Hotel is an even distance between town and the park. It's a modest three-story building that is a little rundown, but because there isn't any competition, the owners see no reason to maintain the joint.

After pulling into a spot, we both climb out of the car. The first-floor rooms lead straight into the parking lot, and it appears the Cranes have taken up residence in the farthest room available.

The hotel is eerily silent, meaning all the guests are already camped outside Pineland's turnstiles. That, or the place is empty because no one wants to spend Halloween at a theme park where people keep disappearing and dying.

While leading me to Room 120, Asher digs in his pocket for his key. I guess he doesn't keep it in his wallet. In the glow of the flickering overhead light, I spy a "privacy please!" sign hanging from the door.

"We keep it on the knob 24-7," Asher remarks when he catches me staring. "Not that it stopped HPD from barging in while we were out for lunch."

"They searched your room, too?"

"Can't blame them for being thorough now that someone important has gone missing," Asher grumbles bitterly before scanning his room key on the pad on the door. "Sorry, this will only take a second. I'm sure my folks will love to meet you."

The sudden sound of blaring sirens has us both turning around. My eyes widen as four squad cars shoot past the hotel, their blue-and-red lights piercing through the darkness.

"They're headed toward the park," I breathe out.

My stomach plummets. Did they find Jenna? Is she alive or is she...

"We should get inside," Asher prompts, opening the door. When he realizes my feet have been rendered entirely useless in my panic, he tugs me over the threshold. He locks the door after me, swiftly moving the chain in place, as well.

It takes me a moment to register that the room is completely dark. And empty.

"Your parents must've gone out." I should be filled with ease that I don't have to face them, but I can't get the sound of the sirens out of my head.

"Probably got hungry." Asher flips the light switch, and I blink until my eyes adjust to the golden glow. The room slowly comes into view. There's a wastebasket full of tissues. Bouquets of wilted flowers stand in vases with murky water. Three small suitcases rest on luggage racks. I bet the family has visited Dad's laundromat at least once to have clean clothes throughout their extended stay.

While Asher heads for his wallet on the bedside table, my eyes scan over the pair of queen beds. The bedspread on one is completely rumpled, like someone just woke up. The other is still made-up with pillow mints resting atop it.

I frown. The staff at Hathaway Hotel prides themselves on impeccable house cleaning, but they would never disregard the privacy sign on the door. A sign that's apparently on the doorknob all hours of the day. So why does one bed look completely untouched? Who isn't sleeping here at night? Asher... or his parents?

My pulse begins to pound in my ears. Something's wrong.

You're in a hotel room with a guy you met a week ago. Of course, something feels off.

"Do you mind if I use the restroom?" I ask, mostly so I can take a deep breath in private.

"Totally," Asher says easily, pointing towards the door on the far side of the room.

Opening it and snapping the light on, my eyes widen at the chaotic scene before me. The sink is splattered red with blood. No—hair dye. There're plastic gloves, a squeeze bottle, and a stained towel on the counter.

A muffled sound to my right has my head whipping toward the shower. Pulling back the plastic curtain, a scream rips through my throat.

There's a boy, bound and gagged, in the shower. His bruised eyes widen with shock before he begins shaking his limbs, begging to be freed. He has hair identical to Asher's.

"They were right, Gwen," Asher says icily, coming up behind me. He's so close I can feel his warm breath on the back of my neck, and it makes the hair stand on end. "You always believe them."

I freeze when the cool barrel of a gun presses against my temple. Asher uses his free arm to wrap around my chest as he pulls me against him.

"Believe who?" I fail to keep my voice from shaking.

His laugh is cruel as it rings in my ears. "The liar."

Before I can react, he bludgeons the side of my head with the butt of the weapon, and the world disappears before my eyes.

The last thing I hear before slipping away is the sharp ring of gunfire.

CHAPTER
TWENTY-SIX

I DON'T WAKE up in the hotel room.

Blinking at my shadowy surroundings, I try to make sense of where I am but come up with nothing.

Plastic cables bind my hands behind my back and my feet together, leaving me to lay limply on the surprisingly clean linoleum floor. My body screams in protest as I try to observe my environment without making any noise. It's clear I was not relocated gently.

There isn't much to see without shuffling. The walls of the little square room are wooden and covered in paper notices. With my head still spinning, I can't read much from here, but every single one bears the Pineland logo—an acorn with the park's name in vibrant green across it—and the word "WARNING" written in bright red. What I'm supposed to be warned about, I cannot tell.

What I do know is I'm likely somewhere in the park. How I got here, however, is still up for debate. I highly doubt he walked me through the main entrance turnstiles. He must've brought me in through the back of the park. Maybe he has a key to one of the chain link fences that surround the property?

Somewhere the security cameras are not as necessary or reliable.

My pulse quickens when I spy him. With his back to me, the boy who calls himself "Asher" sits at a desk, which rests below a window with the shades drawn shut. A nearby lamp just barely illuminates a shining metal desk.

He told us he was Alice Crane's brother. We had no reason to not believe him. And yet, we never once saw him with his parents. He didn't have any online profiles.

And that poor boy back in the motel. The one who "Asher" shot and killed. I'd be willing to bet anything that was the real Asher Crane.

So who the hell am I dealing with?

Doesn't matter. Focus on figuring out where you are so you can escape.

There are very few places toward the back of Pineland with available land to build a new structure. If I had to guess, I'm not in a guest area. Then a forceful wind shakes the shed, and I hear the unmistakable creak of a rusting metal attraction outside.

I realize exactly where I am.

"Give me three chances to guess the ride," I croak, startling the imposter to his feet.

That's when I notice the dark lump stashed below the desk. Immediately, the sensation of a thousand spiders crawling over my body tickles my limbs.

Jenna.

Unable to take my eyes off her, my heart stops. Dried blood mats her short blonde hair. I don't have to see her face to know it's as bruised as the back of her neck. She's not moving.

Dread pools through me. I'm about to be next.

How did she get mixed up with this? Why her?

Regaining his composure, Fake Asher grins at me. "Bet you could do it in one."

How will he kill me? Will he make it quick with a bullet through my head? Or will he draw it out and make a statement with my death?

Crossing the small room in two quick paces, he squats in front of me. Before I can squirm away, he grabs a fistful of my shirt, keeping me so near I can feel his hot breath against my face.

"She's dead?" I stammer.

Fake Asher cocks his head to the side, not bothering to look over his shoulder at the body slumped behind him.

"I thought you wanted to guess rides, Gwen Gardner."

"Was killing Alice and Asher not enough?" I spit back. "You had to kill Jenna Thatcher too?"

He chuckles under his breath. "If you ask me, my girlfriend had it coming."

Those bright eyes linger, waiting for it to dawn upon me. This imposter is Jenna's secret boyfriend from out of town. He's probably Alice's secret beau, too, and then posed as her brother. How did none of us realize the color of his hair was fake?

"Who are you?" I scream into his smiling face. "Why would you kill them?"

"No one can hear you," he assures me, releasing my shirt to caress my face. "You blend right in with the park's background shrieks."

"They'll find me," I bite back, jerking away from his hand.

"With what? Your lousy burner phone?" He offers me a look that begs me to stop acting delusional. "They'll find it smashed on the side of the road alongside Dev Vishwakarma's and Thrill2Kill's remaining stash."

"Why are you doing this?"

"You're not going to get me monologuing, Gwen. I know better."

"What?" I scoff. "I thought you wanted to 'clear the air about last night?' Are you trying to prove to your little *Liar-*

land buddies that you can do what Luca could not? Write a better ending because you and your freak friends think we simply exist to play a part in some horror movie you don't find entertaining enough? You're out of your mind!"

"And, as usual," he shakes his head, "you have it all wrong."

He talks with the confidence of a man who knows me, which means I'm dealing with someone who has completely lost their grip on reality.

"What plot point am I missing?" I ask, desperate to keep him talking. Dev saw me leave with the person we know to be Asher. I have no idea how long I was unconscious, but if there are guests in the park, it's been long enough for someone to notice I'm missing.

Maybe this was the clue Weegan unearthed during our undercover operation last night. Hopefully, he's realized I'm dealing with a phony and has been tailing us. But then why hasn't this place been stormed by the Hathaway Police Department?

Just the thought makes me deflate. I'm on my own.

"Unfortunately, the truth is none of your concern, Gwen Gardner."

"Give me a break—" I start to groan before a figure bursts into the shed.

At the sound of the door flying open, Fake Asher leaps to a dark corner.

For a split second, behind their large, shadowy frame, I'm granted a peek of the rundown Ferris Wheel looming outside.

The imposter was right about one thing. I knew I was near the Old Wheel, the out-of-service Ferris Wheel that closed in the nineties after the tragic death of sixteen-year-old Walker Andrews. But that was not the only death to plague this attraction. This is also where I discovered Chase's body last summer.

The Old Wheel is the setting of all my nightmares. Now, it's where I'm going to die.

"Is she in here?" the intruder demands.

Wait—

I practically sag with relief.

Weston found me.

"Help!" I shriek. "Asher is a fraud!"

"Oh my gosh, Gwen!" Weston races over to me and raises my bound body so I'm sitting upright. He scans over me, searching for any injuries, before locking our eyes.

A chill shoots down my spine as a pitying smile stretches his lips.

"Damn, Gwen, how many times are you going to fall for this?"

CHAPTER
TWENTY-SEVEN

No. *No.*

This has to be a prank. A misunderstanding.

Weston was on my side. He helped keep my head on straight.

Now, it's spinning so wildly that I barely register my temple slamming against the ground as Weston pushes me back onto my side.

I never asked for his *Liarland* handle, and all along, it was Thrill2Kill.

You know me. You know who I'm going to kill next.

You know me. You know me.

I know him. Weston.

"It's starting to get a little embarrassing, Gwen. Like, really? How many bold-faced liars are you going to trust in your lifetime?" He clicks his tongue, studying me like I'm a puzzle missing one too many pieces. "It's almost a shame that we'll never know."

The cool floor presses against my cheek as I strain to look up at him. "That's it then? You're going to *kill me?*"

Loping back into the light, Fake Asher crosses his arms and leans against the desk. Just how long have they been planning this together? It's no wonder they were so comfortable and trusting of each other from the get-go. They fooled us all.

Weston huffs with disappointment. "We gave you all the chances we could to prove us wrong. How many hints did Ethan and I need to text you?"

Ethan. Asher's real name is Ethan.

Weston and Ethan didn't use Thrill2Kill to play with me. It was a test to see if I had what it took to outwit them, and I failed. But what was the point? Why are they doing this?

Barely giving me any time to process, Ethan rattles off all the clues I missed. "We told you Thrill2Kill was someone you knew, we showed you the *Liarland* chat room, then we sent you through the haunted house where we dumped Mr. and Mrs. Crane's bodies—"

My eyes widen at the confession. The smell in the *Play With Us* house. Surely, that was not...

Nausea consumes me. They killed the entire Crane family. How could anyone be capable of something so *vile*?

I'm not dealing with humans. These boys are monsters. Soulless monsters who have completely lost their grip on reality. There will be no reasoning with them.

Which means I'm as good as dead. I wonder where in this park they'll dump my body. How long will it be before Dev and my family find me?

"It was easy to do," Ethan says, noticing my expression of disgust. "To kill them. Weegan permitted the Crane family to return home and bury their daughter days ago. Her body was relocated to a morgue back in Ohio, but the rest of her family didn't cross state lines before I caught up with them."

Now that Weston's around, it appears Ethan has decided to monologue after all.

"I met Alice on *Liarland,* but after she learned how passionate I was about this place, she decided to end things between us. She didn't understand how the Pineland murders finally gave my life purpose. I didn't have anyone until I joined

Liarland. I belong here. But when I told Alice, she called me a 'delusional fanboy.' I promised her she would come to regret that."

"So you murdered her entire family?" Just saying it aloud sounds ridiculous, and yet, the boy before me made it very, very real.

"Am I delusional if I succeed?"

"Succeed at what?"

"Inserting myself into the story and rewriting it into one the world respects—starting with the main character." Ethan's head shakes with disgust. "I've never seen such a pathetic lead before, Gwen. You don't have the chops to be a final girl."

"I didn't ask to be your final girl!"

"Don't worry! You won't be for much longer. We're on a bit of a time crunch because Weston's on his break."

I blink between them with disbelief. "You're kidding. You've done all this work to better the story and now you want to rush the ending?"

Weston crouches down before me and brushes a strand of hair from my face before speaking. "Maybe for some, this is about a better ending, but trust me, I'm ready to skip ahead to the new beginning."

"What new beginning?"

He shakes his head. "What happens after today won't be any of your concern, Gwen."

"What did I ever do to you? After everything we've been through together, I thought we were—"

"*Friends*?" he finishes for me, barking out a laugh. "Friends don't watch friends lose everything and not check in on them! Friends don't ignore warning signs that their friends are really suffering. Friends don't incorrectly accuse their friends of murder!"

"I didn't—"

"Last summer, you thought I killed Luca!"

"Not for long!" I sputter. "And in case you need a

reminder, I'm not the one who framed you! That was Jenna and Valerie!"

"One of whom has already been dealt with," Ethan chimes in, dramatically gesturing toward Jenna's body like he's a ringleader and she's his prized circus act. "The silly girl thought I actually loved her, just like *you* thought I was actually Asher Crane."

My mouth grows dry. They plan to kill all three of us. Someone has to warn Valerie. Hopefully, Milly was wise enough to get her out of Hathaway the moment I went missing.

Weston huffs out a low laugh. "The girls in this town will believe anything."

"You can't just kill the people who upset you!" I remind them of the obvious despite knowing it's fruitless. These boys are delusional and desperate—a dangerous combination.

"Why not?" Weston rises angrily to strut around the tight quarters. "They killed me first!"

"You seem pretty alive and well to me."

"There is more than one way to kill a person, Gwen," he mutters. "My whole future was stolen from me. My scholarships. My spot on the team. My hope of ever making a collegiate roster. Now I don't know if I'll even be accepted into a school!

"I've lost my teammates. My parents have never been more disappointed in me for losing control of the life they worked so hard to provide for me. I've never felt more alone, Gwen. Do you know what that's like?"

Before I can answer, he continues. "It wasn't until I joined *Liarland* that I finally found people who understand me. People who believe I was left to suffer alone by all you 'survivors.'"

He stops his pacing to shake his head at me. "So yeah, I may still be alive, but I'm no longer living."

"You still can!" I screech back at him. "We're so young,

Weston. Right now might not look as you expected, but that doesn't mean you give up! Most of us are still trying to figure out what we want."

"That's exactly what I'm doing, Gwen. I'm taking back control of my story. I'm getting my life back."

Scoffing, I fight in my bindings. "*This* is getting your life back?"

"It is." His eyes narrow with determination. "I want everyone who ruined my life to cease to exist, starting with Pineland. Unlike Marty Boone, Wendy Thatcher has a soul. She'll close this hellscape of a park after she finds her daughter's body inside it. And then, one by one, every single one of you who stood by while my future vanished will do the same."

"All our lives fell apart, Weston! None of us have had it easy!"

"You have Dev. Valerie has Milly." Weston's voice lowers as he meets my eyes. "I've had no one."

"*Liarland* will always have your back, bro," Ethan chimes in. "You didn't deserve to be forgotten by the people who were supposed to be your friends."

Weston nods like this is a true statement, and that's when the last of my hope of making it out of this alive disappears. These boys have completely convinced themselves into believing they deserve vengeance.

"Please," I stammer as tears lick my cheeks. I'm not above pleading, even if it is hopeless. "I'm so sorry for not noticing what you were going through. I'm sorry that you suffered alone. But don't let this place ruin our lives more than it already has, Weston. Please."

A beeping sound echoes from his pocket, making us all startle.

Weston pulls out his phone and turns off the alarm.

"Damn it! This is why I told you not to move them to the Old Wheel," he grumbles to Ethan. "It's too out of the way. I spent half of my break trying to get out here!"

Ethan's attention jerks back to me with a wicked grin. "But don't you think it's fitting, Gwen? Where I picked for your life to end? Maybe your death will finally be the one to earn our community the regard we deserve."

"You've moved their bodies too many times," Weston snaps. "Enough risks. This ends tonight."

"Let me take care of her, man," Ethan negotiates. "You won't have to worry about the mess anymore!"

"She's mine," Weston says with such absolute certainty that Ethan immediately nods.

The boys share a determined look. Both are so desperate to change this story that they've lost their senses. Ethan believes fans of this true crime terror deserve further recognition and respect. Weston longs to put an end to it. At their loneliest, they found each other.

The jock turns back to me with a disappointed shake of his head. "The horror story that ruined my life couldn't even have a decent leading lady. You're pathetic, Gwen, and no one will be surprised when you die."

With that, he storms out of the shed, but not before hollering over his shoulder at Ethan, "Don't you dare go into the park. The place is swarming with cops looking for you. They've got security stationed at every backstage entryway, so they don't know you've already snuck back here. Keep it that way."

And then he's gone.

Ethan turns back to me and huffs out a breath.

I scoff, realizing I'm stuck with the one playing second fiddle to the real mastermind. "Aw, were you hoping to snag some cotton candy before killing me?"

He checks to ensure my bindings are tight enough in response. I only see his silence as an opportunity to speak more. Weston's already made it abundantly clear there are some holes in Ethan's decision-making.

Maybe there still is hope.

"So, what was your last ride?"

"My last ride?" he asks back.

"Yeah, like what ride did you choose to make your last ride ever? Because after they catch you, you're never going to step foot in a theme park ever again. Hell, you might never see the outdoors again."

I do my best to shrug, which proves to be a challenge while slumped on the ground with my hands bound behind my back. "Anyways, I hope you made it a good one and not something dumb like *Sybil Saves the World*."

After an agonizingly long pause, Ethan finally mutters, "It was *Deciduous Divers*."

"Yeesh." I make a show of holding back a laugh. "That was a choice."

"You don't like *Deciduous Divers*?"

"In a park that has *Wolverine Racers* and *Pine-ageddon*?"

Ethan puffs out a breath. He might not say anything, but he's still told me everything I need to know. I'm in his head now.

"But hey, *Deciduous Divers* is a fine last ride. A little basic, if you ask me, but to each their own."

"I'll get to ride *Pine-ageddon* again," he mumbles to himself.

"Um, tonight is the last night of operation until next summer. And with how things are going, it could be Pineland's last night ever."

I watch the cogs of his mind turn as he processes this. Ethan may have lost his humanity long before I met him, but who says monsters don't like roller coasters?

He jabs a finger at me. "Stay here."

I wiggle in my bindings to prove I'm stuck.

After grabbing a staff baseball cap from the desk, the boy gives me a final once over before making what I can only hope is the last mistake of his life. He leaves me alone.

"Where are you going?" a deep voice calls as soon as Ethan slams the door after him.

My pulse thrums in my ears. There's someone else helping them? And why does that voice sound so familiar?

"Weston messaged. He wants me to see if I can get Valerie alone, too."

"I thought we were only dealing with Gwen and Jenna tonight?"

It hits me. This guy was at the *Liarland* group outing. PineBanned. Bobby.

How many people in this chat room have lost it? Bobby is a full-blown adult, for goodness sake! Why is he helping teenagers commit murder? Surely "fixing" the end of this story cannot be worth the consequences.

But clearly, to them, it is.

At this rate, all I know to be true is there is nothing more terrifying than a man who has lost his mind.

"I'll just be a minute," Ethan says firmly, making the chain of command clear. Weston's the ringleader. Ethan is his right hand. They're current characters in this story, after all. Bobby is nothing more than back-up. The guy who keeps watch outside the door.

"Want me to go in there?" Bobby asks.

"No," Ethan orders. I hear him fiddling with something metallic before the doorknob jiggles as it's locked. "Stay outside and deal with anyone who wanders back here."

"But what about—"

"You're lucky to be here at all, Bobby," Ethan bites back. "Do not ruin this for us."

That's rich coming from him.

After the longest pause, Bobby finally complies. "Fine— but word of advice? You don't want Weston beating you back."

"No shit," I hear Ethan say, but his voice is already quieter. I see him strutting away from the Old Wheel so clearly in my mind. The tall grasses that are never cut back bending beneath his feet. The shadowy Ferris Wheel left to rust towering behind him. I probably can envision it so easily because it haunts me every night in my sleep. The nightmares usually start with me climbing the ancient attraction and end with me screaming at the feeling of Chase's corpse beneath mine.

Just the thought makes the phantom spiders return to my limbs. Though, I'm not sure they ever left after I laid eyes on Jenna.

Heart hammering, I remain perfectly still in case Bobby decides to check on me—or worse, Ethan sees the error in his ways and returns. I'm not about to piss off a person who's already killed five people. Ethan's gone off the deep end. Weston too, for that matter.

I may have fallen for their lies, but I refuse to go down without a fight.

Staying frozen for what feels like an eternity, I wait until I hear Bobby start watching something on his phone before daring to exhale.

"Like hell am I going to die in here," I mutter to myself, scooting toward the metal desk. Surely one of the triangular table legs is pointy enough to saw through the cables around my wrists.

I flinch when another voice slices through the silence.

"Like hell are *we* going to die in here."

CHAPTER
TWENTY-EIGHT

My head whips toward the only other body in the room.

It's all I can do not to scream. "You're alive?"

"You thought I was dead?" Jenna Thatcher hisses back.

"You looked pretty dead!"

"News flash! You don't look much better."

The sounds of Bobby shifting outside has us both freezing. But after he doesn't shove the door open, we breathe out.

"Whose plan do you think is better?" Jenna asks me. "Because I think mine is pretty good."

I'm too ashamed to admit I don't have an idea that even remotely resembles a plan aside from cutting our bindings, so I prompt her with a "Let's hear it."

"You didn't wonder why there are so many boxes in here?"

Despite my body's protests, I adjust myself to face the darker corners of the room. Not wanting to confess I hadn't even noticed the boxes, I simply respond, "No?"

"Remember the big Halloween firework extravaganza Mom planned to cap off the first ever Hauntland season?"

My eyes widen. "You're kidding me."

Just when I didn't think things could get much worse. We're surrounded by *explosives*.

"I wish I were kidding. They planned to shoot off the fireworks from back here. Apparently, it's the only place the fire marshal would approve."

"I thought the show was cancelled."

"You gotta buy fireworks pretty far in advance," Jenna says like this is common knowledge. I guess being the daughter of a theme park owner makes you an expert in pyrotechnics. But now is not the time for a lecture.

"What's our move?" I ask her.

Jenna stares pointedly at the boxes of fireworks before looking back at me like it's obvious.

My lips part. "You want to use the fireworks to signal where we are to the cops?"

"No, I want to shoot fireworks at the dumbass boys who used me!" She rolls her eyes. "I've been waiting days for the authorities to find me. I'm done relying on them."

"Detective Weegan searched every inch of Hathaway." I study Jenna as she worries at her lip. That's when it hits me. Jenna cared for Ethan. There's no way he and Weston were able to hide bodies in this park without the help of someone with a set of keys, something I'm sure Jenna happily handed over. "Did you know Ethan was going to kill Alice?"

"Of course not! I thought he was breaking up with her."

"And you didn't tell the cops when you realized he killed her instead?"

"Not after I was the one who handed him the key!"

It's Valerie and Luca all over again. A girl trusts a boy to help her and he takes it too far by killing people. "Did you learn nothing from last summer?"

"Clearly not," she huffs, "so can we focus on escaping right now?"

"I'm just supposed to trust you?" I bite back. "How do I know you're not still helping them?"

I don't need to hear a confession to realize Jenna's been privy to Weston and Ethan's scheme all along. Of course, she was. I was such a fool not to see it before. This whole mess started with Jenna drawing Dev into Wetlands. I'm sure all the "clues" pointing to Dev being Thrill2Kill was just another one of their tests.

Jenna blinks at me. "I'm not asking you to trust me, Gwen. But unless you also have a lighter hidden in your bra, I fear we're better off working together in this instance. You do want to live, don't you?"

I swallow hard. What if this is another test? Is this another lie they all want me to fall for?

What difference does it make if I fail again? Death is the outcome either way.

My lips pinch when I realize I'm likely no wiser than the other girl tied up in here. We're puppets, and we both have the strings around our wrists to prove it.

Not anymore.

"How'd you get a hold of a lighter?"

"I figured things were going south when the boys started obsessing over you," Jenna grunts, starting to rub the plastic cable binding her wrists against the pointed corner of the table's triangular leg. "I realized their priorities had shifted away from simply closing the parks to wanting to write the 'perfect' ending."

"You want to close Pineland, too?" I ask, inching closer to start sawing away at my own cables. These boys may think themselves some sort of experts in the field, but I think a proper murderer wouldn't have used such thin plastic ties to hold us hostage. Not that I am in any position to complain about their skill level.

"I don't know what it is about this awful theme park," Jenna mutters, still working on her bindings, "but it turns people into monsters. The team members, the guests, the owner..."

She trails off, clenching her jaw.

"I don't know how the Boone family survived," she finally continues, referencing the original owner.

"They didn't."

It's funny how the Boone name used to command this entire town. Now, everyone's too afraid to speak it. I wonder how long it will be before the Thatchers are given the same treatment. Seeing what happened to the Boones, I'm sure Wendy's put the utmost pressure on herself and her daughter to not meet the same fate. It should've been the easiest task.

But maybe Jenna's right. Something about this theme park does turn people into monsters.

There's the faint sound of snapping plastic before Jenna whispers victoriously, "I'm free!"

"That was fast."

"I had a head start," she acknowledges before fishing under her shirt. "Want me to burn yours off?"

"No, thank you," I swiftly answer. "I think I'm close."

I might have no choice but to work alongside Jenna right now, but I'm not letting her get anywhere near me with an open flame.

"Suit yourself," she says, pulling her hand out from under her shirt to free her ankles from their bindings with an enviable snap. "I'm gonna go survey our ammo."

Increasing the speed at which I drag my wrists up and down the table leg, I ask, "How'd you even meet Ethan in the first place?"

"On *Liarland*."

This truth messes with my rhythm for a moment, but I recover quickly. "What on earth were you doing on there?"

"Collecting reasons to prove to my mother that buying Pineland was a terrible idea, and inventing Hauntland was an even worse one."

So that's how Jenna got roped into this. Ethan and Weston believed in her cause before twisting it into their own nightmare. One that suddenly involved me.

A fire burns through me that I've never felt before. I'm so done with people roping me into whatever narrative they see fit for me. This is the last time I play a pawn in someone else's story.

From now on, I'm writing my own.

With a satisfying snap, my wrists break free from their bindings. I could've probably been finished quicker had I allowed Jenna near me, but there's something empowering about doing it myself. I think it's the fuel I needed to finish the job.

To destroy them, I must become them.

It's a role I never expected to embrace. But how long can someone be a victim before they eventually become a villain?

I guess I just found out.

Joining Jenna in the back of the shed, I delicately eye the boxes of fireworks, like one wrong look could make them blow. There are at least a dozen boxes, all carefully labeled with signs warning that explosives are inside. They all appear unopened, aside from the box Jenna is carefully rifling through.

"How do we know which ones won't explode everywhere?"

"We don't," she answers far too calmly.

"Awesome."

"But we can probably use our best judgement based on the firework names." Jenna carefully withdraws a rocket cylinder from the box. On the side, in bold red letters, is the word "Brocade" above the enormous warning label.

"Brocade? Like lace? What does that even mean?"

"Does that sound big or small to you?"

"I don't know!" I hiss. One wrong move and we burn to death.

"Then let's find one with a name that sounds like something that's gonna shoot straight."

"We can try," I grumble, already feeling helpless.

Quietly as possible, we rip the tape off the boxes. If Bobby hears our scuffling and unlocks the door, we're done for. With the loosest grip possible, we gently remove the different rockets from the boxes. There are fireworks labeled as chrysanthemum, waterfall, and spider, none of which sound like they're going to shoot the way we want.

We both startle at the sound of Ethan's voice outside. "Anything to report?"

"Nah, man," Bobby responds coyly. "It's dead back here."

"I wondered if anyone would try to sneak off to the Old Wheel. Park is packed with teenagers."

"What about cops?"

"Didn't see any."

My stomach sinks. Aren't they looking for me? Why aren't they searching the most obvious places to hide someone?

"Just pick something," Jenna whispers, waking me from my spiral.

"This one," I say, pulling a long cylinder out of a box. A shooting star with a long tail is printed on the side, and over the illustration, is a single word.

"Comet," Jenna murmurs over my shoulder.

Our wide eyes meet. If we're going to bet on anything, it might as well be the shooting star.

"Give me the lighter."

Her lips part, but before she can protest, I hold out my hand.

"I mean it, Jenna. If you want to make it out alive, you're going to give me your lighter. Now."

No one else is taking control of my story. Not anymore.

"Weston's on his way back," we hear Ethan say outside, followed by the sound of the lock clicking open.

"Now, Jenna!" I whisper fiercely

"Damn, Gardner. Fine." With eyes like saucers, Jenna fishes into her top and withdraws the rectangular lighter. "Just don't blow us up."

I practically balloon with relief. She wasn't lying about the lighter.

"I'll do my best."

I steel myself with a deep breath, shifting the cylinder into one hand and grasping the lighter in the other. I don't dare test it. A prematurely lit fuse will doom us.

My heart leaps into my throat when the doorknob jiggles.

One shot. I get one shot at taking back control.

"Hey, dumbass!" I call as the door flies open, and Ethan's figure appears. "How's this for final girl material?"

I ignite the lighter.

CHAPTER
TWENTY-NINE

SETTING the end of the fuse aflame, I hold onto the canister for as long as I dare before throwing it directly at Ethan.

Faster than I expected, golden sparks begin to shoot out of the canister, which streaks through the air.

"What the hell?" is all Ethan can get out before the screaming sparks ram into him. Then all we can hear is *his* screaming.

Faster than I'd like, the firework whizzes past the boy and explodes through the night.

Not waiting a moment longer, Jenna and I shove past a howling Ethan, who is busy swatting at the sparks singeing his skin and burning holes through his shirt.

We race into the open air in time to see the firework burn up in front of the Old Wheel.

"Hey!" Bobby screams, chasing after us.

"Toss me the lighter!" Jenna screams, and wasting no time to think, I comply.

"Get them!" Ethan cries.

As we run through the wild grass surrounding the forgotten attraction, I spy Jenna fumbling with a canister.

"Which one is that?"

"I don't know!" she yells back. "Duck!"

I lower my head and quicken my speed as she lights the fuse. To my surprise, she doesn't aim the rocket at our captors but tosses it straight into the air. A moment later, it explodes overhead into an enormous golden cloud with glittering tendrils.

The bang freezes everyone, but not for long enough.

Rough hands grab my waist, wrenching me back.

"Got her!" Bobby bellows over my screams.

I thrash as hard as I can, but it's no use. He's double my size and strength. One hand abandons my waist and rises to squeeze my throat. Already out of breath from sprinting, I instantly begin to struggle for air beneath his grasp.

That's it then.

The ending I wrote for myself.

Bobby tightens his grip even harder, making it nearly impossible to suck in any air at all.

As I fight for one last breath, Jenna bolts past me. And why shouldn't she? In a world of villains and victims, it's everyone for themselves.

"We're done waiting for Weston," Ethan grunts, limping into view beneath the still-golden sky. "After that pathetic show of strength, Gwen Gardner, I fear the world has seen enough."

Refusing to look at him, I keep my eyes trained on the glittering firework above. My ending isn't going to be him. I redirect all my thoughts to those who brought me peace during this chaos. Mom, Dad, Gil, and Dev.

Sweet Dev. More than anything, I wish we could have fixed things before reaching this conclusion.

I will him to know how sorry I am. And to know he was the best part of this actually-not-so-horrible town. And that, despite all the odds, I think he's the first boy I've ever loved.

Now he's the only boy I'll ever love... and I think I can be content with that. With that truth, I let my eyes close.

"Gwen!"

I squeeze my eyes harder, allowing myself to relish the sound of his voice conjured by my mind.

"Gwen!"

CHAPTER
THIRTY

My eyes fly open only to immediately narrow against a dozen beams of harsh white light.

He found me.

I don't have to write this ending alone.

"Don't come any closer or she dies!" Bobby barks at the officers behind the lights. His grip on my throat tightens. Out of the corner of my eye, I spy Ethan making a run for it, but Bobby's constricting hand makes it impossible for me to warn the others.

"Gwen!" I can't find Dev behind the bright flashlights but take solace knowing he's somewhere in front of me. "Hold still!"

As soon as the words leave his lips, I hear the electric hiss of a taser followed by a gurgle of agony from Bobby. His body shakes uncontrollably before he drops limply. Someone yanks me out of his grasp before he takes me down with him.

My lungs burn as I finally inhale.

"Gwen, are you hurt?" I hear Officer Mulligan ask, inspecting me for any serious injuries.

"I'm okay," I rasp between coughs.

Before Sarah can examine me further, I'm pulled into another set of arms. It's this tight hold that feels like home.

"You're okay?" he asks pleadingly. "How badly are you hurt?"

In Dev's safe arms, I melt into a puddle and allow him to burden my weight. "I was wrong," I croak against his chest. My tears seep into his shirt. "I'm so sorry."

"It's okay." He tries to calm me down. "You're safe now. That's what matters."

"Ethan!" I gasp suddenly. "He's pretending to be Asher Crane. Did they—"

"They got him, babe," Dev interrupts. "You torched the shit out of him. The guy could barely run away."

"What about Weston?"

Dev pulls back to look me in the eyes. It's the first time I can properly see his face. His midnight eyes narrow when he asks, "*Weston*?"

"It was him, too."

I've never seen Dev look so furious as he turns to Sarah. "Did you hear that?"

"Already radioing it in," she calls over her shoulder while jogging toward the other officers. "Don't go anywhere until you talk to Weegan and the paramedics clear you!"

Judging by the sound of sirens wailing in the distance, an ambulance isn't far off. A member of the Pineland first aid team hands Dev and me water bottles as we go to sit at the base of the Old Wheel. I immediately gulp down half of it, allowing the cool water to soothe my burning throat.

"Are my parents on the way?"

Dev nods, shifting so his arm still hugs me close to him. "They had a search party combing through the woods, but they're coming."

My lips pinch at the thought of my parents desperately trying to find me. It makes tears prickle at the corners of my eyes again, but I don't want to cry anymore. This Ferris Wheel has seen enough of my tears to last a lifetime.

"I can't believe we trusted Weston," Dev mutters, glowering at his feet. "I was so preoccupied trying to figure out if *Jenna* was the one framing me that I didn't think to look at anyone else."

"Jenna, Weston, and Ethan fooled all of us."

"Excuse me?" Dev demands.

After I explain, his grip on my waist tightens as he squeezes me closer. "I can't wait until we can escape this terror of a town. Everything and everyone here is doomed."

I breathe out a laugh at the irony. For the first time in our lives, I'm the one who feels safer here than I do surrounded by strangers.

"What is it?" he asks, brushing a strand of hair from my eyes.

"I'm just happy it's all over."

Glancing up at Dev, I find his lips twisted with uncertainty.

"You don't think it is." I know Dev well enough not to frame it as a question.

"Is it ever? Or are we caught in some cursed cycle? It may slow down at times, but does it ever truly stop spinning altogether?"

"Maybe it does now."

"You know it won't. There's always going to be something."

Glancing up at the rusting wheel above us, Dev considers his response, but that pause is long enough for me to feel every possible emotion. Apprehension that he knows something I don't. Relief that he still cares enough to worry so intensely.

Finally, he shifts so that he's facing me. "Gwen, the last five months have been impossibly challenging. You've struggled to know who to trust—and for good reason. I'm not going to hold that against you."

"But?"

He shrugs helplessly. "But, if you really want this to be the end, you gotta get off the ride. It's never going to stop spinning, but who says you have to stay on it?"

I nod, understanding what he means. I'm the one giving power to these monsters. They're never going away. It's my responsibility to figure out how to block them out. Otherwise, I'll spend the rest of my life drowning in lies. And that's a pretty quick way to lose myself and everyone I love.

Tell him.

Now is not *the time. He'll think it's just a reaction after everything that happened.*

"I can tell you want to say something," he says, a puzzled look on his face as he inspects mine.

Of course, he always knows what I'm thinking. "Are you a mind reader or something?"

"What is it, Gwen? Whatever it is, I can take it."

My head shakes. "It's not the right time. It can wait. I promise it's nothing bad."

Realization dawns upon his face before a sly smile begins to tug at his lips. "Gwendolyn Gardner—Miss Anti-Commitment herself—was going to say *it* first at the most cliche spot in all of Hathaway? The Old Wheel, really?"

I go to cover my face, but Dev captures my hands with his.

"It does seem fair for you to say it first, considering I'm the one who bravely confessed his feelings way back when. Not that it went well for me, but I think things might work out better for you."

"Will you shut up so I can say it already?"

He grins cheekily. "Say what?"

"That I'm in love with you," I breathe out. "I believed I was going to die back there, and all I could think about was how devastated I was that I never got the chance to tell you."

The corners of his eyes crinkle. "Tell me what again?"

"That I love you!" I groan, gently elbowing him. "Give me a break here!"

Dev's thumb gently rubs my cheek. "If we have it my way, I'm never giving you a break from saying that. Not ever."

"Saying what?" I tease back.

"Please, this doesn't go both ways. The whole world knows I've been in love with you since we were eight."

"And recent shortcomings haven't changed that?"

His head shakes adamantly. "Never. I've always loved you, Gwen. At this point, I don't think anything will change that."

For the first time all night, I feel like I can catch my breath. And in the spirit of turning the evening around, I lean in, because the only person I want taking my breath away is him.

"Gwendolyn!" I can hear my mother's hysterical cry from across the field.

"Later," Dev mouths, helping me up so I can meet my parents.

Mom looks like she hasn't stopped crying since I first left the house, and my father doesn't appear much more put together.

They don't have long to hold me close before the paramedics arrive. After checking my vitals, they relay the good news that I'm okay but warn us to brace for the bruising that'll likely appear around my neck. Apparently, Ethan's already been taken to the hospital, where he will receive treatment for his burns before going into police custody. Wendy Thatcher, who was as distraught as my parents, insisted Jenna be checked out at the hospital, as well.

"Are you sure you don't want to be admitted?" my mom asks.

I shake my head. "I just want to go home," I say before turning to the nearest officer. "Can I just give my statement here? It's not like you don't know where to find me if you need to ask me anything else."

The officer looks like they want to protest, but after

glancing over at my father, they concede and step away to make the ask into their radio.

A moment later, the officer returns. "Weegan's on his way to talk with you."

"Here?" I ask.

"Here."

"Good," Dev chimes in.

It's not too long before Weegan walks up, hands clasped behind his back.

"Did you find him?" I ask immediately. "Did you arrest Weston?"

The detective remains stone-faced while delivering the update. "Ethan Hall and Robert Dunlap remain in custody."

My eyes narrow. "And Weston McCray?"

Weegan clears his throat, but to his credit, he doesn't break eye contact when he says, "Ethan and Robert insist they were working alone."

I balk at the man. "But they weren't! Jenna Thatcher and I can both attest to that. Are you waiting for my statement to bring him in? Because I can assure you, Weston is Thrill2Kill and was planning on killing me tonight."

Weegan continues like he didn't hear that last part. "After hearing Ms. Thatcher's statement, she's being taken into custody, as well."

I blink with surprise. Between being the daughter of one of the most powerful people in town and getting kidnapped, I guess I assumed Jenna would be absolved of her earlier involvement with Ethan and Weston.

"But you're not bringing in the McCray boy?" my father demands.

"We did, Jonah," Weegan says to him. "But Ethan, Robert, and Jenna are insistent that Weston was not involved."

"*And* Jenna?" I roar. Does she have a death wish? Weston was going to murder the both of us. Why is she covering for him? "She might not have killed anyone, but she knew everything those boys did from the start. Ethan *and* Weston."

Weegan's jaw clenches. "I'll have another word with her. But Weston McCray worked nearly a full shift tonight before the park closed early after your fireworks went off."

"Well, you're going to need to check the security footage because he snuck away during his break."

"There are video feeds that confirm he went into Crew HQ when his break started and left when it ended."

"Well, he ducked out a side door and came to the Old Wheel. I promise!" Feeling like I'm losing my mind, I look around helplessly. "Aren't there still cameras out here? Surely, they caught him walking by."

"This camera's feed was not recording this evening."

"Of course not!" I laugh wildly. "What a coincidental glitch!"

"And we've heard alibis from many other individuals. Multiple witnesses can attest to Weston's presence." Weegan taps his pen on his notebook, like all the answers lie in there.

My lips curl with disgust. How many monsters are there? How many are willing to lie for *him*?

"Do these alibis happen to be coming from his team-mates?" I ask.

"Weston McCray isn't on the Hathaway High hockey team anymore."

"That's why he wanted to close down Pineland. This park ruined his life."

"Every piece of evidence points to Weston McCray clocking in for his shift and working it as normal."

My voice raises. "Are you calling me a liar?"

"Gwendolyn," my mother warns under her breath.

"I understand the frustrating position you are in, Gwendolyn, and I'm sorry for it."

"Weston McCray tried to kill me. That's the truth."

"I'm not ignoring your side of the story," Weegan

responds far too calmly. "But there are processes that I must follow. I cannot keep Weston McCray in custody without multiple pieces of evidence that corroborate what you're telling me. I simply do not have enough information yet."

"Hopefully my death will be enough to bring him in for another round of questioning," I snap frustratedly. "Because with Weston walking free, it could happen at any moment."

"In the meantime," Detective Weegan says, redirecting his attention to my parents, "I do believe it would be in Gwen's best interest to be accompanied when out and about."

"Of course, she will be," my mother scoffs. "We believe every word of our daughter's statement and take that very seriously. I can only hope your force will do the same."

"We're going to do our jobs, ma'am."

"That remains to be seen," she snips back.

"I'm going to see this through," he promises my parents. "And while this remains an open investigation, an officer will be stationed outside your house."

My father nods, and judging by his clenched jaw, it's the most controlled response he can manage.

"You should have someone outside Valerie's house, too," I pipe up, looking Weegan dead in the eyes. "She was who they planned to target next."

Weegan jots this down in his notebook before closing it. "I appreciate you all staying so late to speak with me. If I need anything else, or have any updates, I'll be in touch."

And with that, we're dismissed.

As we all numbly walk away from the Old Wheel—the scene of yet another tragedy—I can't help but think of Dev's concerns from before. Maybe we are caught in a cursed cycle. One that truly never stops spinning.

Because I may be going home to fall asleep in my own bed, but so is the liar. And unlike me, I bet he sleeps soundly.

CHAPTER
THIRTY-ONE

When a week passes, and Weston McCray is present at school every single day, I know I'm screwed. There is nothing but my word that incriminates my almost-murderer. And in a town full of liars, I look like the biggest one. Because my statement is the opposite of everyone else's.

"I still don't think we should be here," Dev whispers in my ear as we stroll into the last place either of us wants to be. Pineland.

Now that her daughter is home safe, Wendy Thatcher wanted to still find time to thank her crew members for their tireless dedication to making Hauntland an immediate success. Despite it being a week too late, she rescheduled the staff Halloween party for tonight. It's all to save face, if you ask me. She probably hopes some new drama will arise from tonight's celebration to take the spotlight off her daughter.

"Jenna hasn't been to school all week and isn't returning my messages," I grumble. "How else am I going to get a hold of her?"

"She's not going to stop lying now," he says, trying to get me to see reason. "If she decides to throw Weston under the bus, that'll mean admitting she lied to the cops in the first place."

"She wasn't under oath."

"There are still consequences, Gwen. Jenna knew they killed Alice and her parents but told no one."

"None of us are safe as long as Weston walks free," I huff, not that Dev needs reminding. He's bared witness to every single one of my spirals since we were reunited a week ago. "Let's just get in and out like we agreed."

"Good," Dev says, clasping my hand tightly in his, "because I can think of about a dozen places I'd rather be with you than here."

Only a small portion of the park is open for the evening's festivities. A few snack carts are being manned by upper leadership. With all the crew members off-the-clock, there aren't any rides running, which is just as well. After a long season, I think everyone has had their fill of attractions.

A DJ is set up beneath the Fake Oak and an impromptu dance party has broken out in front of it. Never mind that one of our classmates was found dead inside this very tree last summer. Who cares that he became a martyr for a bunch of murder-obsessed mouthbreathers on the internet?

Focus.

"Do you see her?" I ask, searching through the mass of people.

Dev shakes his head. "The costumes don't help."

He's right. Everyone is dressed up in every kind of costume imaginable, and it seems a majority have inconveniently donned an accessory that disguises their identity. Between the wigs, masks, and inflatable hoods, it's going to take all night to find Jenna.

"We should split up."

"Absolutely not!" Dev looks at me incredulously.

"The sooner we find her, the sooner we can leave."

"No, Gwen," he says firmly. "This is the last place I'm leaving you alone."

I know better than to argue, so I tug him closer to the crowd. The pulse from the speakers thrums in my chest in time with my heartbeat. Just being in the park makes me want to crawl out of my skin, but I won't know peace for as long as Weston McCray walks free.

I need Jenna Thatcher to understand we're all in grave danger unless she corroborates my side of the story.

We walk a full lap around the exterior of the dance floor but there's no sign of her.

"Let's try some of the picnic tables," Dev suggests over the blaring music, and I let him pull me in that direction.

The temperature drops at least ten degrees as we depart the dance floor, and head toward the partygoers resting their feet and munching on kettle corn.

Valerie and Milly wave us over. They're wearing matching vampire costumes, and when we walk up, are dipping two straws into a fizzling pop. When Valerie smiles at me, I'm impressed to find faux fangs glued to her canine teeth. I guess I can't be surprised. Valerie was never one to miss out on the opportunity to dress up.

"Didn't expect to see you two here," she says, making room for us to sit.

I politely shake my head at the offer. "We aren't staying long."

She nods with understanding. "Looking for someone?"

"Have you seen Jenna?"

On cue, Valerie rolls her eyes. "Thankfully, no. That girl has wisely kept her distance from us."

"Jenna's antics have dredged up some pretty bad memories," Milly says, her glossed lips pinched. "My comment sections have been brutal."

"I wish I could say I was surprised," I say with a frustrated shake of my head. "Do you still have an officer outside your house?"

"Not since Thursday."

My eyes squeeze shut with fury. There's still a squad car at mine, but with Ethan and Bobby gleefully confessing to everything, I doubt it'll stay parked outside for long. Those boys got the glory they were looking for. They'll go down in Pineland infamy as the ones who pretty-successfully wrote a sequel.

"I'm sorry, Gwen," Valerie murmurs.

"It's not your fault."

"But I'm the one who started all this."

My head shakes again. "You are not responsible for the monsters who are dragging out this story. None of us are."

Valerie's creased forehead tells me she believes otherwise, but I'm not going to place any blame on her. It's people like Ethan, Jenna, and Weston who continue to make my life a living hell.

"We're gonna keep looking for Jenna," I say, giving the girls a nod goodbye before pulling Dev away.

There's no sign of her at any of the other picnic tables, nor at any of the snack stand lines. I'm beginning to question if she even showed up at all.

"We could try the dance floor again?" Dev suggests. "Maybe we missed her last time."

"No costumes?" I hear a voice ask behind us.

Before we turn to him, I mentally throw a mask over my face. He isn't getting a single emotion from me. "I'm a bit sick of Halloween."

This brings a grin to Weston McCray's face. I fight back a grimace of my own. How dare he plot to kill me and then smile like it was all some big misunderstanding? I guess I shouldn't expect much from a boy who turned up to a company Halloween party wearing scrubs splattered in what I can only hope is fake blood. He would dress up as a sexy nurse.

Dev immediately shifts himself to stand more in front of me. "You need to stay away from us."

"Why?" Weston asks, cocking his head to the side. "I'm not going to hurt you, Gwen. That was all Ethan."

"You can drop the act with me," I say dryly. "You're really going to let Ethan have all the glory?"

"What glory? He failed."

"He beat Luca's body count. Pretty sure that makes him a legend in some circles."

"I never wanted to be a legend, Gwen," Weston says with an easy shrug. "I just want my life back."

"So do I," I hiss back.

"Doesn't that make us on the same team then?"

"Not even if we were the last two people on Earth."

Weston's booming laugh makes Dev's hand tighten around mine. "Whatever you say, Gwen."

He might no longer have immediate plans to kill me, but what if he changes his mind? There's no guarantee he won't snap again.

The sound of a microphone crackling draws all our attention back toward the DJ platform, where Wendy Thatcher has taken her place.

"Gather round, everyone!" the woman chirps into the microphone. "All I request is a moment of your time."

Dev gives my hand a squeeze when Jenna walks onto the small stage to stand next to her mother. Like us, she's one of the few not wearing a costume. Just an evergreen Pineland polo like her mom.

Returning our attention to Weston, we find him leaning in closer to speak.

"See you on the other side, Gwen," he gets out before Dev yanks me back. "Whatever happens, know the show is far from over."

My mouth grows dry at the threat. It brings me right back

to the night all this started in the haunted house, the hooded guest walking by over and over again.

"Sit back and enjoy the show," they had said.

I never did identify the owner of that voice. Maybe I never will.

And that's the real threat, isn't it? There's always going to be someone out there who thinks I don't deserve to live. Who agrees with Weston's cause. Who are like Ethan and Bobby—willing to give up everything to be part of the narrative themselves.

With one last stony look at Weston, we join the crowd in front of the platform.

"I didn't like that one bit," Dev mutters under his breath as we find a place to stand.

Neither did I, and if we don't convince Jenna to confess that she lied, we better get used to threats like that being tossed our way.

"So sorry to interrupt the party," Wendy says, not sounding even remotely apologetic. "I just wanted to share an important operational update with you all before it's released to the public."

At this, the crowd goes completely silent.

Realizing she officially has a captive audience, Wendy continues, "It's hard to put into words how much this park means to me. I grew up in Hathaway, so all my free time was spent here in Pineland. It's what sparked my initial interest in the themed entertainment industry, which eventually led me to opening a water park of my own nearby. I'll admit, when the opportunity arose to take ownership of Pineland's operations, it was a dream come true. I knew it would be a demanding task to run both parks, but I was up for the challenge.

"But recent events have made me realize I would rather aim my efforts toward different endeavors. While I firmly believe this industry can provide a lifetime of memories and joy for everyone who steps foot inside a theme park, I'm no longer confident our parks meet that standard."

I feel Dev press closer against me, and I realize it's because my breath has hitched as I hold onto every one of Wendy's words.

"And please know, that is not a commentary on the hours and hours of hard work you have dedicated to these parks. You, the crew members, are the ones who have kept the joy coming for our guests day in and day out. I am grateful to each and every one of you for that.

"But I fear the public's vision for our park has changed, and if I may be frank, it is not a vision that I wish to embrace."

She pauses to glance over at her daughter. It's at this moment I realize Jenna Thatcher is beaming.

I already know Wendy's next words before she says them. "And so, after great deliberation, I have made the difficult decision to close Pineland and Wetlands."

Hushed conversations break out between shocked crew members.

"I will *not* be selling Pineland to a new owner," Wendy goes on to say over the murmuring crowd. "Therefore, tonight will be its last night open."

Everyone's reactions grow louder as Wendy fights to keep the attention of the crowd.

"I want to thank you for your dedication to this company. It has been an honor to work alongside you. Now, let's celebrate our accomplishments together!" she finally concludes, as if anyone is still listening.

As Wendy and Jenna climb off the platform, the music awkwardly turns back on at full blast, but no one seems to be in the mood for dancing any more.

"Now's your chance if you want to talk to Jenna."

My head shakes. "There's no point. Jenna got what she wanted. She won't stir up another mess for her mother now."

Across the crowd, I find one set of eyes locked on me.

Realizing he's captured my attention, Weston smirks victo-riously.

His earlier words echo round and round in my mind, threatening to drive me into a full-blown spiral.

Whatever happens, know the show is far from over.

DEV and I don't say a word to each other while he drives us home. We left the party immediately, but we weren't the only ones with the same idea. Some angry crew members also left following the conclusion of Wendy Thatcher's speech. More sentimental ones vowed to stay in the park until the very last minute.

It isn't until we pull into my driveway that Dev finally speaks. "We need to get out of here, Gwen."

"Do you want to come inside?" I reach for the door handle before he stops me.

"That's not what I mean, and you know it."

Glancing out the window at the squad car parked on the street, I'm not surprised to find it empty. My mom's likely convinced the poor officer to come inside for a quick cocoa break.

Gnawing on the inside of my cheek, I turn to meet Dev's eyes. "Do you want to go for a walk?"

His forehead creases. "After dark in Hathaway?"

"Yeah, after dark in Hathaway."

After a long pause, he blows out a surrendering breath.

"Fine, but when your dad gets pissed, I'm throwing you under the bus."

"Deal."

As we start walking down the street, Dev wraps his arm around my shoulder, hugging me close to keep me warm. We should've listened to his mother and worn our winter coats, but we chose to live in denial instead. Before we know it, our street will be blanketed in snow.

We may not speak our destination aloud, but we both know we're heading toward the park at the heart of our neighborhood. The place where everything changed for us. It's where I realized I had to stop fighting the inevitable. Dev was never going to be simply a friend.

I just had no idea how important he would become.

When the shadowy playground lit only by moonlight comes into view, Dev makes it clear we won't be staying outdoors for long by steering us toward the swings. We each claim one and start gently swaying in sync.

"I mean it, Gwen. We can't stay in Michigan. Mom and Dad won't like it, but they'll get over not seeing me at Griswell in the fall. We can find an affordable school near the coast. Or maybe, somewhere out of the country."

I laugh at the absurdity. "We're not moving to another country, Dev."

"Why not? We could make it work!"

"I'm sure we could, but we're not going to."

"Gwen, if you stay in Michigan, there's no telling what could happen to you. What if these freaks decide to blame *you* for the closure of their precious theme park? They're all out of their minds. There's no telling what they'll do!"

"Dev, babe, you need to breathe."

"Stop acting like I need to calm down! You're not safe here, so we can't stay!"

"I'm not safe *anywhere*, Dev!" I plead with him to listen carefully. "The story is already out there. No matter where I go or what I do, it's never getting erased. And I don't think it's healthy for me to act like I can rewrite what happened to me." I rise from my swing so I can stand and face him. "I can't, Dev. It happened. If I keep pretending like it didn't, I'm never going to figure out how to live with it."

He climbs off the swings too so he can grasp the sides of my arms. "You shouldn't have to live like this!"

"I know I shouldn't, but I don't have a say in the matter. This is my life now. The new normal. If I don't accept that, I'm going to live every single day in paranoia that everyone is lying to me or mocking me or plotting to murder me. I can't live the rest of my life with fear."

Chewing on his lip, he shakes his head with frustration. "How do you come to accept it?"

"By embracing the truth." My chest rises and falls as my breathing spikes and tears tease the corners of my eyes. "I'm Gwen, the girl who cares so much that it sometimes leads her to make horrible decisions. Everywhere I go, there are going to be people who know that about me. Some are going to think it's embarrassing. Others might consider it an opportunity to take advantage of me. But hopefully, there will be a few decent humans who don't give it a second thought."

Dev gently brushes a strand of hair from my face. "But how are we going to know who is who?"

I shrug helplessly. "We won't."

"I hate that."

Scrunching my nose, I ask, "While you're hearing things you're gonna hate—"

Dev sighs deeply before gesturing for me to go on.

"I don't think I'm going to leave Hathaway in the fall."

Nervously, I watch as his throat bobs, and when he doesn't speak, I take that as my cue to continue.

"For the most part, I know what I'm up against here. And even when I discover the people I've chosen to trust are bold-faced liars, at least I'll have my parents and my brother to lean on. I'm all for embracing the cruel truth about my new reality, but I'm not sure I want to do so without people I know I can trust nearby."

Dev's quiet for a long moment, and just when I worry he might never speak to me again, he leans in to press his lips against mine. Gentle and grounding.

"I'll stay with you," he murmurs against my lips.

I pull back immediately. "No, you aren't. You're going to Griswell. It might only be forty minutes away, but I'm going to need somewhere to escape to when Hathaway starts to feel like... well, Hathaway."

We stare at each other, carrying on with a silent argument. But I'm not going to be the one who caves first. I'm not letting Dev change his story for me.

"Fine," Dev breathes out finally, pulling my chin back toward him so he can kiss me again. "You win."

"That's a nice change of pace," I whisper while swirling with relief. "The odds were definitely stacked against me."

"And despite those odds," Dev promises, brushing his lips against mine, "I am always going to bet on you."

THIRTY-THREE

WITHOUT PINELAND, it was the strangest summer of our lives.

I never realized how powerful of a cornerstone the park was for our town until it was gone. Even now, ten months after Wendy Thatcher announced it would not reopen for another season, people are still struggling to accept the new reality.

A lot was forced to change without the parks. Mayor Dillard had his work cut out for him when it came to addressing the rapidly changing economy and job opportunities. Like most, my parents are stressed, and while I know they'll never say it to my face, I'm sure it's a relief I've put off college in the interim. Even after a school year full of sessions with the guidance counselor, I still don't feel called toward a particular career yet. I know I'm going to have to figure it out, but I'd rather not waste money on tuition while I do so.

It was weird to not spend every day at the park, but Dev and I found plenty of ways to fill our time. In fact, all things considered, it may have been the busiest summer of our lives because we were determined to enjoy every last day of us both living in Hathaway.

Still, faster than I would've liked, it became August.

"You can probably still fit back here," Dev says while surveying the stuffed bed of his truck. The cover barely fits over top, and if the tailgate will shut remains to be seen. "We can pack you away and none will be the wiser."

"Sounds good to me." I nod, pretending to crawl up into the bed. "You'll have to drive me back for my shift at Cheezy's in a few hours, but I'm up for a ride."

Laughing, Dev pulls me out and places my feet back on the ground. Without a word, he simply holds me close while we both study the boxes of clothes and cello case crammed into the back of his truck. I'm afraid if I look at anything else, I might cave and be the one to cry first.

Forty minutes away didn't feel very far until right now.

"Two years ago, if you had told me I would be the one moving away and not you..." The hoarseness of his voice gives him away.

"You would've been like," I say with a watery laugh before dramatically lowering my voice, "'I'm not even talking to that girl anymore. What do I care?'"

"I do not sound like that." Dev cackles in my ear, hugging me tighter. "And, of course, I still secretly cared."

I pretend to be shocked by this admission.

"Oh please, get over yourself," he groans. "Who professed their love for the other first?"

I turn to face him. "Yeah, well, who wanted to say it first?"

"Me," he says proudly, pecking my forehead.

We grin at each other, both realizing we won't have much longer alone. Dev's parents only left to refill the family's water bottles before starting the drive to campus.

"I'm going to miss you," I murmur, rising on my toes.

"Not if I have any say in the matter," he insists, pressing his lips against mine.

I draw him nearer, committing every detail of him to memory. My best friend. The boy I love. We can handle the space to grow separately. He's going to master his craft and I'm going to figure out mine.

Just as his fingers begin to tangle in my hair, his parents loudly open and close the front door. I can't help but smile at the tormented groan that escapes Dev's lips when I rock back onto my heels.

"Are you sure you don't want to squeeze in?" He gestures toward the bed once more.

I move around him to close the tailgate. "In a few days, I expect to hear a piece you composed about how much you miss me."

He grins. "I'll play it for you when you come visit next weekend."

"You have yourself a deal." I risk stealing one last kiss. "I love you."

"I love you, too. I'll see you soon."

And after the tightest hug, he's climbing behind the wheel and pulling away from our neighborhood with one final wave.

Not allowing myself to cry, I hurry back to my house a few doors down. Everyone else is out, so I have the place to myself. Mom's taking Gil back-to-school shopping, and Dad's working on finding new customers for the laundromat.

I still have a few hours before my shift at Cheezy's, so I head upstairs to my room and open my laptop.

Clicking away from the *Liarland* tab, I return to the document that houses the script I've been writing. If people want to dissect what happened to me, they might as well hear it from someone who will tell the truth. The script shouldn't take too long to finish with all the free time I now have on my hands. Then all I have to figure out is the best way to share it.

There may be those who disagree, but whether they like it or not, I *am* the final girl in my story, and I have every intention of taking back control of the narrative.

ACKNOWLEDGMENTS

As soon as I finished writing *Liarland*, I found it impossible to say goodbye to this thrilling world. I'm honored you feel similarly. With that in mind, my first thank you is to you, the reader. I'm so lucky you want to go on this ride with me.

I have the great fortune of working alongside two humans who are fantastic editors and even better friends. To Andie Smith, thank you for being utterly brilliant and continuously excited when I throw a new draft at you. And thank you to Kaitlyn Katsoupis, whose stroke of genius absolutely bettered this story.

Thank you to Katt Phatt for creating another remarkable cover. I am forever in awe of your talent. And thank you to Nancy Moore for helping make it possible.

I'm so grateful to the booksellers in Orlando and beyond. Your kindness and enthusiasm are gifts I'll forever cherish.

To Taylor Maloney, my dearest friend. The best thing to ever happen at a theme park in the middle of the night was meeting you.

I grew up a theme park fan because of my family. Mom and Dad, thank you for falling in love with the parks (and *at* the parks!), and for sharing that love with us. And to Adam, who always sang along with me to park soundtracks while driving to school.

In the *Liarland* acknowledgements, I shared that I met the love of my life in a theme park. It seems fitting to expand on that now... I met the love of my life *at a Halloween event* in a theme park. Taylor, my darling husband, thank you for making every day an adventure.

ABOUT THE AUTHOR

Madison Rupp
writes young adult thriller and horror-romance novels. Based
in Orlando, Madison can usually be found scribbling in a
quiet corner of a theme park. She's a firm believer that riding a
roller coaster cures writer's block. Madison is also the author
of *Liarland* and *Death Dates*.

You can connect with her online at madisonrupp.com.

 instagram.com/madisonrupp
 x.com/madisonrupp